Bonds of Love & Blood

Short Stories

MARYLEE MACDONALD

Praise for BONDS OF LOVE & BLOOD

Exploring topics of personal authenticity, the need for solitude in which to grow, and the painful and confusing clash between diverse personalities and cultures, MacDonald applies insight, power, and delicacy to create characters between whom the psychic space virtually sizzles.

FOREWORD REVIEWS

Readers walk the streets, farms, and countries of each of these twelve individuals and their circles and will find these very different journeys engrossing.

MIDWEST BOOK REVIEW

With elegant prose enlivened by shards of mean humor, MacDonald captures how hard it is to love and/or trust abroad or at home.

KIRKUS REVIEWS

Author Marylee MacDonald has done an absolutely masterful job of presenting her readers with short stories so beautifully written that the characters will stay in your mind long after the story, and indeed the book, is done.

READERS' FAVORITE

In her collection of twelve brilliantly-written short stories, MacDonald explores the pain and beauty of human relationships. MacDonald's writing is raw and visceral, creating a strong emotional connection between her characters and the reader.

US REVIEW OF BOOKS

Bonds of Love and Blood is brilliantly written and nothing less than emotive.

HOLLYWOOD BOOK REVIEWS

Bonds of Love and Blood is poignant, honest, and compelling, as are all of these stories. Highly recommended.

PACIFIC BOOK REVIEW

MacDonald dares to question which is the greater, more unsettling risk: the alluring intimacy of foreign terrains, or the intimate dangers of domesticity?

TARA ISON, author of *Reeling Through Life* and *Child Out of Alcatraz*

Her characters remind us of our universal and contradictory longing for solitude and for connection. Savor this book. Enjoy being in the hands of a generous and visionary writer.

EILEEN FAVORITE, author of *The Heroines*

These elegantly crafted stories brim with emotional wisdom and eloquence. Bearing you around the world, they will imprint themselves, deeply, indelibly, upon your heart.

MELISSA PRITCHARD, author of *Palmerino*

In stories linked by themes of journey and displacement, each character is backed up "right against the precipice..."

ADRIA BERNARDI, author of *Openwork* and *Dead Meander*

Marylee MacDonald writes with wisdom and patience and dramatic power in presenting converging inward and outward journeys. At each turn, the imaginative storytelling guides you into the riddling hearts of people who appear to be out of options but become ready to learn to try again.

KEVIN MCILVOY, author of *Little Peg* and *The Fifth Station*

Tight, interesting, and evocative, these are stories that surprise and delight.

MOLLY GILES, author of *Rough Translations* and *Creek Walk*

"The Pancho Villa Coin" is an absorbing and troubling read. The story manages to soak the reader in a pleasingly foreign atmosphere while building a feeling of threat.

MICHAEL SIGNORELLI, Judge, Faulkner-Wisdom Competition

People who avoid short fiction in favour of novels may complain that too much is left out or too much is compressed into a small space. Marylee MacDonald's splendid collection is an antidote for both objections. Like two virtuoso short story practitioners named Moore—Newfoundland's Lisa and America's Lorrie—MacDonald masterfully reveals exactly what we need to dwell memorably with her characters at decisive crossroads and to revel in the prime benefit of short fiction: imagining her characters' prior lives and the outcomes of their crises. Her fiction takes us on a Mexican holiday with an abusive husband and his wife and daughter and to an encounter between a young male tourist and a trans-gendered tourism worker in a Southeast Asian resort. We are with Anna searching for her vanished son in Prague, an African-American Vassar grad arrested in a Baltimore bar, and Leslie when her workaholic-scientist husband Ashok brings his widowed Indian mother to live with them in Ontario. MacDonald's savvy understanding of human relationships, and her lucid, vibrant, and ruggedly poetic prose, make for riveting stories you both can't put down and must pause at length between, imagining what came before and what comes next.

RICHARD LEMM, *Shape of Things to Come* and *Burning House*

Bonds of Love & Blood

Short Stories

MARYLEE MacDONALD

Grand Canyon Press

Copyright © 2018 by Marylee MacDonald
All rights reserved.
Tempe , AZ: Grand Canyon Press [2018]

www.grandcanyonpress.com

Library of Congress Cataloging-in-Publication Data
MacDonald, Marylee
Bonds of love & blood : short stories / Marylee MacDonald.
228 pages ; cm

ISBN: 978-1-7320787-3-4 (paperback) | 978-1-951479-18-3 (Amazon pa-
perback) | 978-1-7320787-5-8 (Kindle) | 978-1-7320787-1-0 (epub) | 978-
1-7320787-2-7 (pdf) | 978-1-7320787-4-1 (audiofile) | 978-1-951479-09-1
(audiofile)

1. Interpersonal relations—Fiction. 2. Solitude—Fiction. 3. Short stories.
I. Title. II. Title: Bonds of love and blood

LCC: PS3613.A2714255 | DDC: 813/.6—dc23

Printed in the United States of America

Cover design by: www.tatlin.net

4 5 6 7 8 9 10

For Bruce

For happiness one needs security, but joy can spring like a flower even from the cliffs of despair.

ANNE MORROW LINDBERGH

Love is something far more than desire for sexual intercourse; it is the principal means of escape from the loneliness which afflicts most men and women throughout the greater part of their lives.

BERTRAND RUSSELL

TABLE OF CONTENTS

THE BEAN GROWER

——————◦——————

HER PRECIOUS VALENTINES! With the snipped fingers of her mittens, Fabienne Drummond felt the six-inch bean-pods. Leathery. Beneath the planting beds, rubber tubing coursed with solar-heated water, but the heat wasn't sufficient. Wilson Turnrow—a widower she had known since childhood—worked at the opposite end of the greenhouse, packing straw around the pole beans' roots. Icicles hung from his mustache.

"You look like a walrus," Fabienne said.

"Suppose so." He clapped his brown snowsuit with gloved hands. "Done here. Need to head out to the sugar bush."

Wilson and his damned sugar bush.

"Can you turn on the propane?" she said.

"Don't think it'll do much good."

"I have to try."

He let the door slam. A moment later, she heard the whoosh of the propane burner and felt the downdraft of heat. Registers hung just above the grow lights.

The Scarlet Runner, a bean from the 1800s and one of the earliest in her seed bank, had hooked a tendril up and around a hanging fluorescent. What she loved about beans was their active, urgent lust for light. She climbed a step-stool, pulled the tendril down, and made the plant more compact. In another week, the speckled pods of Wrens Eggs would be ready to harvest. The best she could do for the Commodores and Old Homesteads and Pencil Pods was to pack straw around their roots, and she'd been at that all day. If the power stayed on and the sun shone even a little, the straw would hold in enough heat to keep the pods from freezing. The beans might be smaller than average, but they would be good enough for the canvas bags of soup beans she sold at farmers' markets.

Outside, the sky had turned the color of pewter. She closed the greenhouse door and looked back. "Goodbye, my friends. Good luck."

Shoulders hunched, hands tucked beneath her armpits, Fabienne stepped carefully down the icy path. Wind came first from one direction and then the other. Smoke curled from the chimney of the white, gabled house where Wilson stood, looking up.

"You see them birds yet?" he said.

"I thought you were going to see about your trees."

"Look there." He pointed to the side of the house.

Up by the louvered, attic vents, she saw finches, nuthatches, robins, and jays, the birds that had returned a week ago for spring. The triangular, delicate marks of their feet looked like ivy suckers. In defiance of gravity, they were walking as if suction held them to the wall.

"It's a wonder they don't fall." Her words huffed out a vapor balloon.

"Reminds me of what the Bible says about the end times."

"I never read that part."

A brown bird that looked like a fat cigar coasted in. The little birds made room.

"I never seen a jay hawk mixing it up with them little birds," he said. "This storm's going to be a doozie."

"With good effort, we protect ourselves," she said.

"Look there." Wilson pulled her sleeve with his mitten. "Blade's off the windmill."

Gusts carried the shriek of ball bearings. The windmill limped.

"Can you fix it?" she asked.

Wilson's eyes widened. "Are you out of your mind?"

"You could fix it before the true cold sets in."

"It's barely above freezing."

"I thought you could fix anything." That's what he'd claimed. If it's broke, I can fix it. "Oh, just forget it." She turned back to the house. "If it goes, we can melt snow." Bucket flush for the toilet. No more showers.

"I best go drain the pipes," he said.

"Leave the downstairs toilet," she said.

"You sure?"

"Just do what I tell you."

His eyes touched her face and then moved to the sugar bush. From atop the distant hill, the maples' fingered branches waved like spectators looking down on the white house, the weathered barn, and the greenhouse, its fabric luffing like sails. She walked around to the kitchen door. Wilson had helped her roll up the parlor rugs, spread plastic, and carry in all the seed flats. She could think of nothing more to do, apart from waiting for the storm to hit.

HALF AN HOUR later, Fabienne watched Wilson change the batteries in the portable radio. He had his mental list, too. He placed the radio on the floor between their recliners and then warmed his hands at the wood stove. The fireplace had been blocked off with a piece of sheet metal. The Scandinavian stove, with its splayed feet and a blue ceramic finish, threw a tremendous shot of heat up the stovepipe, where Wilson had recently installed a warming oven. Near the ceiling, the pipe disappeared into the wall, and the wallpaper had turned brown as pie crust. Beneath the stove, a black tomcat with pieces torn from its ears basked in the heat, paws curled beneath its chest.

"I wish Mama would bring her kittens in the house," Fabienne said.

"She won't." Wilson pressed his thick fingers against his eyes and let out a groan as he sat down. Below the fold of his stomach, she saw a strip of long johns. He turned on the radio.

"The storm is expected to be the worst in a hundred years," the announcer said. "In parts of Saskatchewan, power lines are down, and all traffic is halted on the roads due to ice. Somerville has opened a shelter at the high school. Bring food and bedding." The governor had declared a state of emergency.

"Instead of staying here, how 'bout we head to town?" Wilson kicked down the footrest. "Your friend Laura would let you lay out the flats in her garage."

No reason to believe the governor. Fabienne had ridden out many a storm right here. "*Pas nécessaire.*"

"Whatever you say, boss."

"Don't call me boss," she said. "You've got a stake in this farm."

"Phhh!" He snapped open a newspaper. "The 4x4's in your name, and so's the sugar bush."

"You've got the use of one and the income from the other," she said.

"I may not even get any syrup out of them trees," Wilson said.

"Certainly you will," she said, "what with all that new piping you put in."

Sit tight, and they'd be fine. She pulled off a glove and wiped condensation from the windowpane. No snow. A sunless sky.

"Maybe the forecast is wrong," she said.

"Don't count on it," he said.

A laugh-trill pealed out from the radio: Dr. Ruth with her stupid Kissinger accent giving advice on sex. Everywhere but in New England, the world went on with its trivial, stupid business. Sex! Sex! Sex! What was so hard about it!

Wilson folded his newspaper. "What say we do it?"

"Where?"

"Here," he said, pointing to the rug in front of the stove. "We ain't got nothing better to do."

The room was only sixty-five degrees and his hands were chapped, but sure, why not? She unbuttoned her flannel shirt.

Her grandmother had been a midwife, a *sage femme*, and as

a child, Fabienne had seen breech births, miscarriages, teens in trouble, and Catholic women with sixteen children. It was only when she'd passed menopause that she dared have unprotected sex. Wilson was good that way. A good worker; a good pal. Fabienne felt freer than she'd ever felt in her life, free very deeply in herself. She didn't mind that a corner of her conscience protested that she was using Wilson. Men had been doing that to women for years.

AT FIRST THE sky showered them with snow, and it seemed the worst of the storm might pass to the west. Then, a steady rain began to fall and turned to sleet before it struck the ground. Beyond the one window Wilson had left unshuttered, a curtain of water slanted down. The pump went out and the electricity failed, but she felt reassured by the jackhammer of the greenhouse generator. That would keep the lights on and the water pump running for a while. With a little heat, her winter crop might yet be saved. As long as the house stayed warm, the seedlings would survive.

Ash built up in the stove. Wilson shoveled it into buckets and carried the glowing embers outside, where they sizzled. "Devil take this rain." He slammed the door, then tramped through the darkened second parlor, crowded with overstuffed chairs, a horsehair sofa, and assorted end tables. He opened the door to the garage. "We're going to be needing a deal more wood."

"I can help," she said.

He had stacked two cords of wood against the far wall, but the wood was hard to reach on account of the cars. He slid between his workbench and the bumpers. "Shut the door and stay inside," he said. "You're letting the heat out."

A grapefruit-colored cat meowed around her ankles. "Pamplemousse!" Fabienne closed the door, poured evaporated milk in a bowl, and opened the door; but the cat rubbed back and forth against the jamb, her tail flicking like a whip.

"Can you hear the kittens?" she called over the truck's cab.

"Don't worry about them," he said. "Worry about you'self."

"We'll be fine." She stood aside to let him pass.

Back in the parlor he kicked aside the seed flats and dumped the firewood next to the stove. "I wish I'd brought the barrow in."

"What else is there to do," she said, "but carry wood?"

He gave her a look and slumped down in his chair. "The cold's making me winded."

Since the sleet started, she'd hardly taken a moment to sit. She'd arranged and rearranged her propagation flats, moving the frost-prone species further from the walls and the sprouts and cuttings to the middle. She had a nursery of babies on her hands, and the little squares of soil around their roots drank up water; she ran in and out of doors with big tubs, collecting run-off from the gutters. One water tap worked, the soft water from the cistern, but they needed that for bathing, and as soon as the tank emptied in the attic, they'd have to melt snow. The temperature in the room dropped to fifty-five degrees, and the room smelled damp and clammy.

Later, sitting before the stove with a plate balanced on her lap, she heard shots ring out.

"Hunters?" she said.

"Trees." Wilson ate left-handed and sopped up beans and rice with the last of the store-bought bread.

His mouth moved ever so slightly under his mustache, a silent conversation with himself. Then he got up and went to the bathroom. When he came back, he smiled hard. She could see his teeth.

"Shitter's froze," he said.

She jumped up to see. An inch of yellow piss steamed on a layer of ice. She jammed the plunger through. "Get more anti-freeze."

Not waiting for his answer, she went to the root cellar, and in a back corner, found two old white-steel slop jars with red-rimmed lids. Wilson would hate them. She hated them and remembered how embarrassed she'd felt as a child, knowing her grandmother would see her bodily waste. She put the slop jars in the bathroom and labeled them his and hers.

Then, back in the parlor, breathing hard, she made herself

sit down. On the windward side of the house, the shots sounded closer. The volleys reminded her of duck hunters shooting from blinds. She had always feared hunters when they snuck past the no-hunting signs posted around the perimeter of the sugar bush, but these were not hunters, she reminded herself. The trees were splitting under the burden of ice. Wilson put down his magazine, looked over at her, and reached for her hand.

ON THE MORNING of the second day and before he'd even made coffee, Wilson turned on the radio. Sleeping and eating in the same room reminded her of the time she'd had measles and been allowed to lay on the daybed in the parlor and listen to her grandfather's tube radio. "Fibber McGee and Molly" or "Ma and Pa Kettle." But the radio did not reassure her today. Wilson had tuned in WEBB out of Augusta. Randy McCoy, on "The Morning Buzz," said the governor in Augusta had put out a call for able-bodied men. Power companies from several states were sending teams, and men who could climb a pole or handle a chain saw were urgently needed to assist crews trying to restore power. The pay was triple time.

Wilson put his bowl of oatmeal on the floor and wrote down the address.

"I guess I can still shimmy a pole," he said.

"Why didn't you fix the windmill then?"

"Would it have made you feel better to see me go up there and scratch my head?"

"You said you could fix anything."

"What if I fell?"

"You wouldn't fall."

"People do," he said.

"Then don't go work on that power crew."

Wilson added logs to the fire. She noticed the magazine on his chair. It had palm trees on the cover.

Gusts of wind banged and rattled the front door. The wind had changed direction. Plastic tore off the windows. Beyond Wilson's reclining hulk, she saw the windmill, a bride with a great, unmanageable train. The plastic had caught on the tower.

Wilson's eyes closed. She placed her hand on his.

"I think the San Juan Islands would be a nice place to live," he said.

"Why do you say that?"

"It's warm."

"Near Seattle, right?"

"They have Butchart Gardens. I been there once. Lots of flowers."

"How about beans?"

"Don't you have customers out west?" he said.

She had customers everywhere, but this was her farm. "I'm not interested in moving."

"I'm taking you to the shelter," he said.

"I can't go," she said, "but you go if you want."

She didn't have to say "and don't bother coming back." He must know that. There were limits to their commitment. Survive together until one or the other of them got cold feet. Apparently he had.

He stoked the fire, scraped the oatmeal pan, and scribbled a phone number on an envelope.

"Are you that desperate for money?" she said.

He put the envelope under his coffee mug. "Matter of fact, I am."

But why? She wanted to ask and didn't. He had zipped himself into his snowsuit and put on his hat and gloves.

Through the bottle glass next to the door, she watched the truck back down the icy drive.

WIND KNOCKED ON the door. She pulled the blinds and stoked the stove. Needing to hear a human voice, Fabienne turned on the radio: "roads slick as skating rinks;" "power out across Quebec;" "Pepco crews making their way up from Maryland."

She wondered what it was like out there, that world Wilson had ventured into. She raised the blind. Rain and sleet had washed away the snow, and as she stepped out the front door to gather icicles hanging from the eaves, she slipped and crashed down on her coccyx, about driving her spine through the roof of her head. She crawled back inside and lay panting in the hall.

Wilson called on the cell phone to make sure she was all right. "I'm just fine," she said. "You don't have to check on me." She tried to sound her usual irritated self to disguise the little seed of worry planted in her stomach. She had his work to do plus her own.

Every few hours she brought in more logs and grew irritated at the cat mewling about her legs. Last thing she needed was to trip again. The fall had bruised her ribs, and when she bent to water the plants, she could hardly catch her breath.

That night, the outdoor temperature dropped to minus twenty, not counting the wind chill. To keep up with the demand for heat, the stove needed to run full blast. She set an alarm that woke her every three hours and stumbled from sleep to add logs to the firebox.

If Wilson came home, she would forgive him for leaving, but she would not beg him to come back.

THE NEXT DAY she opened the garage and took a hard look at her Honda. It would never make it to town. At first, she'd been worried about the plants. Now she worried about herself.

"I'm with a road crew clearing trees from Route 25," Wilson had said, his call miraculously making it through the ether. "Are you sure you're safe?"

"I'm fine," she said, almost a reflex, and was about to add that she wasn't fine, but exhausted and freezing. "I keep towels in the warming oven, a kettle on, and when I feel too cold, I wrap my hands around a cup of tea."

"What's the temperature in there?" he asked.

"Ninety," she said. "I'm walking around in shorts."

No matter how much wood went into the fire, the temperature in the house never rose above forty. After a trip to the garage to gather wood, she wrapped warm towels around her neck.

ON THE STORM'S sixth day, three days since Wilson had been gone, she could stand her own filth no longer: peeing in the slop jar, recycling her underwear, her armpits' reek. She heated water for a sponge bath and ventured upstairs to find clean clothes. A thin layer of ice coated her furniture. She could not see her reflection in the frosty mirror. A pane had cracked, letting in a stream of cold. Wilson had left duct tape on the dresser. She closed off the leak and stared at the headboard of the Eastlake bed—the indented pillows—and pictured the two of them huddled together, the orchestrated turning of their bodies as they settled down to sleep.

In the parlor, so close to the stove she burned her thigh, she washed her crotch and threw her dirty undies in the fire box. That time they'd had sex on the floor had been average, his pole burrowing her from behind. If she'd known he was deserting her, she would have demanded five stars.

Dressed in her parka, she sank back in Wilson's chair. The plants needed water. Pots should go outside to catch the sleet, but the thought of getting up was more than she could bear. She was dead tired from feeding the stove and melting ice. Her mind felt foggy, but she was clean. Prepared for the hospital, the old "what if you were injured in a car wreck and the ambulance..." She should let him know he could have the farm if she died.

She picked up the phone and called the number on the envelope. A woman answered. "Does anyone know where my husband is? He's not really my husband, just..." She could not bring herself to say "hired man."

The operator asked, "What's his name?"

"Wilson."

"Is that his last name?"

"No," Fabienne said. She could not remember his last name. She never thought of him as anything but Wilson.

HE STOOD OVER her. Wood chips fell from his mustache and eyebrows. He stoked the stove.

"How long you been like this."

"Dunno," she said.

"I couldn't get back," he said. "The roads was blocked."

"All right now," she said. She put her arms around his neck. "I missed you."

"You let the fire go out," he said. "What was you trying to do, kill yourself? You near froze to death."

"Under control," she said. It had been pleasurable to sink down into darkness, not scary at all.

He shoved plants out of the way and made a path where he walked her up and down, one hand around her waist as she shuffled her feet. Floating up near the ceiling, she looked down, mildly amused. The lame and the gimp. Or maybe the halt and the lame. Then he pushed her chair right up to the stove, took off her boots and wiggled her toes.

"You're tickling." Her foot jerked back.

"I'm sorry," he said. "I made a mistake, and I'm sorry."

"Nothing to be sorry for." She thought he meant abandoning her; but he'd come back, so it was all right.

"The truck slid just as I pulled in the garage."

"And hit my car?" she said. "Oh well."

Cat. Kittens. Warmth beamed toward her like heat from the sun. His big body, his breath. She wanted him to pick her up and carry her upstairs. She wanted his body on her like a human quilt.

"The cat finally moved them kittens," he said. "Right up by the door. I think they was froze before I squashed 'em."

She was so sleepy, she didn't care. She slept and slept, toasty warm from the fire Wilson fed, and she woke up when the Mama cat jumped on her lap. It was as if she'd woken from a pleasant dream into a bad one.

"What happened to the kittens?" she said.

"I cleaned 'em up." Wilson stood above a fry pan on the stove. Pieces of chicken sizzled in hot oil.

"What are you doing?"

"Cooking a chicken," he said.

"But we don't eat meat," she said.

"I do." He looked at her in a challenging way, a thumb hooked over his hip pocket, as he plunged a fork in the cooked flesh. Whatever tiny hole of interest she'd allowed herself to have for him closed tight. She threw off the comforter and got up to check her plants. The tender shoots had shriveled. The leaves felt like lettuce frozen in the crisper. She walked silently around the room, shoving the flats with her toe, picking up a pot, turning it around, looking at the frozen, wilted leaves that hung from the stalks. Dry and brittle, her plants were gone, a whole room of plants that she had diligently watered. She tried not to think of the danger she'd made herself vulnerable to on their behalf.

THE NEXT DAY a cold sun spread a seductive brightness across the sky, and even though the temperature had not lifted, Fabienne let herself be lured outside to survey the devastation. Wilson went toward the windmill. Carnivore! she thought, watching his humped back.

The eaves dripped icicles. Those near the front door joined at top and bottom like organ pipes in caves. Along the driveway, ice encased the hedge-apples. The weight of the ice pushed limbs apart. Near the greenhouse, ice sugared the red berries of a Pyracantha. The door of the greenhouse had frozen to the threshold. A stout branch broke as she wedged the door open.

Light filtered through the fabric ceiling, blotting the sun's glare. A half-used bale of straw blocked one aisle. The layer of straw on the bush beans had not crushed them, and she felt her spirits momentarily lift. The beans might have survived. She slid her hand through the foliage. Leaves crackled. Below ground, the fuzzy tap root snapped. Her forehead fell against a wooden tripod. What a job to clean all this up, replanting everything from scratch. She would have to be like Scarlett O'Hara and think of it tomorrow.

She closed the door behind her and walked toward the windmill, wanting to see how soon Wilson could get it turning. As she rounded the corner, she saw him picking up loose blades knifed into the soil.

Then she glanced down. By the cellar door, where the contents of the slop jar—feces and frozen piss—had been tossed, she saw a paste of bloody fur and flesh.

She caught her breath. "Wilson! Cover these kittens up with straw. It's disgusting."

Wilson straightened up and turned on her a face of such longing that, for a moment, she had no idea what was on his mind. Then she knew. It was somewhere warm. The Northwest. Maybe British Columbia.

He walked slowly towards her, his boots crunching the frozen furrows. In his glove, the windmill's metal blades fanned out like over-sized cards.

When he stood next to her, she felt again his size, not just his height but his mass, what a bulwark his body made against the cutting wind.

"Don't you never use that tone of voice with me again," he said. "It reminds me of how you was always bossy."

"But Wilson..."

"Not now. I'm trying to sort things out." He handed her the blades. "Take these on in the house. I'll count how many new ones you need."

"You" need. Not "we" need. And he was trying to sort something out. As long as they had known each other, she'd never once thought of him reasoning with himself. But of course he had thoughts. He'd just never shared them. It seemed odd that one could live with a man for seven years and still not know the interior of his mind, but that was what she liked about Wilson, his ability to work side by side without demanding conversation.

PAMPLEMOUSSE HAD STEPPED on a thorn. With the cat squirming on her lap, Fabienne plucked out the thorn and felt the cat's loose belly with its pink, distended nipples. When she lowered the cat to the floor, Pamplemousse continued to limp. A mother, wounded by the First Hand of Nature, what Fabienne thought of as the destructive hand.

She carried all the frozen flats from the house back to the greenhouse, every live plant gone. The house emptied, she made herself busy cleaning up the dirt. Still no electricity. All done by hand with broom and mop.

Out in the sugar bush, the syrup taps needed attending to. She knew the trees weighed on Wilson, but he refused to confront the damage until she had the house put right. He plowed the drive, and with a winch off the back of the 4x4, dragged fallen trees to the barn. He thawed the water pipes with a propane torch. The toilet flushed. The oil truck refilled the fuel tank. Finally, he drove to town and bought new blades for the windmill. When he returned, he went out to the barn, where she found him repairing the broken rope on the extension ladder.

"Are you still thinking about moving west?" she said.

He looked up. "I won't leave till I do right by you."

In his eyes, she saw something she had not seen before. Good-bye.

THE WEATHER WARMED and a mud-bog surrounded the house. Wilson cut his hair and shaved his mustache. His jaw was strong, his chin white compared to his leathery cheeks and nose, and he looked ten years younger. How handsome he was, now that he no longer hid behind that walrus mask; he seemed to know it, too.

"It's time I faced the sugar bush," he said.

"Time indeed," she said.

Head down, his hands fists, he started across half a mile of fallow land. She saw him from the kitchen window, the sun on his back, the shirt tail of his camouflage jacket covering the hip pockets of his overalls. In one hand he carried a red canister of gas and in the other, a big chain saw that dragged on the ground. She didn't see his goggles.

Maybe he had left them on the workbench. If she brought the goggles as a peace offering, it might thaw things out between them—the safety glasses for some conversation about whether he really meant to leave.

Hurrying across the field, she reached the border of the sugar bush and saw him a hundred yards east, heading into the bramble. An impenetrable thicket, like something from a fairy tale, blocked the trail. Empty syrup buckets lay crushed on the ground. Sap dripped from bore holes, trees pumping their lifeblood. Wilson stared at the damage, the saw hanging by his side. His work pants were rotten around the tops of his boots.

"Wilson!" she said.

"What?" He didn't turn around.

"We need to talk."

"Can't you see I'm busy?" His face flushed, and the tendons stood out on his neck.

She reached for his hand, but he pulled away. She grappled with his coat sleeves, aware of the chain saw by her leg, his finger on the trigger. His arm tensed.

"Stop it," she screamed.

"The storm could have killed you, Fabienne." He pulled the rip cord of the chain saw, and she jumped back. He threw the whir of teeth against the nearest fallen branch and struggled to push the blade through the pulpy fiber. The motor's roar stopped. Blade stuck.

He was angry at the trees, not her. What a relief.

"Wilson," she said.

He took his finger off the trigger and turned around, his face empty.

She said, "Why don't we sell the downed wood to a timber company?"

He shook his head, tears in his eyes. "It's all brash. The wind twisted them trees every which-away. Ain't worth a dime."

"Come in the house. We need to talk."

"Let me load them beans in the truck," he said. "You can move your whole operation west."

"Sell the farm?"

"There's other farms." He nodded toward the field. "With soil a whole lot better."

"You're sick of me," she said.

"I'm not sick of you at all. I…" He dropped his eyes to the saw.

She did not want him to complete his sentence. It scared her, what he might say. Instead, he followed her, docilely, back to the house. Slime popped on their boots. Final words would be spoken. Life was no longer a matter of mere survival. It was coming to a point where they would either reach a new understanding or part. She stopped at the border of the kitchen garden.

"Look at this." She squatted down and ran her fingers across the loam, turning the clods until she found a small unfolding leaf with a white tendril folded like a thumb across a palm. The Second Hand of Nature, the force that brought new life.

He shook his head and turned away. "Your fucking beans." His eyebrows drew together, and his jaw tightened. "You're the only stupid fool stayed put."

"Was it foolish?" Tears came into her eyes, and she stood.

"I'm going to Vancouver," he said.

"When?" she said.

"Tomorrow, next week. Soon, anyhow."

"What will you do?"

He looked at her. "Find some other rich lady to live off."

"Am I a rich lady?"

"Rich enough," he said. "What I make's spare change."

"Do you have enough saved?" She sounded so falsely supportive.

Wilson held up his hands. Frost had burned off the hair. "This is what I have. My hands."

She took his hand and led him inside. She had unrolled the rug and put the parlor furniture back in place: her grandmother's settee, the rocking chairs. With a stick, Wilson reached up to twirl open the cast-iron grate that let heat to the bedroom.

She said, "Can you really imagine yourself … well, with someone else?"

Avoiding her eyes, he snorted and shed his coat, hooking it behind the door. "I must be crazy."

"Why are you crazy?"

"Either you are or I am," he said. "I thought you wanted me to go."

"Why?"

"Them kittens."

"Kittens!" she said. "I forgot about the kittens. It was my fault anyway. I let them freeze. We should have taken the beans to town like you said."

Fabienne felt the garage cat Pamplemousse nuzzle her ankle. The cat had taken up residence inside the house, and she was consorting with the old tom.

Wilson sat down on the bottom stair and pried off his boots. He held up the sole. "This place is a peat bog. I don't know how you'll manage."

"I guess I'll find me another man," she said.

"Bull shit!" Wilson peeled off his socks and dropped the suspenders from his shoulders. "You're too old."

"I don't feel any older than seventeen."

"Ha!" he laughed. "You got a young body, but your face looks old." He pushed her toward the hall tree and squeezed her chin, forcing her to stare at the reflection of her crosshatched wrinkles.

"You're not even nice." She liked her face. "I didn't make you come back. There's nothing holding you here."

"I sure as hell didn't come back for the trees!" His pants fell around his feet. His long underwear was yellow with sweat, tops and bottoms.

"I turned on the water to the upstairs bath," he said. "I want a shower the worst way. After that, I think I'll take a snooze. Work can wait a day."

He didn't mention sex. Fabienne felt strange that they had slept in the same bed for so many years, and now he found her old.

She picked up the cat and ran her fingers through its belly fur. The cat pulled away. She turned the cat on its back. The nipples were pink and tender. Pamplemousse might be pregnant again.

At the head of the stairs, Wilson turned and called down. "If I was to stay, I'd want to take a month off and go down south in winter and lease out the sugar bush to hunters till I could get it cleared. I was talking to some guys on the crew said their club could make us a good offer."

Hunters on her land? Never.

The water came on with a gush. She put the cat down and stumbled up the stairs.

On the flowered linoleum of the upstairs hall, she saw his wet footprints, padding to the bedroom and back. Irritated, she took a towel from the linen closet and swished it across the floor with her foot. When it dried, it would be just as if he'd never moved in. Then she saw his long johns in a heap on the floor, and as she picked them up, the smell of earth and sweat and wood chips came rushing at her. Oh dear.

Pushing open the bathroom door, she inhaled the steam. Water pelted the plastic curtain. She undid a barrette, shed her clothes, and pulled back the curtain. Wilson stood, soaped up, his hair flattened.

With her hand on the small of his back, she pushed him forward. "Make room for me."

"Is that an order?" he asked.

"Please," she said.

He paused a minute, then she slapped him on the butt.

"Ow!" He ducked forward and straddled the drain, bracing his arms on the tub's curled rim. "What's this supposed to mean?"

"It means I want a shower, too."

He straightened up, and she realized she'd said the wrong thing. If they were going on together, it was not just Wilson who'd have to change. Slowly she wrapped her arms around his waist and slid her fingers through the hair on his belly. Her cheek pressed the skeleton of his back as she held on for dear life.

"It means I'm not opposed," she said.

"Good," he said. "Now we have something to talk about."

THE AMBASSADOR OF FOREIGN AFFAIRS

———○———

SUN FILTERED THROUGH the redwoods and fell on the hotel balcony where Kiyoshi Tanaka held a black mug in his palsied hands. Stretching his legs to rid them of cramps, he blew on his tea, sipped, and hoped the caffeine would carry him through dinner. Only three hours before, his plane had landed in San Francisco; he'd made it safely to the eastern shore of the Pacific, his first time in America, and tonight, he would meet the family of the groom. His daughter Mayumi, thirty-seven, shivered and buttoned her sweater.

"Up here in Marin County," she said, "it's always foggy."

"Is it warmer where you live?" he asked.

"Much," she said. "But in Sunnyvale, the sky's so brown you can hardly see across the bay."

Despite the fog, it was beautiful here in Mill Valley. Mist rose from the stream below. Gauzy shrouds wrapped the trees.

"Do you know what they are?" she said, nodding toward the forest.

"*Sempervirens,*" he said. Always living, but fossils, like himself. *Japonica* or *sequoia*? He put his cup on the table. After huffing on his lenses and wiping them with his handkerchief, he stood and peered into the dusk. *Sequoia*, no doubt. The trees grew admirably straight and joined at the sky. Birds twittered. He felt a haiku coming and patted his pocket. Regrettably, his notebook was in the room.

"I remember..." Mayumi whispered.

He knew what she was thinking: her mother's love of redwoods, the sacred *sugi* that sacrificed themselves to provide the beams of ancient temples. An old poem came to mind.

I see her only from afar
For she is lofty
Like the divine *sugi*
By the shrine at Miwa.
Many are the nights I sleep alone.

Resting against the balcony, he folded his arms. Caring for Chiyo had worn him out. Seven months had gone by since her death, and his enthusiasm for life had not returned. At Mayumi's urging, he had decided to extend his stay, but he could not stay forever.

Mayumi looked up at him. "You're not drinking your tea."

His tea was cool by now. "It tastes..."

"Stale?"

"A little." He leaned over for his cup.

"You don't have to drink it." She snatched the mug away and threw the contents over the rail.

This was an unfamiliar tone.

"The tea was only slightly bitter," he said.

"No, no, no. Very bitter." Mayumi dumped out her own cup, doubled over, and began rocking. Through hair hanging around her face, he saw her wipe her eyes. "I do not have to drink the bitter cup!" she said. "No one can make me."

"No one is forcing you to marry."

"Immigration is."

Not another disrupted engagement! One had been enough. He handed her a folded handkerchief. "Here once again at the *basho* tree, my sleeves are soaked with tears."

She sniffed a laugh. "So do you think the frog should leap in the pond again?" she said.

"That depends."

"Father, ever the diplomat."

"He is a *gaijin*," he said, "but not all of them are boorish."

"If I want to marry, this is my last chance."

"*So desu*," he said.

Like hulls of rice in a burlap sack, weariness shifted through Tanaka's body. During his wife's long illness, he had begun seeking truths in the poems he had memorized as a young man. Basho wrote that it was rare for anyone to reach the age of seventy. The period when mind and body truly flourished was not much more than twenty years. In anticipation of his flight to California, Tanaka had reread the poet's great works, "Account of a Weather-Beaten Skeleton" and "The Narrow Road to Oku," preparing himself for this separation from the one person who meant most to him. His wife was gone. Mayumi was all he had left.

"What should I do?" she said.

"You came here to live with him."

"Live, yes."

"But not marry."

"He is weak."

"*So desu*," he said.

"I need someone solid." She looked up, eyes glittering. "A rock."

He waited. Maybe she had decided to come back to Japan. But what would be her future: her old job at Berlitz, dinner with her father, watching her girlfriends raise their children? His life was nearing its end, but there was much she had left to experience.

Sighing, Mayumi stood. "We should go. Ian's mother bought tickets to this dinner-dance. 'Real America,' she calls it."

Tanaka picked up the chairs. "First, the rock must wash his hands."

THE AMERICAN LEGION Log Cabin Post 179 met in a large, two-story building made from pine trees notched at the ends. Behind the log building, smoke, infused with the smell of fatty pork, turned the sky an eerie white.

Hesitating to cross the parking lot, Tanaka asked, "Is the building on fire?"

Mayumi laughed. "No. It's a barbecue."

Barbecue. His nose tingled.

Mayumi flipped open her cell phone. "Ian, where in hell are you?"

Mayumi was angry. That was a bad sign. If she did not treat her fiancé well, he might walk away. Her first fiancé, brother of Mayumi's best friend, had not been patient with the outbursts, and shortly after Tanaka had put down a deposit on the wedding-hotel, the groom's mother had called to "discuss the future." She had witnessed too many of Mayumi's tantrums.

Mayumi had stayed in her room for months, claiming she would never fall in love again. Young people! This word "love"—what did it mean? His circumstances had been different, a matter of survival after the war. For his wife Chiyo, a widow four years his senior, marriage had been a chance to start over. Many decisions in life came from opportunities that landed in your lap and not from choice at all.

As they approached the building, he looked through the downstairs windows into a noisy, crowded tavern.

"Don't worry," Mayumi said. "We're going upstairs."

"Fine," he said, looking up at a balcony. He heard music.

The stairs were steep. Halfway up he paused to catch his breath.

"Are you okay?" Mayumi said.

"*Daijyobu*," he said, though in truth, the smoke hurt his lungs.

Mayumi flipped open her cell phone. "Come help my dad."

He put up a hand. "*Iranai*." He did not want to show weakness before his son-in-law. There were only ten more steps.

Shortly before her mother's death, Mayumi had brought Ian to the apartment. He was one of her "tutees," Mayumi said, and she wanted him to practice his Japanese. For the occasion, Tanaka had dressed Chiyo in a silk bathrobe and brought her to the living room. To keep her bones from coming through her flesh, he put two cushions on the floor. Ian arrived, a slight young man: round-eyed, pink-cheeked. Polite, Tanaka thought, but unremarkable.

When they departed, Chiyo said, "He is more than her student."

Tanaka said he was too young. "They will learn to care for each other," Chiyo said, sighing with relief as he placed her down on the futon. "We did."

UPSTAIRS, TANAKA STOOD at the door. Men shouted. Chairs screeched. It was like the Tokyo Fish Market. On the stage, three cowboys with guitars stood at microphones. A man played a violin, but badly, bowing across several strings at once. Tanaka saw a hundred metal tables with folding chairs and a U-shaped space near the stage for dancers. No one had started yet. People were eating.

Ian came toward them, his smile a reflex, like the kick after a doctor's knee-tap, and Tanaka remembered that Americans always smiled, even for no reason. Tanaka bowed.

"You made it," Ian said, clasping Tanaka's hand in both of his. "Great to see you again."

Tanaka had forgotten Ian's curly hair. The boy looked like a politician. So undignified: men with permanents.

"Come on," Ian said, turning back the way he'd come. "My mom is dying to meet you."

"*Ashi de matoi*," Mayumi muttered.

A drag? Ian's mother? This was disrespectful.

Ian took her hand and smiled. "I missed you," he said.

Mayumi turned her cheek and he kissed it.

They were headed for a table near the stage, where Tanaka saw an attractive woman with hair like yellow cotton-candy. She was seated and staring at him.

"That's my mom," Ian said. "She's had ants in her pants all day."

Tanaka thought of his *haiku* teacher, Yoko Sugawa, who taught that an ant was like Basho's frog. Ten poets looking at the same ant would write ten different poems. In seventeen syllables, he had described his ant, an exoskeleton in three parts—the head, thorax, and abdomen. When he had read his poem, Mrs. Sugawa sat in silence. Then, finally, she said, "Let us look not *at* our ants but rather into them. If we pay attention, surely the ant will speak to us." So far, his ant had remained silent.

Ian's mother scooted back from the table and stood, hands on hips. Her smile snapped into place. Even a small ant, like the sugar ants that found their way to his fourth floor walk-up, could not have managed to crawl up the leg of her jeans. She wore a white, long-sleeved shirt. Two pointy cones that looked like water-cooler cups stood out from her chest. Ian introduced them. His mother's name was Carol.

Tanaka bowed.

"Get outta here!" Ian's mother grabbed his hand. "Mayumi, you didn't tell us your father was so *galant*."

There were four places at the table. She pulled her chair around to his side and, once seated, he felt her thigh press his leg.

"By the end of the weekend," she said, "we're going to be bosom buddies."

Bosom, he thought, nearly breathless, but managed to gasp out the phrase he had rehearsed. "This is a momentous occasion for both our families."

"Darn right!" she said. "I'm so tickled Ian met a sweet little girl like Mayumi."

"She is woman," Tanaka said, a woman well beyond marriageable age, he could have added, but didn't. At home, thirty-seven was "old Christmas cake."

"Well, she looks like a girl to me," Carol said. "How old are you, honey? Ian's such a gentleman. He won't say."

"That is private information," Mayumi said. "I wish you would not keep asking."

Carol held up her hands. "Hey, hey! No offense."

Ian's lips stretched sideways like large rubber bands, and when he looked down, his chin disappeared inside the collar of his shirt.

Poor boy. Tanaka wondered if he should do something.

Ian ran his fingers through his hair. "I didn't realize you spoke English, sir."

"Oh, yes," Carol said. "Your English is perfect."

"My written English is better than my spoken," he said.

"He worked in the Ministry of Foreign Affairs," Mayumi said.

"That sounds like our State Department!" Carol clapped her hands. "We'll have to call you Mr. Ambassador, the Ambassador of Foreign Affairs."

"But I was only a—"

Don't swallow the worm, Mayumi said in Japanese. He looked at her, frowned, and cocked his head. She looked back, thin-lipped. He was only going to explain that he was a low-level bureaucrat, stuck translating agricultural treaties.

"Did you bring a tuxedo?" Carol said.

Tanaka nodded.

"Good," Carol said, "because you're mine now, and I get to show you off."

"How do you mean?" Tanaka said.

"You're a status symbol," Mayumi said. "A trophy."

"My father is rich," Ian said.

"That's putting it mildly," Carol said. "He's filthy rich. And, he ran off with my best friend. They bought this place up at Sea Ranch and left me with a crappy, three-bedroom condo in Mill Valley."

Tanaka thought about the word "valley." It was hard to pronounce. Double "els" had always given him problems. He wanted to thank her for placing him near the *Sempervirens sequoia*. The mist, the creek, everything was wonderful, and tomorrow, he would wake up and look at the view with the benefit of dawn.

"I am enjoying Mill...the hotel you arranged," he said. "The bed seems very comfortable."

"Well, good," Carol said. "Make me an offer I can't refuse."

An offer? What sort of offer? Tanaka looked at Mayumi. She shrugged and rolled her eyes.

Two men in black leather jackets took a table by the dance floor. One had a long, white braid and a mustache like a Chinese emperor. The man glanced over.

Carol jerked a thumb at them. "That's my old beau," she said. "I seem to have a way of picking them." The old boyfriend folded his arms and turned his back.

"Let's annoy him." Carol put two fingers in her mouth and whistled.

A heavy woman in a stained apron came to the table, looking at them with a smirk. "Had a few, Carol?"

"We'll take the barnyard platter." Carol held up four fingers. "And bring some brewskies."

"I didn't even have a chance to look at the menu," Mayumi said.

"The barnyard's what everyone's having," Carol said. "This here's a fundraiser they do once a year. The vets set up smokers out back, and it's the best damn barbecue you'll ever eat."

"Vets?" Tanaka said, looking from Ian to Carol.

"War veterans," Carol said. "But don't worry. You're safe— unless you're a *kamikaze* pilot. You're not, are you?"

"I was fourteen when the war ended," Tanaka said. "My first job was working for the Army of Occupation."

"What is this 'barnyard platter?'" Mayumi said.

"You're not a vegetarian, are you?" Carol said. "If so, there's corn on the cob."

"I hope it's not spicy." Mayumi looked at Ian.

"Not too," he said. "Oh, and Mr. Tanaka, with barbecue, it's polite to eat with your fingers."

"Thank you for explaining," Tanaka said. He had never heard of anyone, with the possible exception of Koreans and Africans, eating meat with their fingers.

Ian leaned over. "Did Mayumi tell you about my mom?"

"Tell him what about your mom?" Carol said.

"That you're a party animal," Ian said, looking at her.

Party animal. Tanaka frowned. Was this related to "barnyard?"

"What you see is what you get," Ian said.

"She is out of control," Mayumi muttered under her breath in Japanese.

"I believe the expression is 'free spirit,'" Tanaka said. "Is that correct?"

Carol shrugged as if trying on new clothing. "I'll take that as a compliment."

Ian laughed. "Truly, you are a diplomat."

Carol gestured toward the stage. "We're being watched."

A lone cowboy sat on a stool. He was chewing a toothpick.

Tanaka straightened himself and picked up his beer. A full liter. "What time must I be ready for the wedding?"

"Noon," Ian said.

"I am curious to see the ceremony."

"It'll be outdoors," Ian said. "All our friends are coming." He took Mayumi's hand and gazed at her with a look of longing. "I wish your mother could have lived to share our joy."

Speaking Japanese, Mayumi said, "He doesn't know this is inauspicious."

"Poor lady," Carol said. "Did she suffer at the end?"

Tanaka looked at the ceiling. There were several dark stains, as if a bottle had exploded, and smoke rings around the circular vents.

"I understand. It hurts right here." Carol thumped her chest. "You Japanese hold everything inside. Sometimes, it's better to let it all hang out." She shook her hands as if they were limp rags.

"Mom," Ian said, "I don't think this is something they want to discuss. Besides, dinner's here."

Carol moved the saltshakers. A stack of paper plates, a pile of rolled-up napkins, and a metal platter landed on the tabletop. Tanaka stared at the wings and haunches, but watched what Ian's mother did; and when she reached with her fingers for a quarter chicken—no hot towels to clean hands, no trips to the washroom—he grabbed a steak as big as his shoe. At home, a steak this size would feed a sumo wrestler. However, he was in America. He bit off a corner, then saw Ian's mouth gape open.

Mayumi giggled behind her hand. "You should use a knife and fork."

He looked at the napkins. Rolled inside, the plastic silverware was white. He hadn't seen it. Tanaka put the steak down and wiped his fingers. His lips burned. The sauce must contain hot pepper. He gulped beer, but that made the burning worse. He wiped his lips, cleared his throat, and pulled at the knot of his necktie. There was no food in Japan, not even pure *wasabi* squeezed from a tube, that could burn a hole in your tongue this fast.

The man Carol said was watching them approached the table. He removed his hat. "I just came over to say '*Kon'nichi wa*' and '*Sayonara*.'"

Tanaka stood and bowed. "Good evening." He wondered why the man was wishing him "good afternoon" and "goodbye." Strange *gaijin*, Tanaka thought, sitting down. What an experience this was!

Carol finished her beer, looked at the stage, and, catching the eye of the lead singer, jerked her thumb toward the dance floor. "Let's get the party started."

"I don't feel like dancing," Ian said.

"If you dance," Carol said, "I'll limit myself to one glass of champagne at the wedding."

"Okay, one dance, Mom," Ian said. "Then we're going. You've had too much to drink."

"One beer?" she said.

"And three bourbon sours while we waited."

"Come on, Mayumi," Carol said. "Don't be a stick in the mud. Dance with the Ambassador."

Tanaka had seen his daughter throw a plate across the room. She looked as if she were about to do that now. "It's only a cheap one," she had reassured her mother, who had risen up on an elbow to see what shattered. Mayumi, as reliable as a hand-wound clock, was also sprung-tight. An invitation to a baby shower had triggered her outburst. One by one, her friends had married, and when babies arrived, they could no longer go out with her. Before she'd met Ian, Mayumi had spent most evenings at home. Tanaka stood and offered his hand.

Mayumi started to refuse, then looked at Ian.

He had a pleading look in his eyes.

"Oh, all right," she said; and then in Japanese, "I'm just

humoring him."

"Small gesture, large kindness," Tanaka said.

Other women scooted their chairs out, wiped their hands, and pushed the piles of bones away. A song began. It was one he recognized: "The Tennessee Waltz." Tanaka had learned ballroom dance as part of his Ministry training and enjoyed the waltz. Mayumi had never learned, and she moved like a Bunraki puppet, hands limp, arms like wooden sticks. The only time he'd ever seen her dance was in her bedroom; her mother had been in the hospital to have a lump removed. Mayumi had turned up the phonograph's volume and pumped her arms until her eyes rolled and she fell on the floor, exhausted. It looked like a seizure, but when Tanaka knelt and brushed back her bangs, she smiled. "That felt good."

He did not understand why she had these periodic explosions. Her mother never had them. America might be a better fit. When the music stopped, Tanaka bowed and walked his daughter to the table. He tucked a napkin in his shirt and fell to the task of scraping sauce off the steak. His top denture had come loose. The adhesive was back in his suitcase, and he pressed his thumb against his plate, trying to get it to reattach.

Ian, holding a chicken drumstick and pointing at the food, asked a busboy to "box up a doggy bag." Tanaka knew about this tradition. In the years he worked at the Ministry's Tokyo office, he had often played host to delegations of chicken farmers, and they never left food on their plates. The busboy returned with the leftovers.

The lights dimmed. A mirrored globe began to revolve and throw sparkles. "Let's pick up the pace," the lead singer said. "This next one's for all you Two-Steppers." The band began to play. The tempo was fast. Ian's mother went over to the man on the stool, and after a brief conversation, he joined her on the dance floor. Catching her hand, he dipped and swung her around. As Tanaka watched her footwork, he decided that the dance steps were not a fox trot, but closer to a cha-cha-cha. Every few steps, she took a little hop and swung around, guided by her partner, who flung her away from him, then yanked her back so that she curled into his arm. He was not exerting himself, and his posture was not the normal dance position: erect. When he expected to receive her, he curved his back slightly at the shoulders, and when he flung her away, he straightened up, the heel of his cowboy boot coming down on the floor, as if to say, There! Take that!

Under the table, Tanaka's feet began to move. Carol was an excellent dancer; she knew how to follow a man's lead. The band changed tempo. A waltz again. He stood, determined to cut in.

Ian intercepted him. "I'm sorry, Mr. Tanaka. This is dragging on. We'll get you home."

"It is a good party," he said.

"I'm tired," Mayumi said. "Ian, call your mother."

Tanaka frowned. That tone in his daughter's voice was getting under his skin. He wanted to dance.

OUTSIDE IN THE parking lot, the full moon cast shadows.

"Are you all right to drive?" Ian asked his mother.

"Fine," she said. "You take Mayumi and the Ambassador back to the hotel."

Tanaka wished Carol a good night's sleep and bowed "good night" to her dance partner. The two headed toward a black, Ford F250 truck. Ian ran across the gravel and demanded to know where she was going. Tanaka stood by his daughter's Camry. The mother, he gathered, was arguing that they might go to another place and dance.

"Drive your own car, then," Ian said.

"I'll come back for it," Carol said.

Mayumi called across the parking lot. "Ian, my father is tired."

That was true. Tanaka got in the back seat, the leather sighing beneath him. Reaching in his pocket for his pill-box, his hands shook. He pried the top off and put the pills in his mouth, one at a time, then spread his fingers and hoped to see the shaking stop. Across the top of his skull, he felt a prickling sensation. Until just this instant, he hadn't thought about his frailty or whether there was any point to life. The evening had been remarkable.

"Ian!" Mayumi shouted. "I'm leaving." She stood by the open passenger door, then slammed it, and stomped toward the driver's side.

Ian ran to the car, jumped in, and revved the engine.

"Get in!" Ian's voice changed octaves.

Mayumi slid into the front seat and closed the door.

Roaring out of the parking lot, Ian followed the truck. "Write down that license number!"

"The hotel's the other way," Mayumi said.

"I have to follow them," Ian said.

"Turn around. Now, Ian, before I get angry."

"Just write down that license."

"The truck is making too much dust," Mayumi said.

Tanaka felt a bump and heard the hum of tires. When the Camry emerged from the cloud, he saw they were on a winding, mountain road.

"Did you get it?" Ian screamed.

"Get what?" Mayumi said. "I couldn't see anything."

"I think they went the other way," Tanaka said.

Ian turned into a driveway. "I'll drop you off and go find her." Then, looking in the rear view mirror, he said, "Do you need anything, Tanaka-*san*?"

Tanaka could not avoid the frightened eyes that sought his understanding. His stomach growled.

"*Udon*," he said.

"Why don't you give it up?" Mayumi said.

"That guy could be a serial killer," Ian said.

"The guy's in more danger than your mother," Mayumi said. "She's just making a fool of herself."

No, Tanaka thought. She was bringing shame on the family. Only a man could understand the power a woman had to rob him of dignity.

AT THE HOTEL Tanaka saw that someone had been in his room. The lights were dim and on the white quilt sat a small square of dark chocolate. Grateful, he unwrapped the foil and felt the chocolate melt on his tongue. The sweetness lasted through his shower. He toweled dry, put on pajamas, and after filling a water glass, removed his teeth. He was about to turn out the light when he heard a drawer slam. It was from Mayumi's room. A second slam shook his mirror.

He sat on the bed, his feet dangling above the rug. He listened. Silence. He slid off the bed and into his slippers, padding around. He rubbed his chin. There was a mole. From it, long hairs grew. He had depended on his wife to snip the strands with her manicure scissors. He hoped his daughter might be willing to do it, but now he was afraid to ask. She needed to calm down.

He put on a robe and then remembered his dentures. Outside Mayumi's door he gave three brisk raps.

She looked out. "Oh, it's you."

"May I come in?"

She stood aside. "I'll make tea."

"Black will keep me awake."

"I have *o-cha*."

At a double sink by the closet, he saw a coffee maker; she poured in water, and he heard the water hiss and drip. Suitcases stood beside the dresser. Ian's clothes lay heaped on the bed. Sitting on one of two chairs by the door, Tanaka rested his elbow on the table.

"When do you expect him back?" Tanaka said.

"Soon," she said.

"What will you do then?"

"Leave." Mayumi carried over two cups and sat down.

"Where will you go?"

"The hotel's not full. I have money."

"Tomorrow is your wedding."

"He can have it without me."

Tanaka brought the cup to his lips. In the steam, he could smell a hint of grass. This was the way Chiyo would have prepared it.

Nodding to his tea he said, "A man and a woman need each other in many small ways."

"I cannot go through with the wedding," she said. "I'm too upset."

Tanaka looked into his tea cup. Sediment had escaped the bag and collected in the bottom.

"If you do not marry him, you will bring dishonor on your family."

"What family?" she snorted.

"Me," he said.

"I thought you would be happy."

"I will be, if you are content."

"I want to come home. I miss my country."

"When you came here, did you love him?"

"After mother's death, I would have done anything to leave that apartment."

"Why?" he said.

"It was dark and sad."

"Did you love him when you accepted his proposal?"

"I guess you could say, I hoped I could."

"I wondered about the age difference."

"He doesn't know my age."

"How old does he think you are?"

"Twenty-nine."

"How fast the clock turns back."

Mayumi shrugged. "I don't think he would care."

"Then what is the problem?"

"His mother."

"She is busy with her own life," Tanaka said. "She will not interfere." He put his cup down, then turned, drew back the curtain, and saw the Camry pull into an empty space. He watched Ian open the trunk and take something out.

"He can't stand up to her," Mayumi said.

Tanaka dropped the curtain. "This is women's business." Women's business was generally ill conceived and petty, and he had no patience for the minor hurts and intrigues of women who did not like their husbands' mothers.

A key turned in the lock.

"Ian!" Mayumi stood and threw her arms around him.

So much for not loving him. Mayumi looked happy, Ian pleased. What was love but a smile at the end of the day? It was simple.

"Hi, you two," Ian said, placing three white bags on the table. He unpacked wax containers of soup and handed out chopsticks. "I drove down the hill to a Japanese place. They were closing, but I pounded on the door and convinced them to give me some *udon*."

"Did you find her?" Mayumi said.

"She wasn't in the usual places," Ian said.

"The slut," Mayumi said in Japanese.

This had to stop, Tanaka thought. His daughter's displays of temper were a disgrace. He was fed up. *"Sonna koto iwanai de kure. Kotchi made ki ga makeru ja nai ka."*

Mayumi blinked as if she'd been slapped. Tears welled in her eyes. She looked at him.

He shifted his eyes to the bed. Move, he thought, and make room for your husband. To make sure she understood that she was not to use that tone of voice again, added, *"So darou."*

"So it is," Ian nodded, "but the other thing you said, I didn't get."

"He was reminding me to have better manners," Mayumi said, moving to the bed. "Please. Take my chair. You have had a stressful day."

She looked at Tanaka.

He nodded.

"Thanks, honey," Ian said. "You didn't tell me your father was such a kind man."

Tanaka watched his future son-in-law. Ian dipped chopsticks into his *udon*. The boy should lower his voice, not let it change register. He could turn his head and hide his feelings of upset, even if he could not make them go away. Mayumi must show respect for her husband.

Ian bit the noodle in half.

"Do it like this," Tanaka said in a gravelly voice, pulling the worm of a noodle through his lips. "*Tsu-rup, tsu-rup.* That is the verb for eating noodles."

Trying to recall a Basho poem, he sucked another long one and moved his feet so that the three sets of knees touched.

The poem came to him. For Ian's benefit, he translated.

"In this world of ours, we eat only to cast out, sleep only to wake, and what comes after is simply to die at last."

He licked his lips. The noodles tasted good.

WEEKEND IN BALTIMORE

———○———

BEFORE BALTIMORE, LIFE looked like it might be heading someplace good. He was done with school. Had a decent job. Friends. Then, Friday night came. Fog drifted down the harbor district's bumpy streets. He and his buddies walked three abreast, just looking to fill the time, maybe find some women. At the club, a bouncer blocked the door with his arm. Terrell Duncan handed over his ID and looked at the mess of twenties in his wallet. Should have brought some ones. The bouncer waved his buddies through, but Terrell hung back, looking for women of color. None on the dance floor. None at the tables. Maybe he should wait in the car. Sean, his former college roomie, had disappeared into the mosh pit. Nathan had the keys. Terrell put away his license. He hadn't wanted to come out tonight, leastways here, and the prickly feeling at the back of his neck wouldn't go away. He was just being paranoid. Nothing bad was going to happen—his buddies would look out for him—and so, he went in.

On a platform near the entrance stood a wooden barrel with a galvanized washtub. Iced beer. A blonde in a leopard-skin bikini popped the caps off Millers and Heinekens. From sticking her hands in the washtub, her fingers had shriveled. He couldn't pull his eyes away from her breasts. No blue veins. Probably implants. He looked around for a table.

"Hey, what about your drink?" she said.

"I'm not all that thirsty."

"There's a one drink minimum." The blonde wore a black, velvet baseball hat with rhinestones that spelled out her name in cursive. *Misty.* Dropping her chin, Misty batted her long eyelashes and fake-smiled.

"It's not necessary to flirt," Terrell said. "You're just demeaning yourself."

"Don't be fresh."

"I'm not being fresh," he said.

"Yes, you are."

He could hardly hear her above the din. "Let me have a Heineken."

"That'll be ten bucks," she said.

"Ten buck beer?"

"You got it."

"What a rip!" There wasn't even live music, just some rockabilly crap.

She leaned back and stretched, pooching out her belly. Her navel looked like a wad of old gum. He took out a twenty. She reached in her canvas apron and gave him two fives back, then held out her palm.

"I don't have any ones," he said.

Later, in jail, he remembered the hard look she gave him; but right then, he didn't care. Money was money, to him as much as anyone else. Too bad for her.

Terrell brushed fries from a table and hunkered down to nurse his beer. A DJ behind a soundboard spun tunes. Misty, in her sparkly baseball cap and skimpy swimsuit, grabbed folks as they came through the door. What a job. Every day, dressing up in a leopard-skin bikini. One step up from prostitution, not that he didn't feel prostituted in his current job. The low pay sucked. Fax and file. That's all he ever did. A think tank, supposedly, although nothing he did for the Urban Institute required a modicum of intelligence. He had a BA, *summa cum laude*, and his brain was rotting.

He felt a hand on his shoulder: His buddy Sean grinned down

at him. Terrell motioned to the empty chairs at the next table. Sean pulled one over and sat backwards on it. His best friend was always doing things backwards. The backwards baseball-cap thing. Putting his socks on inside out. Even sweaters, so the label showed. Sean had duded himself up in khakis, a long-sleeved shirt, and tie. And for what? This place was a dive. Terrell looked down at his XXL pink, Vassar sweatshirt. He had wanted something comfortable, not one of the suits he wore to work, and now, he was wishing they'd gone to one of the college bars out in College Park. Would have, if Sean hadn't been desperate to get away from campus. Nathan, loosening his tie, came toward them. "The women are Barbies," he shouted.

"I hate their stupid hair." Sean made a barking motion with his hand. "They should wear dog collars."

Terrell looked at the women. Teased hair. Like Italian girls from the Jersey Shore. He laughed and shook his head. It took all kinds. Nathan waggled his eyebrows in the direction of the barmaid.

Sean looked at Terrell. "Can you front me some cash?"

"Forget to stop by the ATM?" Terrell said.

"Yeah."

Terrell pulled out another twenty.

His eyes ached and he rubbed them. Too much time standing at the copier, a flash of light blinding him every few seconds. Maybe he should go back to school. It wouldn't be out of the question to start a master's. Maybe sociology or psych.

Sean put down two Millers. Nathan took one. Sean, the other.

"Guess I don't get change," Terrell said.

Nathan pulled out a ten.

"I'll pay you back." Sean sat.

"Sure you will."

"What's that supposed to mean?"

"Nothing. Come on." Terrell planted his elbow and reached for Sean's hand. Sean squared off. Terrell felt the pressure of Sean's fingers against his. He gave a little ground. His part-time job, personal trainer, was a lot more fun than his day job; but his mom, an actuary for Met Life, kept saying he should go for a PhD and not waste his math ability. Maybe so. He ratcheted Sean's hand back to vertical. The length of his forearm gave him the advantage. He slammed Sean's hand onto the table.

Sean flexed his fingers. "This is a stupid way to spend Friday night."

"There's no one for me here," Terrell said.

"How about Georgetown?" Sean said.

"A blues club would suit me better."

"The review made this place sound a lot cooler than it is," Sean said.

Standing, Terrell saw Misty, the barmaid in the leopard-skin bikini, jerking a thumb for him to come over. Terrell pointed at his chest. She nodded. Yes, him. He made his way to the platform where she stood, hands on hips, the way his mom did, ready to come down on him about an unmade bed. Misty looked foolish there on her platform, lip-syncing words he couldn't hear; he was about to turn away. From the wads of bills crumpled in her canvas apron, she dug one out and held it up. Somehow, he knew she was trying to say, "You gave me this!"

He put his hand to his ear. "I can't hear you."

Her lips moved again.

"You gave me a twenty," she said.

"Yeah, so?" he shouted. That's all he'd had in his wallet. He walked around to the side of the platform and placed one foot on it. She reached over her head and pulled a dangling rope. A spinning blue light came on and a disembodied voice said, "Blue light at station six." Dancers stopped moving.

Terrell took his foot down. "What's the problem?"

"It's money out of my paycheck," Misty said.

Two beefy guys with bulging knit shirts grabbed Terrell's arms. A man in a green blazer appeared. He had a walkie-talkie pinned to his shirt. He pressed a button and opened a corner of his mouth. "Call me a wagon."

"What is going on?" Terrell said.

Hands vise-gripped his arms, right above the elbows. Bouncers led him past the restrooms into the kitchen, where he exchanged a glance with a Mexican busboy heaving a plastic tub of dishes onto the counter. Behind him, he heard Sean. "Hey, where are you taking him?" The music started up. A door opened to the alley. Outside, dumpsters overflowed. Terrell smelled garbage. Parked in the glow of amber lights, a white panel truck idled. The paddy wagon looked like a bread van—no city insignia, no flashing light. Maybe this was some kind of kidnap situation. But then Terrell saw the uniforms: two cops, one a veteran with a gruff voice, and the other a young, light-skinned brother.

"There's been a misunderstanding," Terrell said.

"You can't arrest him for no reason," Nathan screamed.

The light-skinned cop grabbed Nathan's elbow and escorted him across the street. In college, Nathan had been an introvert. No surprise he didn't know how to handle the situation. "Relax," Terrell called. "I'll get this straightened out."

Sean pushed through the bouncers. "What's going on?"

The bouncers released Terrell and dragged Sean across the street. "Why don't you go find some real criminals?" Sean shouted, his feet windmilling.

"Stay cool, Man," Terrell said. He felt a tic at the corner of his eye, and when he started to press it, the white cop grabbed his arm.

Put down on the sidewalk opposite, Sean cupped his hands. "Remember Rodney King. Don't worry, Buddy. You didn't do anything."

"I know," Terrell said.

The white cop shouted, "Shut the fuck up, or we'll throw you in the wagon."

Across the street, Nathan paced up and down, tearing his hair. Terrell had thought that was just an expression, but he saw, now, that people really did it. Fists clenched, Sean looked like a bull about to charge. It was pretty funny watching the two of them freak out, because just as soon as he explained, this bullshit would all be over. Then Terrell felt the white cop's hand against the middle of his chest and his back against the wagon.

"Let's see some ID."

Terrell pulled out his driver's license and slid his college ID toward the man.

"Put it away," the cop said.

"But I just graduated from Vassar. Jane Fonda went there. Jackie Kennedy. Meryl Streep."

The cop looked at him for the first time. "Are you some kind of queer?"

"Are you some kind of homophobe?" Terrell said. "No, it's an Ivy League institution. One of the Seven Sisters. In Poughkeepsie."

The man looked at him for a minute. No smile associated with that stare. Then, he wrote down Terrell's drivers-license number and pushed his shoulder, spinning him around. Metal slid around Terrell's wrists and the latch clicked, pinching his skin.

"Watch him," the policeman said.

Terrell laughed. "Where am I going?"

"Other guys have tried to run away," the light-skinned brother said.

Terrell gave the brother a look. Surely, the guy could tell what kind of person he was—a college graduate, not some criminal scum. When he started to explain, his mouth went dry. They stood in silence by the van.

When the other policeman came back, Terrell expected to see the bar girl with him, bar *woman* he would have said at school, where it was politically incorrect to call a female over the age of sixteen a girl. The cop was alone. He opened the wagon's double doors and made Terrell take a big step up. The door slammed. The air inside smelled of urine, smoke, and vomit. The engine revved and the wagon bumped over potholes.

AT THE STATION Terrell found himself inside a small booking area, the yellow walls smudged from the shoulders and hips of criminals. He wasn't one. They'd see that. Behind the counter, a weary policeman stood doing paperwork. "Sit down," he said, nodding toward the room's single chair. Okay, the policeman was busy. Terrell just had to be patient. In a couple minutes, he could explain. An old schoolroom clock had a red second-hand. Terrell watched it. His pulse beat twice for each tick. His heart thought he was running; yet, here he sat—stock-still. It was 12:20 A.M. and he felt irritated because he would only have a few hours of sleep. Tomorrow, Saturday, his first client, Bill Thomas, a wimpy little accountant at the general accounting office, would arrive at five of 10. He always wanted his money's worth. At Gold's Gym, when you were their "Man," you had to be on time, or they would hire another trainer. Sean better be raising hell with the bar's management and getting this nonsense dismissed.

The cop who'd brought him in returned. "Come with me."

Terrell followed him to a small room where coffee cups had left ghost rings on the table. The cop left. Carrying a sheaf of paper, a policewoman paused by the door. "First time here?"

"Yeah." Like, welcome to the hotel.

"You're not one of the regulars," the policewoman said.

"Obviously not."

She nodded and walked away. Just making conversation.

A moment later, the cop who had put him in the van returned. Big gut and capillaries on his cheeks. If he had to chase down a real criminal, he'd be in trouble.

"You should reduce the alcohol consumption," Terrell said.

The cop frowned, his mouth fixed. He swallowed a bee-bee of saliva.

"Could you loosen my cuffs?" Terrell said.

The cop looked over Terrell's shoulder. "Your cuffs are plenty loose." He put a clipboard in front of Terrell's face. Snapped under the clip was the funny money. Someone had photocopied the corners of a twenty and taped them over the ones of a dollar bill.

"So, where'd you get it?" the cop said.

"It's not mine."

The policeman snapped his ballpoint. "Would you care to make a statement?"

"I bought a beer at 10:30," Terrell said. "There were three hundred people in the bar. That bill didn't come from me."

The policeman pulled a dirty phone from a nook in the wall. "I'm calling Secret Service."

Terrell laughed. "Let them come."

The policeman cupped his hand over the receiver and mumbled. Pretending to talk. The guy was so obvious.

The receiver slammed down. "They'll be here by morning," the policeman said.

"The sooner the better, Barney Fife."

"Okay, smart ass," the cop said. "From here on out, you may refer to me as the 'arresting officer.'"

"Am I being arrested?" Terrell said.

"What do you think?" the cop said. "Stand up." Back in the booking room, he unlocked the cuffs. "Take off all your personal items—coins, shoelaces, belt, watch, and rings. Put them here." He patted the counter. "Cell phone, too."

Terrell worked his Vassar ring over his knuckle. The officer pointed to the silver cross with the clasped hands of Jesus. A priest had persuaded his mother, a high-church Episcopalian, to enroll him in Stepanic High School where Jon Voight and Alan Alda had gone; and when Terrell had converted to Catholicism, Father Durocher had blessed the cross and said, from then on, Jesus would be his protector. Since the age of thirteen Terrell had never removed the cross, not even to shower. He fiddled with the clasp.

"Hurry up," the cop said.

"What am I going to do, hang myself?" Terrell said.

"Give it here." The officer held out his hand, then pawed the things into a plastic bag and tossed the bag on a table. On the other side of the booking counter, a door hissed open. The Arresting Officer motioned Terrell towards an old black man in a green uniform. As Terrell approached, the man spun around and headed down a hall that was confined, hot, and damp, like the YMCA in White Plains where Terrell had learned to swim. The door behind him slammed.

His ears plugged up, and he fought the urge to claw toward fresh air. All he had to do was stay calm till Sean showed up.

In a small room with a counter, the janitor flipped open a stamp pad. "Give me your hand."

Terrell let the old janitor take his hand, and in one deft motion, roll each finger. On a white card marked "Fingerprints," Terrell's thumbs spilled beyond the borders of the squares. The janitor pointed to packets of HandiWipes. "Wash," he said.

Thinking of Lady Macbeth, Terrell tore open a wipe. It got dirty and he took out a second. Sweat trickled down his neck. He might be washing more than he needed to.

"Let's go." The janitor showed him the garbage can.

Terrell dropped in the wipes and followed the janitor down the hall. The man, all bent over, walked like Terrell's grandfather, bones creaking with every step. Must have had one hell of a case of acne when he was young because he had a badly pockmarked neck. Terrell looked into a cell occupied by a tall, skinny black man sitting on a metal bunk, his hands between his knees. His forehead gleamed in the fluorescent light.

"Hey," Terrell said.

"Hey," the man replied.

Terrell wanted him to say, "What you in here for?" but the man just leaned forward and looked at his hands.

"You' here." The janitor pressed a red button on the wall. A cell door slid open. Terrell heard a whoosh and stepped in.

On his right, heavy brackets bolted a stainless steel bed to the wall. On his left stood a toilet and sink, all one piece. If he sat on the toilet, his back would be against the sink. There was no toilet paper. He turned. The janitor had vanished. In the space between the toilet and bed, a bright light shone from a wire-covered niche near the ceiling. A small, dirty mirror was below it. Terrell walked over. Not a mirror, a stainless steel panel. He leaned in. His eyes looked yellow, his face wavy. Two steps took him to the door. His fingers curled around the bars. Where the gold paint had worn off, the steel felt ragged. The red button across the hall opened the door. If he could just touch it…he slid his hand between the bars. His forearm caught. Two steps and he bumped the back wall, another two, and his chest slammed the bars. He peeled off his sweatshirt. His shirt was soaked.

"Turnkey!" called the man in the next cell.

So that was what the janitor was called: Turnkey. Turncoat! In the distance, Terrell heard the squeak of a desk chair. The crepe soles of the turnkey's shoes sounded like Velcro.

"Gimme some toilet paper," the prisoner in the next cell said.

Footsteps slowly receded, then returned.

"Zat all?" the other prisoner said.

"Regulation," a voice said.

Terrell tried to force the bars apart—they didn't budge. "Turnkey!" he called.

The turnkey stood in front of his cell.

People couldn't be locked up for no reason. Sean had to get him out of here. Sean was his best friend. He'd better be busting down the door. "What about making a phone call?" Terrell said.

"Have to ask," the old man said.

"Are my friends in the waiting room?"

"Ain't no waiting room." He ambled off.

Terrell heard a chair scrape. His legs began to shake. He tested the bed with his hand. He weighed a lot more than most guys, certainly more than the skinny-ass dude in the next cell. If he was lucky, the bed wouldn't fall off and kill him. Forcing himself to stay in one place on the steel and not scrabble around like a desperate little dog on a vet's examining table, he curled up. The steel smelled like disinfectant. Same smell as deodorant cakes in urinals. Heat drained out of him. He arranged his sweatshirt to cover his shoulders. Once, his mom had been down in Jamaica visiting his grandmother; he had been staying at his aunt's place in the Bronx and his tonsillitis flared up. He'd felt the same kind of cold—teeth chattering, face burning. Shit, he would give anything for a blanket. If he'd let Sean go off on the cops, they'd be lying end to end, the furnace of Sean's body-heat warming him. Sean would do everything in his power to make bail. He knew, better than any-one, how Terrell had a thing about prison.

TERRELL WOKE UP, frozen through. Metal clanged; men laughed and joked. For a moment, he thought he was in a locker room. No. Jail! He leapt to his feet. Pressing his cheek to the bars, he looked down the hall. The turnkey was leading in two new arrivals: a red-haired college student and his drunk friend, who staggered and scraped the wall. The red-haired dude, who wore a Maryland football jacket, begged to call his uncle, a hot-shot lawyer in the Justice Department. He promised the jailer a tip. Instead of walking toward the cells, the turnkey reversed direc-tion. The two disappeared back toward the booking room, and a few minutes later, returned to enter their cell. An hour later, the turnkey led them out.

As they passed, Terrell grabbed the football jacket. "I need you to call my friend Sean."

The big guy looked down at Terrell's hand. "Don't mess with the threads."

"Sean O'Brien." Terrell let go. "He lives in College Park."

"What's his number?"

Number one on speed dial. Terrell hadn't memorized an actual number in years.

"He just got a land line," Terrell said. "Call new listings."

"Yeah, sure," the football player said.

"Sean O'Brien," Terrell shouted. "Like Sean Penn."

"Okay, okay."

"Move on out, boys," the turnkey said.

"Or like Conan O'Brien," said the football player's friend.

"Not Conan!" Terrell shouted. By then, they were gone.

"Hey, Turnkey," the inmate next to Terrell screamed, "why you letting that college kid kiss your ass?"

College kid. Sure! That was the angle. Terrell waited a few minutes. "Mr. Turnkey," he called, "I wonder if you might bring me some toilet paper."

The man appeared with three folded sheets. Terrell took the paper and stared down in the turnkey's doleful eyes. "I have not had an opportunity to make a phone call yet, and I believe I have the right to legal representation." He was a college kid, too, the old man ought to realize. Plus, the man was a brother.

The turnkey smiled. "I know what you're saying."

"The policeman didn't read me my Miranda rights."

"This ain't like on TV." The turnkey sauntered off.

No kidding, Terrell thought.

SECOND SEMESTER OF senior year, Terrell had gone over to Green Haven Correctional, the state pen that had once housed Old Sparky, the electric chair. For one unit of Community Service, the easiest A of his four years at Vassar, he'd tutored a guy named Larry, who was in for dealing hash out of his girlfriend's apartment in Queens. A three-time offender, Larry had a high Afro. The first time they'd met, sitting in the meeting room at a round table, Larry had a cold. They wouldn't give him anything to dry up his sinuses. Terrell wished he'd brought some cold tabs. Larry said it wouldn't have done any good because the guards would have confiscated the pills. Terrell nodded. He guessed there had to be rules.

By the end of the term, Larry had made progress. He could read a paragraph clear through. He knew how to use the dictionary's index words. Terrell explained how he'd be graduating, and he told Larry about his job down in Washington DC. "What kinda job you gonna have?" Larry said. Terrell thought maybe he could inspire Larry to finish his GED. "I'll be working at the Urban Institute," he said. Larry asked what that was, and Terrell said it was a think tank where people came up with ways to solve society's ills. Larry nodded. Terrell was pleased with himself. It was always easier to bring news into prison than expect Larry to come up with something to say. Day in and day out, life in Green Haven was pretty much the same. But Larry had surprised him with some parting words. He cocked his head to one side and made a steeple with his fingers.

"Watch out for The Man," Larry said, jerking his head back toward the guard. "You be a college boy and all that, but to them, you're just another *slave*."

"You've been in jail too long," Terrell said, half laughing. His whole life he'd tried to see himself as an individual, not as a member of an oppressed class.

Larry raised his eyebrows in a knowing way. "It's another world out there, college boy, and you don't know *nothing* about it."

WITHOUT HIS WATCH, each minute felt like an hour, and it seemed as if he had been locked up for days. A cart wheeled down the hall. The smell of breakfast made Terrell's stomach rumble. Saturday morning and still no phone call, but now that it was day, his buddies would spring him. A jailer opened a port in the door and handed him a styrofoam cup and a carton. In the carton Terrell saw a fried egg sandwich. White bread sopped up grease like a paper towel. Terrell took the lid off the cup. Coffee looked like tea. The alternative was tap water: warm and rusty. He sat on his bunk and ate, and with food in his stomach, tried to sort out what had gotten him here.

He must have given the woman a twenty when he bought the beer. The woman was right, remembering the twenty, but wrong in every other respect. Maybe this was a scam she pulled every night, claiming to find a phony bill and then getting a tourist to pony up a real twenty. Then he remembered her saying something about money out of her paycheck. Coffee burned his lips. No, damn it. He'd been at Vassar too long. The bitch had picked on him because he was black, and when he came up in front of the judge, he'd sound just like those cons up at Green Haven Correctional, like Larry: smart, but barely literate, proclaiming, "Honest, Judge, I'm innocent."

After breakfast, Terrell called for the turnkey. A young guy came.

"Has Secret Service arrived?" Terrell said.

"No, they haven't," the turnkey said.

"Can I make my phone call?"

The guy looked at him. "I'll let you know when." He walked away.

Pacing, Terrell heard the turnkey's television. College football season. The first game of the day ended—Michigan, where Sean came from. Then the second game began. Lunch arrived. A hamburger on white bread. Sprite to drink. Dinner arrived a couple hours after lunch, greasy chicken and a biscuit that nearly choked him. None of the food required utensils.

Prisoners demanded to see the Commissioner. Terrell called the turnkey. The old man appeared.

"I've been here twenty-four hours," Terrell said, "and I still haven't gotten to make my phone call."

The old man looked at his watch. "What time was you brought to the station?"

Terrell told him.

"It's not twenty-four hours from the time you brought in," the old man said. "You looking at eight hours for paperwork." The turnkey walked back down the hall. Terrell lay on his bed and his fingers went to his throat. He felt around. They had taken his cross.

SOMEONE WAS SHAKING his shoulder. A green uniform. Finally! Swinging his feet to the floor, Terrell sat up.

"I need your left hand," the turnkey said.

"You have my fingerprints."

"Just do what you told."

Terrell stood. Out in the corridor and cuffed to the bars stood a white guy, plaid shirt hanging, jeans frayed; looked like his highest career aspiration might be working at video rental. Terrell let his arm be jerked sideways. A handcuff clicked shut. The turnkey collected the man next door, as tall as Terrell but way thinner. His pants were falling down because the cops had taken his belt. The three moved like convicts on a chain gang, through a series of doors, and entered an office where three chairs faced the desk of a large woman in a flowery dress. She was plugging away at a computer. So this was the Commissioner. An educated African-American like himself. Finally, he was face-to-face with an authority figure who could rectify this miscarriage of justice. The Commissioner swiveled around to face them and take the first prisoner's information.

The white guy lived with his parents and was charged with possession of one marijuana cigarette. Bail came to twenty-five hundred; he could get out on bond for two-fifty. The man began to hiccup. He blew his nose in his fingers.

"Didn't your mother teach you not to do that?" Terrell said.

The man wiped his nose on his sleeve.

Swearing under her breath because the computer had locked, the Commissioner tapped her nails. When the screen came to life, she took the second defendant's information. He had broken into his neighbor's house; done it before. The court had forbidden him to come within a hundred feet of the premises.

"But I wasn't harming no one," he said.

The printer spit out bail. Exactly the same. Incredible.

Terrell gave the Commissioner his social security number and address. She typed the information. He waited for her to finish. These guys had violated the law, but he'd done nothing wrong. He was out of here.

She spun her chair around, talking to her computer but never looking right at him.

"The charges are forgery, counterfeiting a public document, and theft of a bottle of beer."

"Let me tell..." Terrell began.

"Tell it to the judge."

"Is that supposed to be a joke?" he said.

"Bail is twenty-five hundred and bond two-fifty."

"I'm innocent."

She gripped the top inch of paper rolling from a printer. "This is your paperwork. Hang onto it."

Bitch. He wanted some acknowledgment of his humanity. A smile. A compassionate glance. He looked at a clock above the door. Six in the morning—Jesus!

A different turnkey came to lead them back. Bulge of fat over his shirt collar. Triple chin. Poisoning himself on prison grub. The other prisoners stood. Terrell felt the handcuff tugging his arm, but his legs had seized up, the way they did when he did too many squats. He needed to work out and wondered what Bill Thomas, the accountant from the GAO, had managed to get done. Nothing probably.

"C'mon, move it," the turnkey said. Terrell stood.

They passed an empty cell, and the man arrested for break-ing-and-entering threw his paperwork through the bars. The papers fluttered to the floor. The man laughed. The white guy mumbled that his parents would post bail. If Terrell could only remember Sean's phone number, he could get out on bond. But that uneducated black man? No one was going to save his sorry ass.

The turnkey stopped at Terrell's cell.

"Can I finally make my phone call?" Terrell said.

"How long have you been here?"

"Thirty-two hours," Terrell said.

"I have to put your buddy here back in his cell."

"I need to call my mom," the white boy said.

"Okay," the turnkey said. "I'll take you first."

The cell door slammed. Terrell stood holding the bars. A few minutes later, the turnkey came back and led Terrell to an alcove with a pay phone.

"They took my calling card," Terrell said.

"Call collect."

Terrell stared at the instructions.

"I haven't got all day," the turnkey said. "Dial zero first."

On Thursday, he had called Nathan's to arrange a ride. The last part of the number was 4488. He turned over his wrist. Luckily, the number was still there, faint, but written in pen.

The phone at Nathan's house rang and rang. If no one answered, he'd have to call his mom, but she was up in White Plains, a train ride away from DC. Plus, they might not even let him make a second call. He'd be locked up forever.

"Hello?" a sleepy voice said.

"Collect call for Nathan Finkelstein," the operator said. "Will you accept?"

"Yeah, sure."

"I finally got to make my call," Terrell said.

"Sean figured they'd just let you out," Nathan said.

"Where were you guys?"

"We went to the station, but they said you weren't there."

"You must've gone to the wrong station," Terrell said.

"Sean asked the guy at the bar where they were taking you."

"Didn't he tell them this was ridiculous?"

"Sure, but they didn't listen."

"I need a two-hundred-fifty-dollar bond."

"When? Now? It's Sunday."

"Where's Sean?" Terrell said.

"Home," said Nathan.

"Call. Sean." Terrell spoke very slowly. "Do whatever you have to do, but get me out of this shit-hole."

"Don't worry. You won't go to jail."

"But I'm in jail already."

"No, I mean permanently. I talked to my sister who's a lawyer, and she'll get you off."

"I don't care if I get off. Get. Me. Out!"

The turnkey tapped Terrell's shoulder and took the receiver.

Back in his cell, Terrell sat on the bunk, rocking back and forth. It was Nathan who'd been working the phone. Nathan who'd got on it and called his sister. Terrell pictured Sean stretched out on the couch, chilling and watching football. All through college, he'd put up with Sean's gym clothes stinking up their room. The fitted sheet on Sean's bed had a gray spot in the middle, like a rodent's nest. Like the smell here: rust, piss, grease, and the inmates' mingled, nervous sweat.

TERRELL ATE BREAKFAST. Keys jangled. The turnkey unlocked the door and cuffed him to the white guy.

"My mom's going to kill me," the white guy said.

"Most probably," Terrell said. His would, too, if he ever told her.

The turnkey led Terrell back down the yellow corridor to the booking room where his so-called buddies waited.

"Hey, man." Sean raised a fist.

Nathan gave a timid wave.

Terrell looked away.

A man in an olive sport coat gave Terrell a thumbs-up: the bail bondsman. He high-fived a cop seated at a table. "Hey, Randy. How you doing?"

"All right," the cop said. "How about yourself?"

"Keeping busy."

Yeah, right, Terrell thought.

The cop nodded to Terrell. "Sit down, boys. Let's get you checked out."

"I've been here longer than he has," Terrell said. "I demand to go first."

The white boy turned and looked at his mother, a fat woman in a flowered house dress. She was dabbing her eyes. "That's fine with me," the white boy said.

The officer leafed through some forms. Finally, he tucked them in a cubbyhole and unlocked the handcuffs. Terrell rubbed his wrists. A milk crate held two plastic bags. The officer dropped them on the table. Terrell's bag burst open.

He separated the silver chain of his cross from the coins, and pressed the cross to his lips. The usual warm rush didn't come. Jesus wasn't looking out for him. He put the cross in his pocket.

On the other side of the counter, the bondsman slapped Terrell on the back. "Your buddy Sean, here, racked up two-fifty on his

VISA to get you out."

Sean, with his fly-boy jacket and backwards baseball cap, smiled urgently. "Don't look so scared. You're free."

"At least until the hearing," Nathan said.

Sean held the door.

Terrell slid past. Outside, clouds hung low. Rain spit on him.

Nathan used the remote to unlock his mom's car. Terrell was about to slide in back. The bondsman went around to the other side. The man meant to sit next to him. No way, Terrell thought. Shoving Sean aside, Terrell opened the front door.

"What's that about?" Sean said.

"I'm not riding in back," Terrell said.

"Chill out, man," Sean said. "It's not a friggin' bus."

"That's good," Terrell said. "Because then I might have to kill you."

"I hope you're not going to be one of those blacks with a chip on your shoulder," Sean said.

"One of 'those' blacks?" Terrell waited a moment to see if Sean understood what he'd just said. He looked in the car. The bondsman was taking a cigarette from behind his ear.

"If you're not getting in," Sean said, "close the door. It's raining."

"I ain't riding with no white boys." Terrell pulled up the hood of his sweatshirt, jammed his fists in his pockets, and headed down the sidewalk. The sky opened up. It was a deluge. Behind him, he heard a car door slam. The engine started and Nathan pulled up beside him. Sean rolled down the window. "It's a long walk back to DC."

"I'd rather walk," Terrell said.

"Suit yourself." Sean closed the window.

Terrell felt his socks squish. He wanted to stand in a shower and wash off the jail stink. The rain made him cold.

The car stopped at the end of the block. Through the downpour Terrell saw taillights.

"Hey, Dude!" Terrell shouted. He began to run. "Wait up!"

OREGANO

———◦———

WIPED OUT BY a long day of shooting pictures, Felicia Dawkins slid her camera bag into the kitchen, removed her winter boots, and slammed the door. Laundry baskets, recycling bins, brown bags of junk mail, and stacks of the St. Louis Post-Dispatch filled all but the arc where the door from the garage swung in. She hated coming home and confronting the detritus of married life.

"Hey, Greg," she called. "Why's this crap still here?"

"I'm on top of it," he called.

"You're obviously not." Her sock feet slid across the linoleum and the dining room's parquet floor. In her office (a mess from the manila folders she'd not had time to file) she popped out the memory stick from her Nikon. As it uploaded images to the Cloud, the card reader buzzed, and she tried to estimate if doctoring the photos would take two hours or ten. February was supposed to be her slow month. She'd thought she could get away for a weekend workshop, and now she regretted that she'd crammed too much in.

She found Greg in the bedroom, naked. Light slanting through the window heightened the muscle definition on his legs, and she was tempted to run back and grab the Nikon, and would have, except that ever since the wedding he'd grown shy about exposing his body to her lens.

"I'm sorry I didn't do what I promised," he said. "There's an inch of ice in the truck bed."

"Never mind," she said. "It was just the first thing I saw. I brought the day in with me."

"Where were you?"

"Out in Boone County. Mom-and-pop maple syrup operation. Their web guy wants the photos by tomorrow."

"But you have your workshop," he said.

"Yeah, I know."

Outside, it was five above. Her fingers felt on fire from the cold. She tapped his back, and when he turned, she nestled against the fuzz on his chest. "How about warming me up?" she said.

"Not now, honey," he said, unwrapping her arms.

"Why not?"

"I've got a racquetball game."

What good was it having a young husband if the first thing that went through his mind was racquetball? She was forty-two; he, twenty-nine. They should have been well-matched, but lately it seemed like once a week was all he needed. She sank down on the hope chest at the foot of the bed and watched him dress.

He fished a dingy jock strap from his gym bag and stood on one leg then the other while he hiked it up around his hips. The sagging elastic looked disgusting. She pictured herself with her face screwed up, tongue sticking out, holding the thing at the end of a stick.

"Don't you ever wash that?" she asked.

He put on shorts. "I just took it out of the wash. I did the rest of the laundry too." He pointed to a heap of folded clothes on the bed.

Game or no game, she would have pushed him back onto the mattress, but the clothes were in the way. Sighing in a way that sounded too much like her mother, Felicia picked up a stack of tee-shirts. They felt damp. She unfolded them and draped them across the radiator.

"Didn't I get them dry enough?" he said.

"They're just a little damp," she said.

She wanted to say, Come here, feel this, does this feel dry to you? but she had done that before, and he still never let the clothes get all the way dry.

"What time's the workshop start?" he said.

"Six thirty," she said. "Magic hour."

"Even when the sun comes up, it's not going to be warm. You better wear long-johns."

"I wore them today and it didn't help."

He grabbed the tee-shirt from the radiator, and slid blue sweatbands on his wrists. She waited for him to make a comment about the shirt's dampness, but he tucked it in his shorts and sat down to pull on his socks. "Maybe we could do something fun when you get back."

"Sunday's our day to clean the house." She picked up the clothes he had dropped. There was the bathroom. That had to be done. Should she mention it, or would it occur to him?

"I was also thinking, maybe we could do something mid-week-ish," he said.

"But you're at the store."

"I'll talk to my dad and see if Wednesdays I could make it home by six. That'd give us time to catch a movie or maybe take a class through adult ed. Maybe a massage workshop or watercolor, something that's outside both our comfort zones."

"Have you looked in the paper?"

"I thought you could do that."

"I'll think about it." She wanted to say, let me know when you've got a plan figured out, but instead, she took a deep breath. One thing, one among many, that seemed harder lately, was figuring out their calendars. Hers was complicated because she had jobs during the day and a studio class at St. Louis University three nights a week. Greg worked at his dad's True Value, and if an employee called in sick, Greg had to fill in.

"What are you making for dinner?" he said.

"I need to bond with Photoshop."

"I could pick up a pizza on my way home."

"Get a salad, too," she said, trying to hold back the weariness that threatened to settle in. "What I'd really like is just to have a nice meal together."

"That could be arranged." He smiled and shouldered his gym bag.

She walked with him to the kitchen, where her clay herb-pots lined the sill. A month ago when she'd gone out to Hermann, he'd killed off the basil, sage, peppermint, and rosemary. She stacked the empty pots, handing him the wobbly tower.

He cradled them to his chest. "What do you want me to do with these?"

"Throw them away."

He nodded to the remaining pot. "What about that?"

Only the oregano had tolerated his neglect.

"It's still alive." She clasped the oregano's pot and moved it to the center where the plant would get full sun. Its delicate, heart-shaped leaves quivered when she let go.

"Should I water this or will you remember?"

"I'll remember," he said.

FELICIA HAD NEVER wanted to marry and even joked about how universities, jails, and marriage all fell in the same category: institutions that locked you up until you graduated or escaped. Too many women in her MFA cohort had their creativity extinguished by the demands of married life, and, as she had observed from following the career moves of her Facebook friends, when women felt no urgent need to earn money, they dabbled, never giving their work the attention it deserved. Her mother, a frustrated artist, had a fine hand for watercolor, but she had wasted her life making crafts from *Family Circle* and birthday cakes with seven colors of frosting. Felicia, the oldest, had practically raised her three brothers. No desire to do that again.

Greg had come into her life by accident, and their age difference had made her immediately dismiss him as date material. He was simply the model for the fashion-photography segment of studio class. After his first modeling gig, when he seemed to be wincing from the exposure of so much skin (not nude, but undressing down to his swim trunks) she had invited him for coffee. He was tired, she saw, and wondered if it was because she'd had him moving around. She wanted the students to see what it was like to art-direct, to tell a model how to assume different poses and how long to hold them.

"Was this your first time modeling?" she said.

"Yes, plus I already put in nine hours before coming here. My day job's working at my dad's True Value."

She almost made a joke about working in a hardware store (plenty of screws), but decided not to when she saw his eyes. They were large and blue as opals, a sparkling star in the center of each one, and she felt those stars extend their light around her shoulders.

"Why'd you sign up to model?" she said.

"I wanted to be around creative people," he said, "and I need the money."

It wasn't long before Felicia realized what working in the family True Value meant, before she understood the mixed messages he got from his parents. Work hard. We're leaving the store to you, but we won't pay you what a manager should earn. Greg rarely complained about the hours stocking shelves, pasting on orange tags, or running the cash register when one of the clerks called in sick. He earned little more than minimum wage and had always lived frugally, but after their marriage, he surprised her by suggesting they open a joint account. When she asked why, he said because she should have a cushion. It was no fun groveling. He wanted her to take master classes with leading photographers and use the money in the joint account to pay for the workshop fees.

"Really?" she said, not quite believing he'd be so generous, but even more, astounded that he'd realized this was just what she'd been longing to do.

"Go for it," he said. "Make art."

GROGGY FROM A late night with Photoshop but determined not to let exhaustion ruin her day, Felicia drove along the Great River Road toward Alton. The workshop she'd signed up for had been called "Advanced Nature Photography," a title that made her think of Eliot Porter and Ansel Adams and Stieglitz and that reminded her of how ambitious she had been, coming out of school. It had been ten years since she'd done any work that could hang in a gallery. She needed a subject and a vision. Larry Kanfer, a photographer the department had invited over from Illinois, had claimed the low horizon, dilapidated barns, and dramatic Midwest thunderheads. Inspired and casting about for something besides the Gateway Arch, she'd come up with the idea of flowing water: the Mississippi River in all its floods, freezes, and thaws. She hadn't been over to the locks and dams since grade school, but when she stepped from the warmth of the car into the predawn dark of the Riverlands Migratory Bird Sanctuary, she learned that the true focus of the weekend would be birds.

After her initial disappointment, she reminded herself that nature did include birds, so why not? Greg deserved his money's worth. Stoically, she bayoneted a 200-400 zoom onto the camera body and screwed on the 1.4 tele-converter. She vowed to stick by the instructor's side and catch up every little crumb of wisdom, but felt her resistance mount as she followed eight men (all over seventy, all with lenses that required carrying with two hands) along a trail that led to a duck blind at the water's edge.

"I'm going to walk up the shore a ways," she called, heading north before the instructor could summon her back.

Snow fell into her boots. The rising sun gradually burned off the fog that hovered above the sluggish, sullen water. Eagles made lazy circles above the eddies, but the light was too low to shoot a moving target. Besides, eagles were so obvious. She hated expeditions where everyone came back with the same pictures, and now she hated them even more because she was cold and being overtaken by a bad mood.

Maybe the problem was where she was placing her attention. Since leaving the group, she'd been looking out at the river, fifty yards away in the middle distance. Look far, look close, avoid the middle distance if you can. This advice is what she would have told a class of beginners. She stopped and stared at the grass just off the trail. At last, something worthy of springing the legs on her tripod.

She changed lenses and got to work, looking up when she heard footsteps. The instructor's sun-weathered face and cropped white beard made her think he'd just returned from the Caribbean. Over his polar fleece he wore a many-pocketed jacket like her own.

"Find a nest?" he said.

She had just knelt down in the snow, gloves in her pocket, fingertips already stiff. "I'm not looking at birds."

He crouched beside her. "What have you got going?"

"Just grass," she said, moving aside.

"Wild millet, cutgrass, sprangle top or beggarticks?"

"Grass grass."

"In other words, you don't know." He squinted at the LCD window. "If you're going to shoot birds, you'd better know the names of the grasses, too."

"Why?" she said.

"Because of captions. You can't just turn in a photo that says 'grass' or some naturalist will call you on it." Without disturbing the tripod, he moved his eye to the viewfinder. She hoped he appreciated the seven frozen teardrops clinging to the bottom of the bent blade. He pulled back.

A slow smile spread across his face. "Photography is a way of saying 'I see something and want to save it for myself. I see something and want to show it to you.' Thanks for showing this to me. I would have missed it. Howsomever..." He raised an eyebrow and formed his fingers into the slideable rectangle. "...you missed our early arrival."

"What early arrival?" she said.

"The Black-throated Green Warbler." He put a finger to his lips and looked through the viewfinder again. "Little songbird. Yellow face. Olive green crown. White wing-bars. Zoo-zee, zoo-zoo-zee. If you allow me, I think I can bring him in."

"By all means," she said.

He began to refocus, changing the depth of field. "Argh!

Dadgumit!" He slapped his knee and stood. "He's off."

She saw a bright yellow flash.

Smiling ruefully, he said, "Always, always check your depth of field. I know you wanted a shot of those water drops, but he was not fifteen feet from you. I caught his movement in your viewfinder, and you could easily have bagged both shots. When you're shooting in nature, always give precedence to the shot that moves. Then come back and shoot the static shot for however long you want."

"Okay," she said. "Thanks for the tip."

He laced his fingers together and turned them inside out. Here's the church. Here's the steeple. Look inside and there's all the people. She couldn't tell if he was making fun of her or simply acting like a goofy little boy, which was what all men reverted to if given half a chance.

TWO DAYS OF trooping around behind professional birders who merely wanted to come home with close-ups from their latest bird walk convinced her that wildlife photography was not a direction she would ever pursue. Classes weren't going to turn her into Eliot Porter or Ansel Adams, and she doubted this weekend would give her anything mountable in an exhibition or printable in a book. Frost clung to the hairs of her nose, and she was frozen through.

Home at last she eased open the door from the garage, praying that the crap would be gone, but it wasn't, and the house smelled like onions. How could that be? They had no food in the house, apart from some frozen hamburger and moldy vegetables. Unless Greg had gone to the grocery store. That would be a first.

"Are you cooking dinner?" she asked, walking into the kitchen. The windows were so fogged, she couldn't see out. Greg stood at the stove, whistling and stirring spaghetti sauce. He'd drained the pasta in the sink.

"You want me to put the noodles on a plate?" she asked.

"Sure," he said.

Felicia picked up the strainer. The strands of spaghetti stuck together, a gummy, glutinous mess. She turned on the water and tried to rinse the slime. The noodles felt thick and cold as earthworms. He'd forgotten to put in a tablespoon of olive oil. Had he never heard of *al dente* and the little trick of throwing the noodle against the wall? After plunging the pasta under the hot tap, she separated the strands with a fork.

"You can put the salad on the table," he said. "It's in the fridge."

"I didn't think we had any."

"Oh yeah. I found some tomatoes and lettuce in the bin."

Felicia opened the refrigerator and took out the salad bowl. The lettuce looked like compost. She went straight to the service porch and dumped the contents in the garbage. She didn't say anything. There was no point. Still, the sound of the lid slamming down made its own statement. After moving the colander, she rinsed the bowl.

"What happened to the salad?" he said.

"We can't eat that," she said.

"It's just going to be spaghetti, then." He took a ladle from the drawer.

"It is what it is."

She turned on the tap to wash her hands. On the sill sat the little clay herb pot. The oregano's leaves had turned from green to gray. She sucked in her breath.

Wiping her hands on her jeans, she said, "I'll be back in a sec."

She went in the study. On his roll-top desk she saw a white ring. He'd marred the lacquer with a coffee cup. She rubbed it with her finger, but it didn't go away. He kept the bank statements in a cubbyhole. Two thousand in their joint account. Seven thousand in the interest bearing account, which was still in his name alone.

If she got a divorce, there would be no master classes. That wouldn't be the end of the world. Her days would consist of weddings, bar mitzvahs, catalogs, restaurant menus, Kiwanis and Rotary, plus whatever part-time teaching she found time to do.

She replaced the statement exactly as she had found it and stood for a moment in the hall, her breathing shallow, trying to compose a face.

"Come and get it," Greg called.

She pressed her eyes.

Greg had dimmed the dining room light and lit candles, and now, he was pouring two glasses of Cabernet. Before even sitting down, she reached over and slugged one down. The glass landed hard on the table.

"Thirsty?" he said.

"Dehydrated." Her chair scraped the floor.

Greg went back in the kitchen and returned with plates.

The best way to motivate people was to encourage them. He needed praise, but she could think of few things to praise besides his effort. She watched him eat and forced a smile.

"I appreciate you cooking tonight," she said.

"Thank you," he said. "How was the class?"

"Fine," she said. She was not cut out to sit for days in a duck blind, waiting for some stupid bird to plop down. "I took some pictures of grass."

"No birds?"

"Not enough light. Moving target, you know?"

In fact she hadn't been able to capture a single bird in her viewfinder. Not an eagle. Not a mallard. Not the lone cardinal she'd seen pecking at red, frozen berries. Her fork picked at the edges of her spaghetti. Fresh herbs would have made a better sauce.

"I was wondering why you didn't water my oregano," she said.

He twirled spaghetti around his fork. "What oregano?"

He knew perfectly well the plant had died. He must have seen it while he was cooking dinner. "I was gone two days, and you forgot to water my herb."

"That's its problem."

"What? The oregano's?" She didn't mean to get angry. She hadn't meant to even bring it up. Was he really saying it was the oregano's problem? As if it had willed itself to die? As if it were a sentient being committing plant suicide? "I've told you a million times to water my plants when I go out of town."

"Not a million. Twice. If you want to know, it froze before I could water it, and I thought if I watered it, ice might form around the roots and it would be worse off." He sucked a long strand of spaghetti slowly through his lips.

She put her fork down. "You could have moved it to the counter before you went to bed."

He took a sip of wine. "I didn't think of that."

"You didn't think of that."

"What's the big deal? I'll buy you another."

Maybe the oregano wasn't dead after all. She pushed her chair back, turned on the kitchen light, and took the clay pot down from the sill. With her fingers, she stripped the brittle leaves one by one. He loves me. He loves me not. Or maybe, I love him, I love him not. She stared at the stubble.

"What are you doing out there?" he said.

"Nothing."

She held the plant as if it would speak to her, tell her this is your stop. This is where you get off.

"Felicia, you're on my case all the time."

She waited a moment to see if this tipped the scale. Whining just might. But he said nothing. Carrying the plant she marched into the service porch. Her toe slid toward the shiny pedal on the garbage can. As she pressed down, the can's lid creaked open.

"I hear you doing something," Greg said.

"No, I'm not," she said.

On top of the remains of Greg's salad sat two empty cans of pomodoro tomatoes. The cans should have gone into recycling. He had been too lazy to rinse them. Out in the dining room she heard him clear his throat.

"You are just like my mother," he said. Wine sloshed into a glass. "That must be why I have such a high tolerance for this sort of thing."

"What sort of thing?" The pot in her hand trembled.

"Nitpicking."

Whoa, baby. Like his mother. "So why do you tolerate it?"

"Because I love your creative spirit," he said, "and I don't want to see you crushed."

She bent down and placed the dry little pot of oregano on top of the cans. How lifeless the oregano looked. She did not mean to cry. She should wait until she could talk calmly, maybe after he'd put her name on his account, after she'd figured out if she'd be covered by COBRA if they divorced.

"I can front you a month's rent, or more if you need it. Don't stay with me for money," Greg said. "I couldn't bear it."

She felt a wave of nausea, as if she were a child caught running away from home. He sat an entire room away, but she felt as if the walls had turned transparent. Was it possible he applied to her the same kind of scrutiny she applied to him, that this is what marriage amounted to, this not very flattering reflection? She saw an enlarged snapshot of herself, grainy, with every pore showing, her hard eyes examining his every move.

She lowered the metal lid of the trashcan to keep it from banging shut. She put the plastic recycling bin on top of the dryer to clear a little space. Who needed herbs anyway? They could eat out. They could go to gallery openings and foreign films. She would plan something mid-weekish to help him forget the soul-deadening boredom of the hardware store. She had not meant to be so cruel. In another month Schnuck's would sell flats of herbs, and she could plant them outdoors where they belonged.

BONDS OF LOVE & BLOOD

———o———

IT WAS GETTING on towards dusk, and I had stopped by the rug shop to tell Hamdi farewell. While the tense little Kurd with the shining eyes talked to his boss, Duran Duran, on the phone, I studied a framed photograph of a village somewhere in eastern Turkey. On a rolling, grassless steppe, a settlement of low, domed houses huddled. No water vessels or stacks of wood, no clotheslines or looms, nothing to announce that, here, people needed warmth, light, water, food, or wore clothes or made love or laughed.

In a corner of the frame, Hamdi had wedged a faded color photo of two boys with hollow, black eyes. The older boy was Hamdi. Even then his smile occupied half his face. Or maybe it was not a smile so much as a grimace of anxiety, hunger, and despair. The younger boy, his forehead shielded with bangs, had the perfectly round face of a baby, which told me that he was still under the protection of a woman's care, maybe still fed by her or favored with the extra cup of goat's milk on which the boys must have survived. The younger boy's hair was raggedly cut, and his chin shadowed by the dust ground into its pores. His belly button stuck out of a stomach that looked pregnant, and at the end of his too-long arms, his hands hung limp. Rickets, no doubt.

Why did one child fall through the cracks, and another not? It was a question that had preoccupied me for most of my adult life.

I looked around the carpet shop for the grown-up Hamdi. With a painfully forced smile, he spoke in bursts of Turkish into the phone. Hamdi's face had a gouged, lean look that made him handsome despite his sunken cheeks. Another bad boy to add to the list of men I wished I'd never gotten involved with, Hamdi had immediately drawn me into the orbit of his life. As if this day wasn't already hard enough, I had to deal with my period. The Turkish tampons were useless, and I needed another Motrin for cramps.

"Hamdi, I need something to drink."

"No, no, Angela. I get you tea in half a second." Hamdi put his hand over the receiver and flapped his hand toward the rug-covered bench.

I didn't want him ordering me apple tea or calling little kids to bring a Coke, and I had gone through his album of postcards often enough to realize that I was just one of the many women he had seduced. The door was open. The late afternoon sun spilled down stairs that led up to the plaza. Did I want to leave or not? I wasn't sure. At home nothing waited for me but my job as a postal inspector, and I had an absolutely dead and vacant life compared to the wild ride Istanbul had been. I shouldered my backpack and went outside.

I pointed up to the plaza where Hamdi had first seen me staring into space. Three weeks. A lifetime ago. When he still didn't come, I put my foot on the first step. Finally, he gave me a thumbs-up to show he would soon stop talking to his boss.

Although I didn't want to be rude, I meant to leave the instant I'd thanked him for showing me around. His enormous key chain jangled as he triple-locked the door and came bounding up behind me, squinting at the sun as it fell behind the domes of the Hagia Sofia. His little hop-walk as he tried to keep pace with my long legs made me think about that picture of his brother and of Jamie, the brother I had not seen in many a year.

"Why you run away?" Hamdi said.

"I'm walking, not running," I said. "You don't have to come with me."

"I just want to be your friend, Angela."

Resolutely, I dodged a streetcar on Sultan Ahmet, hoping Hamdi would give it a rest, and sat down near the Hippodrome fountain, listening to the muezzin chant *"Al-lah Akhbar! Al-lah Akhbar!"* from the Blue Mosque's needle-thin minaret.

"Why don't you let me be your friend?" Hamdi said.

"What makes you think you're not?"

"Your eyes."

I turned away and sighed.

"See? That what you do."

I almost believed him, that he wanted to be my friend; but the moment I softened, he would see it in my eyes and try to squeeze my hand with his sweaty palm. If I ever came back to Turkey, I vowed never to set foot in the store again, even if it meant walking a mile around the walls of Hagia Sofia to reach my *pension*. Hamdi had an urgent sincerity that he pressed on you, whether you were up for it or not. I mean, people have their own problems, right? You don't need to be every stranger's friend.

"I really just came to say goodbye," I said.

"That's it? That's all?" When he turned his face to the sun, his pupils shrank. The glitter in his eyes and his half-shaved beard made him look jacked-up, but I couldn't guess on what. He pressed his hands together and looked at his shoes.

"You send me a postcard, or no, just forget about Hamdi?"

"Oh, all right. I'll send you a postcard," I said. "Now I'm going."

"Too bad, Angela, you will miss the night I planned for you."

"Yes, it's too bad." I crossed my arms.

"Kathryn was going to meet us for dinner."

"Kathryn? The mythical Kathryn?"

"I'm sorry. I thought you'd understand."

"What is there to understand?" I said. "I think maybe I'll just stay here and watch the movie."

In the middle of the dirt square, a fountain splashed up intermittently like a geyser. Men in Western dress—jeans and open-necked shirts—herded their wives and children toward wooden bleachers in front of a big outdoor screen. The women wore long gray coats and light scarves tied under their chins. Grandmothers and older sisters guarded small children who ran back and forth to the fountain, dipping their hands in the water and leaning over to see the faces of who they might become. I had not bothered with a head covering, and my jeans had shrunk in a commercial dryer. I was just the tiniest bit grateful for Hamdi's presence.

"Are you not hungry, Angela?"

"What did you tell Kathryn?"

"Nothing. Just to meet us at the store."

I was mildly curious about Kathryn.

"Oh, all right. Let's have dinner then."

"After, we drive up to see lights of the Bosphorus."

"What is it, some kind of lovers' lane?"

"A place to see the view. Your last night I make special send-off."

"No, Hamdi. I've got a 4 AM flight and I haven't packed."

He held his hands up and said, "We'll see, we'll see," and I thought, nobody can make me do something I don't want to do. Jamie had driven that lesson home. To get the $10,000 for the defense lawyer he wanted me to hire, I went to an IVF clinic and donated eggs; but no amount of help on my part could change the direction of Jamie's life. I never should have told Hamdi about my brother. That had sort of spilled out of me one hot afternoon when the air was motionless and the damp sheets called out for some further intimacy. I had offered up a fact about Jamie, that unless he got clemency, he'd be in the slammer till he was seventy-three.

A WHITE FIAT roared up and Hamdi pushed me into the back seat. Neither Hamdi nor the driver moved forward, even though both were half a foot shorter than me. I suppose I represented some sort of conquest for Hamdi, like a short lumberjack and a tall tree.

After a two minute drive, the car jolted to a stop in front of a carpet store. Maybe we'd driven one block. In the rear-view mirror, the driver stared at me. The musty smell of blood filled the car, and I was relieved when Hamdi opened the door and let me out. My work colleague Fred would have told me to go back to my *pension*, lie down, and take a nap. A father with three grown daughters, he can tell from my eyes when I have cramps. I'm kind of lethargic when my period actually hits me, but this time, I was relieved not to find myself pregnant.

Two men waited in the doorway of a carpet store.

"Why are we stopping here?" I said, going inside.

"Kathryn will meet us in half hour," Hamdi said.

"Look, I am almost out of money." The only ATM that would take my card was at the Four Seasons Hotel. "I am not going to buy a carpet."

"You pay too much for carpet in Duran Duran's shop. I do you a favor now and get you low price, so it all average out."

After I went to the bathroom and stuffed toilet paper in my undies, I sat down on a bench and waited. My ovaries hurt and I massaged them with my fingertips. The IVF thing had left me with scar tissue and a longing for the kids out there—if there were any—who looked like me.

The two carpet dealers, light-haired Turks with polyester pants and gold tie clips, spoke almost no English. Their job was to lift the carpets and float them down on the floor, giving the corner a smart snap or brushing the pile so I could see how it looked, light or dark. Hamdi dragged one of the rugs closer and folded back a corner. He re-explained the difference between aniline and vegetable dyes and how the dye went all the way to the bottom of the pile. As the rugs stacked up and I slumped back against the wall, massaging my abdomen and, as Fred says, "zoning out," Hamdi unfolded a brochure that explained the symbolism of creatures from Noah's Ark; he talked about young weavers who worked at the looms until they married. What a way to spend your puberty, I thought, and swung my feet onto the bench. Looking from me to Hamdi, the two carpet guys stood with their arms folded. Hamdi asked me did I like the red or green, and I said red. I did like red. And in a certain mood, I could sit all day listening and watching handsome Turkish men throw rugs down on the floor. It was like having an art gallery displayed at your feet, only your back doesn't kill you from standing.

Kathryn arrived, fifty pounds thinner than the picture Hamdi had belatedly shown me. Like a housewife who'd been vacuuming all day and just run down to the store for cigarettes, she had her hair up in curlers and wore loose, ill-fitting pants. After unpinning her curls, she finger-combed her hair and sat down.

"I'm starving," she said.

"When I finish," Hamdi said.

"I'm not going to buy a carpet," I said.

Hamdi crawled over to the tower of rugs and knelt before me, hands clasped in supplication. "I want to change jobs. I told these guys…" Hamdi jerked a thumb toward the two other Turks. "…I can bring them retail business, and tonight, I must show them how good I sell. That's why I bring you, Angela. You my best customer and friend."

Kathryn lit a cigarette. "Hamdi, she doesn't want to buy."

Hamdi threw out his hands like a comical boy. "No tourist comes to Turkey expecting to buy a rug, but they all leave with one."

"She doesn't want one."

Kathryn, my ally, even though we'd just met and even though I'd been fucking her husband and she probably knew it, stood up. The two men from the shop looked at each other and said something to Hamdi. Some plot they had been hatching had gone awry. Hamdi did some fast talking, and they shook hands. I stood.

"Last chance!" Hamdi followed me out the door. "Last chance for such a good deal. No other tourist come this place. Only Turkish dealer, and I get in big trouble with Duran Duran if he find out I bring you here."

Next door to the carpet shop, a fruit vendor's tilted crates rested on a flimsy table that I bumped, spilling pomegranates. The men from the carpet store and Hamdi scrambled after the rolling fruit; and then, in the mood of general handshaking, the two men from the store, who looked philosophical about the loss of the sale, reached for my hand and wished me well, and I pumped the hand of the dark-haired man who leaned stolidly against the picture window. The setup reminded me of walking down a lineup and shaking hands with felons, not that Fred and I ever booked anyone. As postal inspectors we mostly opened crates with our pry bars and radioed for the police if we saw anything suspicious. The grocer whose hand I held in mine came up to my shoulder, and I looked down on the balding circle of his head and the way the shoulder pads of his jacket squared off the round contours of his chest. His shiny forehead bumped my chin. He rose on his tiptoes, and when someone passed him on the street, pushing his face into my breasts, he jumped back with a look of suffocated dismay. Short men don't usually like a big woman right up next to them. It gave me some sympathy for this poor Turk.

"Pleasure meeting you," I said.

"I'm the driver," he said. "I'm the one who brought you here."

"Oh, right," I said. "Excuse me."

"I am Ahmet."

"Okay, Ahmet, let's move it along."

AT THE RESTAURANT Ahmet sat next to Hamdi and Kathryn sat next to me, and I guess Hamdi had fixed it so Ahmet was supposed to be my date. The restaurant had taken over a quiet street, crowding the sidewalk with tables. To my surprise, Hamdi ordered the most expensive entrée, a feast of five kinds of kebabs, plus köfte and sliced lamb. Enough food for ten. Kathryn ate like she hadn't eaten for a week, and I felt hungry, too; but while Kathryn and I devoured the food, Hamdi and Ahmet turned their heads toward one another, mumbling in Turkish. Ahmet's droopy eyes reminded me of a starving dog's.

I pointed to his plate. "You should eat."

"What? Oh." He looked down at his plate and picked up a kebab, rotating it like an ear of corn and nibbling it with dainty bites, but never putting it down to wipe his chin. Grease dripped on his tie. Finally, when I had sated myself, Hamdi flung his arm over Ahmet's shoulder.

"So, Angela, I am so happy for you to meet Ahmet who is like a brother to me."

"Don't say brother!" Kathryn said.

"It pains me, my darling, when you use that tone of voice."

"Brother this. Brother that." She turned to me. "And where am I supposed to get the money for rent, I ask you that?"

I frowned. "Do you work?"

"Work! It wouldn't be necessary for me to work, would it Hamdi? You would take care of me, wouldn't you, darling?"

Hamdi reached across the table and patted Kathryn's hand.

She removed it, as if she'd touched a hot burner. "Let's ask an impartial observer, shall we Hamdi?"

"Oh, Kathryn, I wish you wouldn't. I'll get the bill." He signaled the waiter, who brought the bill and left it sitting in the middle of the table. Both Hamdi and Ahmet reached for their cigarettes.

Kathryn took out her smokes and showed Hamdi the empty pack. "I'm out, darling. Shall we call each other darling tonight?"

He took a cigarette from his pack and transferred it to hers. "Don't worry, darling. Everything will be all right."

"Where are you from originally?" I said, fanning her smoke away.

"New Zealand. I met Hamdi the first day of my vacation in Istanbul. He scooped me right up, didn't he?" She looked over at Hamdi with a hate glare.

"How romantic," I said. "Quite a prize I should imagine."

"Kathryn has never accepted Hamdi's family," Ahmet said.

His voice had a silky earnestness that reminded me of mobsters in old movies: Edward G. Robinson, parked on a dock and waiting for a delivery of machine guns.

"The truth is..." Hamdi draped his arm over the back of Ahmet's chair. "...Ahmet is like a brother to me."

"When Kathryn came," Ahmet said, "I bought cabinets for her

apartment and helped her find furniture. Now she won't speak to me."

Kathryn blew a smoke ring and looked away.

"In fact, she's jealous because of the time we spend together," Ahmet said. He looked over at Hamdi, who gave Ahmet's shoulder another squeeze and then let go. "Hamdi rescued me. I was a university student, failing all my classes and hooked on drugs. He found me sleeping under a tree in a park and took me to a center for drug-addicted kids, which he supports with the money he makes from his job. The Turkish government doesn't have drug treatment programs. They just put you in jail."

"Is that so?" I said. Now this was interesting. I mean, we don't have enough rehab centers in our country. Addicts wait and wait and sometimes hit bottom, just because that's inevitable, or sometimes they get sentenced for dealing and spend the rest of their lives in jail. The justice system gave Jamie his chance. As had I. He'd slept on my couch, stolen my ATM card, and wrecked my Camaro. In jail he could no longer bring chaos into my life. What I feared was Jamie getting early release, and then me having to teach him about cell phones and bank accounts. He never could hold any sort of job, not even used-car salesman.

"Sounds like they could use Nar-Anon over here," I said to Ahmet.

"We have it," Ahmet said. "Hamdi and I are both involved."

"Too involved, isn't that right, Hamdi?" Kathryn said. "Always money for the derelicts, but not for the wife? Always spending the night out at a meeting, aren't we?" She turned to me again. "You think it's one way when you come here for the first time. What a gorgeous country. What gorgeous men. But when you live here day in and day out, it's another reality. Isn't it, Hamdi?"

"I guess I'll take care of the bill," I said, hoping someone would argue.

"Thank you for inviting us to dinner," Kathryn said. "It's a relief to speak English. Hamdi refuses to speak English with me. Isn't that right, darling?"

Ahmet and Hamdi exchanged a look. I don't think he beat her.

She was acting too bold for that. My brother's wife never would have challenged him with questions, but then again, I never knew until he went to jail what went on at his house.

While I took out the last of my cash, Hamdi cleared his throat and said, "I wondered if you would consider making a small donation to the drug treatment center."

"No," I said.

Kathryn groaned. "He never gives up." She bummed another cigarette.

"Really what I need money for," Hamdi said, "is my brother. He is in a Turkish Army prison, and I must raise $500 to get him out, or he will rot in there for the next twenty years."

"Let him rot," Kathryn said.

"Let him rot," Ahmet said. "Do you not know what the Quran advises? In 2:178, The Prophet says 'Equivalence is the law—the free for the free, the slave for the slave, the female for the female. If one is pardoned by the victim's kin, compensation shall be paid. This is an alleviation from your Lord and mercy.' Think about it Kathryn. Locking him away will only turn him into an unproductive and alienated person. If Hamdi gets him out, we can rehabilitate him and save his family from the shame."

"Shame, is it? There comes a time when a person doesn't deserve a second chance, don't you think?" She looked at me. "What's the law in your country?"

"Three strikes and you're out."

"He's my brother," Hamdi said, looking down at his knuckles. He shook his head. "My *little* brother."

I wished I'd never told him about my brother. Now he had this wedge, and I could feel him prying at the rock in me. I went to the bathroom, and Kathryn followed me.

"Do you happen to have a tampon?" I asked.

From the other stall, Kathryn handed one over. "Don't give him any money," she said. "No matter what he says."

"Does Hamdi even have a brother?"

"Oh yes," she said. "A younger brother. I'm so sick of all this

77

'love you like a brother' stuff. They love their brothers more than their wives." She flushed the toilet. "You know he has a woman in Finland and a seven-year-old child. You'd think he'd want to send the child some money, wouldn't you?"

I agreed that I would expect that. Still, the brother must be the one in the picture. I had pictures like that, pictures inside my head. My hand on my brother's shoulder. Dressed up for Easter. Jumping off a dock at a Wisconsin lake. Years before he got into trouble, he had loved dinosaurs and skateboarding and Parcheesi.

WE PILED INTO the car, me and Kathryn in back. Ahmet drove a few blocks and pulled over to the curb. Hamdi opened his door and flipped the seat forward so Kathryn could climb out.

"Goodnight, you two!" he said cheerfully. "Kathryn's tired, aren't you dear, and Ahmet's going to drive you up to see the lights of the Bosphorus."

Kathryn jerked Hamdi's arm. "Did you warn her?"

"Of course," he said and turned to us. "Enjoy the view."

I was sitting in the back. In case I had to grab the wheel or reach for the key, I moved to the seat Hamdi had vacated. "Skip the Bosphorus," I told Ahmet. "Take me back to my *pension*."

Ahmet sat like a block of stone, and I turned to watch Hamdi and Kathryn enter a dingy alley door. Ahmet's fingers squeezed my knee. I put his hand back on the wheel. He wiggled his fingers and, scowling at me, started the car. It was eleven, and I was dead tired. As long as he didn't have a weapon, I could defend myself. Put him in a head lock. Put two fingers in his eyes or knee him in the nuts. I closed my eyes, lulled by the car winding through darkened streets.

Ahmet pulled into a crowded, paved parking lot.

"Hamdi told me to bring you here," Ahmet said. "It's your last night in Istanbul, and he wanted you to see something special."

"Oh, all right." I opened the door. "Let's get it over with."

There were newly planted trees and fresh sod, some kind of city park on the crest of a hill. Below sparkled the lights of the

Bosphorus, the strait that divided Europe and Asia. The commerce of the world passed at our feet: oil and contraband and arms and grain, massive tankers that, from this distance, looked no bigger than bathtub toys. How great it would be if, somehow, the drug traffic could be strangled here. If Afghanistan's poppies never made it to New York. If dealers like my brother had nothing to deal. Cutting off the supply was the only thing that could have saved him.

Ahmet led me past an outdoor bar of happy drunks. Granite stairs continued down past terraces where entwined couples had taken over all the benches. And no wonder. The moon hung like a silver mirror above the illuminated spans of a bridge. White and red beacons cast narrow beams ahead of ships' prows, and spumes of foam trailed from the sterns.

"It feels like you can see the whole world from here," I said.

A couple vacated a bench and we sat down.

"The Bosphorus Strait connects the Black Sea and the Mediterranean," Ahmet said, crowding against me while delivering his geography lesson. I was not the least attracted to this pudgy Turk whose shirt wouldn't even button. He hadn't one third of Hamdi's energy. Hamdi had fucked me into a state of oblivion.

"What do you do?" I said.

"I'm a customs inspector," he said.

"Is that right? I'm a postal inspector. I work for the US Postal Service."

"Do you carry a gun?"

"At home, but not here."

He shook his head. "We have such an unfortunate problem with hashish and heroin in this country. Not only do we ship a lot of drugs overseas, but many of our own citizens fall victim to this perversion. I feel as though I owe my life to Hamdi. He knows he can call me any time of the day or night and I will help him out. He is like a brother to me."

"You sound like a broken record," I said, "but what's the story with Hamdi's real brother?"

"Did you ever see *Midnight Express*?"

"Sure," I said. "Horrible movie."

"Hamdi tells me you have a brother."

Damn, Hamdi. "I'm feeling cold. Let's go."

"Are you sure you wouldn't like to have a closer view of the water?"

"Take me home or I will go back to the bar and call a taxi."

He made a grab and circled me with his arms, pressing his face between my breasts. Air whistled through his nostrils. He appeared to be smelling me. I drummed my fingers on his back.

"I know you can't breathe down there. Let me go."

"My wife doesn't understand me at all."

I laughed and grabbed his tie, pulling it until his cheeks bulged. "You seem like a reasonable person," I said. "Why do you persist?"

He held up his hands in surrender and I released him. We started uphill, Ahmet trying to catch his breath.

"Hamdi told me, 'Angela is a warm woman. A caring woman. She understands when a man is unhappy with his wife.'"

"That asshole." I regretted every minute I'd spent with Hamdi and every confidence I'd shared, and I wondered how he'd gotten me to reveal myself, when normally I don't. I don't even know what it's like to be married because I've never been. We walked past the bar, Ahmet thankfully keeping his hands to himself.

"Do you work at night?" I said.

"Yes. How do you know that?"

"You're so chipper and alert."

"What does 'chipper' mean?"

"It means happy. Like a bird. Chirp. Chirp."

He laughed falsely. "Chirper."

"No, chipper."

"Shipper," he said.

"Right," I said. "Perfect pronunciation."

In the car I pushed my seat all the way back and reclined it. Maybe I would just sleep here. Ahmet bent sideways and put his head down on my breast, and in spite of myself, I stroked his greasy hair. His shoulders shook and his tears wet my blouse.

"Oh, what's the matter? Is it your unsympathetic wife?"

"Not the wife," he said. "I lied. I'm not married."

Sure, he wasn't.

"I'm thinking about Hamdi's brother."

"Does he have a name?"

"Kemal." He raised his tear-streaked face. "Kemal is his name. He lived with me for two years at the center. My bunkmate."

"You made it and he didn't."

He took a handkerchief out of his pocket and blew his nose. "He fell apart when I left. You know their parents died. Since Hamdi was fourteen, he has taken care of his brother. Begged. Picked cotton. Just the two of them. Kemal never went to school. He has no skills. Hamdi and Kemal walked to Ankara from near the border with Iraq."

"That's a long walk."

"You have sheeps at home?"

"You mean like 'baa-baa black sheep?'"

"What is called the man who looks after the sheeps?"

"Shepherd," I said.

I was prepared for him to grope me again, but he started the car. Very slowly he snaked down the switchbacks.

"Does your Bible not contain a story of the Good Shepherd?" Ahmet said.

In Sunday school that had always been my favorite Bible story, but I had lost my faith.

We drove along the shoreline and passed several hotels where Ahmet offered to spend the night, or the three hours of it that were left, and I accused him of driving me all around hell's half-acre instead of taking me the direct way. Then I noticed the battlements of Topkapi Palace, and knew that he had, in fact, been taking me back to my *pension*.

"Would you mind stopping at the Four Seasons?" I said. "They have an ATM, and I need some cash to get me to the airport."

The car slowed to a crawl.

I grabbed the handle, ready to jump.

"Forget sleeping with me," Ahmet said.

"Fine. I will."

"The money is the most important thing," Ahmet said. "Hamdi only needs $500. You can loan it to him, and he will pay you back just as soon as he pays the bribe and gets Kemal released. You know what Turkish prisons are like. You can't let him rot in jail. Hamdi told me you're his only hope of coming up with the money. He wanted to sell you a rug to make the commission. That's why he pressed so hard for you to buy. That is the honorable way. The business way. Now, he feels so much shame to ask you that he begged me to explain. I must have that $500 tonight. If Hamdi doesn't pay it tomorrow, they will transfer Kemal to another prison, and there will be no way to get him out. 'If one forfeits what is due to him as a charity, it will atone for his sins.'"

What did any of this mean? Why did I have to help?

"This is not my problem," I said.

"Angela, Hamdi wishes to offer prayers for your brother at the same time he prays for the release of Kemal."

"Oh, for god's sake," I said. "I have half a mind to do it just to shut you up."

"You will?" he said. "You will bring me the money?"

"I'll think about it," I said.

"What is your brother's name?" he said.

"Jamie."

"I have my Quran in the glove box." He let the engine idle. "I will wait here till you come back."

The street was dark except for the bright, narrow sidewalk and the spotlights embedded around the perimeter of a high, stucco wall. The Four Seasons was a former city jail turned into a luxury hotel. A giant glass door had replaced the wooden gates.

Exhaustion put me almost in a trance, and I paused just inside the entry to look at the sepia photos of prisoners in striped uniforms and fez-like cotton caps. Leg-irons attached one man to the next.

I crossed the lobby and stood at the desk. The clerk, a young, blue-eyed Brit, asked if he could help me. I hadn't written Jamie in too many years to count, and I didn't want it to be one minute longer.

"I need to write a letter." I said.

"Certainly." He handed me stationery and a pen.

I looked out to the street where Ahmet waited. "That man is following me. I haven't the least idea who he is. I wonder if your security guard could make him go away."

PANCHO VILLA'S COIN

———○———

WITH THEIR THIN arms and caved-in stomachs, barefoot
Indians advanced across the cane fields, hacking left and right
with their machetes. My father drove the highway's centerline
and gestured with his cigarette. "That's where your sugar comes
from, Janet. The sweat and tears of those poor sons-of-bitches. The
world's a tug-of-war between the oppressed and the oppressors!"

I picked up my journal, a spiral notebook with a brown, water-
stained cover.

On the way to Vera Cruz we saw exploited Indians.

This was Mexico, 1958, and even before the trip, I knew a great
deal about these Indians. In eighth grade, we had studied the Aztec
and Mayan civilizations. I even made a *paper-mâché* pyramid like
the one my father had just taken my mom and me to see in Cholula,
but I worked on my project before he came home from the waterfront. The moment I heard him open the door, I slid the pyramid
under my bed. If I'd shown it to him, he'd think I was trying to get
an A, and that would have made him feel bad.

When Father was my age—thirteen—he'd been kicked out of
Roswell Military Academy in New Mexico, and he was sensitive
about his lack of education. That was part of the reason for the
trip, to show me that not everyone in the world had it as good as I

did. With the windows cracked open and two inches of humid air streaming in, I'd had about as much education as I could take.

Insects splatted against the windshield. The car swerved. Then, there was a scrape and a sound like a smashed can.

"Son. Of. A. Bitch!" my father said. "I hope that's not the oil pan." In the rear-view mirror, his blue, washed-out eyes sought mine. "If the oil pan blows, I'm putting you in charge. You and your mother stay in the car with the doors locked. I'll hitch a ride to the next Pemex. Use the steel pipe if anyone tries to break in."

"Fine," I said. Nothing bad would happen. The Mexican people were nice, especially the boys. My mom and me would be stuck in the car, and I would be bored out of my mind. It was hot and I wanted to jump in a pool.

With her arms tightly folded, my mom had been leaning against the window. She looked over at the speedometer, and then, frowning through her glasses, stared at my father.

"What?" he said.

"Is the car okay?" she said.

"We hit another wash-out," he said.

"Are you going to stop?"

"No," he said.

"You could stop," she said.

"As long as the oil pan's not punctured," he said, "I think we'll make it."

"Rex, I'm in quite a bit of pain."

That meant she had to pee.

"Hold it," he said.

"If you see a gas station…"

"There won't be one till we get to Vera Cruz."

I had huevos revueltos *for lunch and a Nehi orange to drink.*

I could have written that I was sick of eating the same thing, day after day. At that age grilled cheese or peanut butter sandwiches would have made me happy, but I didn't dare put my true thoughts on paper.

Although my father was unpredictable, I could absolutely count on one thing: We would never, ever stop between lunch and the place we were going to spend the night. We had taken a lunch break at a roadside stand where two boys charged five *centavos* to let me touch an iguana suspended by a rope around its neck. The heat made my mom thirsty, and she washed down her eggs with two entire Cokes. I had a sip of Nehi orange and poured the rest on the ground so I wouldn't be tempted. Father never let us stop if we had to use the bathroom, and as I had foreseen, once we hit the road again, he blew past every gas station. My tongue felt cottony and my throat burned, but at least I wasn't in pain. I leaned forward, inserting myself between the two of them, and rested my chin on my arms.

"Can we get a hotel with a swimming pool?" I asked.

"I need to stop at a bank and cash a traveler's check," my father said.

"But, Rex," my mother said, "isn't it Sunday?"

Father blew out a stream of smoke in her direction. He tossed me his empty Camel's wrapper. "Here's a camel for your scrapbook."

"Actually, I think it might be a dromedary," I said.

"Then why does it say 'Camel' on the pack?" he said.

"I don't know," I said.

"Then listen to your old man," he said. "It's a camel."

My mother's shoulders shifted, and she cleared her throat.

She didn't have to tell me. I could think what I wanted. Just don't set him off.

I sniffed the pack, tore off the cellophane, and pulled apart the seam so that I could lay the wrapper flat. The sweet smell of raw tobacco reminded me of gingerbread, and I loved the picture of the exhausted, cranky dromedary. Its knees looked like they were about to buckle in the desert's relentless heat. The big pyramid right by the dromedary's tail reminded me of the one Cheops built. But that was Egypt, and all the pyramids in Giza had smooth sides. The Mexican pyramids had steps that led up to an altar where priests performed their sacrifices, tearing the hearts out of young girls.

"How's it going back there?" my father said.

"Fine," I said. Fine, fine, and more fine. Everything had to be fine.

The back seat looked like the inside of my desk back in junior high: colored pencils, a Strathmore drawing pad, scissors, and the red, leather scrapbook where I pasted in postcards, matchbook covers, and ticket stubs. The scrapbook was different from my journal. My dad didn't check the scrapbook, but he insisted on reading my journal every few days, just to make sure I hadn't left out something I would want to remember later. The journal was for him, but the scrapbook was for me. I squeezed mucilage from the angled, rubber top and pasted the cigarette wrapper next to a postcard of a church in Orizaba where we'd stopped the night before.

I liked Orizaba. I remember wishing we could have stayed there longer than one night, but I wrote only the facts he said I would want to remember when I was all grown up.

The Pico de Orizaba is covered with snow. At 18,490 feet, it is the tallest mountain in Mexico.

When we pulled into Orizaba we were still in the mountains, not yet down on the sweltering coast of Vera Cruz, and my mother got busy unpacking her suitcase and told me to go out to the hotel pool by myself. It was cool, and at first, I thought the water might be too cold, but my father would have gotten angry if I didn't get in, so I did.

Backstroking, I could see the volcano. Girl-twins who did not look alike came running out when they heard me splashing around. One year older than me, the twins had just emerged from the jungles of the Yucatan. Their father, an archaeologist, had discovered a new pyramid at Mayapan, and they had held string and helped him take measurements. The red spots on their legs came from leeches.

Karen, the oldest twin by six minutes, noticed the way my breasts were pooching out of my swim top. "Your mom should buy you a larger suit."

"She will," I said, "but they don't sell suits in the local markets."

In the markets, Indian women sit on the ground and sell black pottery, flowered blouses, and rebozos.

"I'll be relieved to get back to civilization," Karen said. "My suit's all mildewy." She snapped her bikini top.

"I prefer the jungle." The other twin, Marion, slipped down into the water and said "brrrgh!" She had on a one-piece like me, but she wasn't spilling out of it. Her wavy, permed hair looked like the mom's on "Father Knows Best."

"I'm going to be an archaeologist," Marion said.

"I want to be one, too." I had wanted to study archeology ever since I was eleven and read *The March of Archeology*. The author, C.W. Ceram, had a lot of stuff about Heinrich Schliemann and the discovery of King Tut's tomb in the Valley of the Kings. There was a curse on the tomb, and two of the three archaeologists had bad luck, like dying. I wanted to stay in Orizaba—These were the only two girls my age I'd seen in five weeks!—but my father said it was a dumpy town with no action.

In Orizaba twins who didn't look alike were staying in our same hotel.

At dinner, the man in charge of the restaurant put our parents at one table and us girls at another. Two weeks earlier, I'd had an attack of Montezuma's Revenge, and ever since then, the only thing my mom had let me eat was scrambled eggs. That night, she thought I was over it and said I could have tamales. I made up my mind to eat in a hurry so I could have another swim. The pool had a diving board, and maybe there'd be some cute Mexican boys. I wanted to practice my jackknife and see if the twins could do flips.

At the grownups' table, their father was saying, "I'm Dr. Arnold Brinkerman, a lowly professor in the Department of Archeology at the University of New Mexico."

"My name's Rex Elmo Stone," my father said. "Don't know if you're aware of this, but in Latin, 'Rex' means King."

"Does he always introduce himself like that?" Karen whispered. She had painted her nails before dinner and changed into a three-tiered, ruffled fiesta skirt.

"Not always," I said. Just most of the time. I tucked my chin and took a forkful of rice.

My mother twisted the hem of her napkin. A rooster *piñata* with curly red-and-blue feathers hung from the ceiling. She kept looking up at it as if she wanted to take a stick and give it a good whack. My father was getting on her nerves.

"Your mother's kind of quiet," Marion said.

"She's shy." I put a hand to my cheek, wanting to protect my mom and hoping they wouldn't examine her face and comment on that, too.

"Our mother didn't come on this trip," Marion said. "We think our parents are getting a divorce."

"Why?" I said.

"She's tired of pulling off leeches." Karen looked at her nails. "Besides, she has a rich boyfriend."

"But she's married," I said.

"What does that have to do with anything?" Karen said.

Marion shrugged. "Grownups. They think they can hide stuff."

"Our mother thought it was a big secret," Karen said.

"He still loves her." Marion looked pityingly at her father.

Wearing khaki shorts and holding the ankle of a leg he'd pulled onto his knee, their father, whose big ears made it seem like he was hanging on my father's every word, rocked back in his chair.

My father was a good head taller and fifteen years older, with broad shoulders and a stomach he liked me to punch to see if he could "take it." His hair had turned white during the war, and he told Dr. Brinkerman he'd been a Marine. Actually, he'd served in the Merchant Marine, loading and unloading cargo. He shifted to another topic: the longshoremen's union, the ILWU. He could go on about the union for hours.

My father had met my mother, an elementary school teacher who'd moved out to California from Colorado, at Playland at the Beach in San Francisco. They'd been put in the same car for the ride through the "Tunnel of Love." Sometimes, my mom would get a wistful look and tell that story, but in Orizaba, my mother sat with her shoulders drawn in, dabbing her weepy eye with a handkerchief. A scar on the right side of her face pulled like the elastic neckline of her flowered dress. Before she met my father, she had been married to a different man, whom she'd had to move out West to escape. She was lucky to have met my father, she said, because, otherwise, she wouldn't have had me. The scar came from right after I was born. My father joked about her running into a door.

"Mom!" I raised my hand.

Marion and Karen looked at each other. Karen whispered, "Do you have to raise your hand if you want to ask a question?"

"It's polite," I said.

My father shook his finger. "You're interrupting an adult conversation."

"Yes, Sir," I said. My father had been born with water on the brain, and his mother died when he was two. Most of his life he'd lived in El Paso with his Aunt Mamie, but she sent him to Roswell Military Academy because she couldn't handle him. He'd been raised without a father figure, my mother said. That was why he was the way he was, and we had to be patient.

My mother smiled lopsidedly in my direction, then folded her napkin and put it on the table. "That was a tasty dinner."

I raised my hand again.

"Yes, Janet?" she said.

"Is my forty-five minutes up yet?"

She checked her watch. "I think it's safe to go in the water."

The twins looked at each other, and Karen whispered, "Do they always treat you like a baby?"

I shrugged. "My mother does."

My father slapped Dr. Brinkerman on the shoulder, almost

knocking him from his chair. "Let me buy you a drink, Doc. Pick your poison. Tequila or mescal."

The archaeologist relaxed the squint of his forced smile, picked up his *Dos Equis*, and took one last swig. He looked at his daughters. "I think I'd better call it a night."

"Oh, come on," my father said. "My wife can sit by the pool."

"Janet will sleep better with a swim," my mother said. "It won't be any trouble to watch your daughters."

"The twins have been in the water enough today," Dr. Brinkerman said. "If they swim anymore, they'll turn into fishes."

My father said, "I never met a man I didn't like and who didn't like me, and I won't take offense, even though I normally do when a man won't let me buy him a drink."

Dr. Brinkerman blanched. "It's just that I've had a long day."

"Rex," my mother said, "you've had a long day, too."

"Party poopers," he said. "All right, Lorrie. You go to bed. I'll be along in a minute."

My mother looked at me. We knew what that meant.

My father pushed back his chair and sauntered towards the cantina. The twins and Dr. Brinkerman were staying in another wing of the hotel, but while Karen ran back to their room to get something to write their address on—so I could send them a postcard—my mother told Dr. Brinkerman we'd just come from Mexico City.

"Oh, really?" he said. "Did you drive down the West Coast, then?"

"Yes," she said. "We stopped in Hermosillo."

"That's not the typical tourist stop."

"I know," my mother said.

We went to a goat ranch near Hermosillo and I got to pet the baby goats. They were very cute.

MY FATHER HAD been coming to Mexico on his own for years, and this was the first time he'd brought us. We'd driven down through the Sonoran desert and stopped in Hermosillo to visit one of my dad's friends, a Yaqui Indian who lived on a goat ranch and who'd fought with Pancho Villa. Then, we'd gone to Acapulco, "where Rex had some business," my mother told Dr. Brinkerman. After that, we'd driven up to the capital, Mexico City, then dropped down to the east coast. Vera Cruz was our last stop before heading home. She traced a triangle in the air. "That's our trip."

"Sounds like you've covered a lot of ground." Dr. Brinkerman looked back in the direction my father had gone. "Your husband's quite the character."

"He is that." My mother dabbed her eye. "Rex is one of a kind. Not many people worry about the world as much as he does."

The political system in Mexico is controlled by wealthy families. Elections are rigged by the PRI.

My father's letters-to-the-editor appeared frequently in the *San Francisco Chronicle*. My mother typed them and checked for spelling errors.

The year before, he had taken us to Washington, D.C. for a lesson in democracy so I would appreciate the many freedoms most Americans took for granted. He showed me the Bill of Rights in the Library of Congress and said any citizen of the United States had just as much right to speak his mind as Joseph McCarthy. The place he wanted to show me the most was the FBI headquarters. The FBI was tapping the phones of his union's leadership. Maybe even ours, he thought.

"J. Edgar Hoover thinks he's such a big shot," my father said. "Let him come out on the sidewalk, and I'll show him who's boss."

My father had spent the entire time we were in Washington being mad.

But this year was different. This year, he wanted to enjoy

himself, and he wanted the vacation to give me an "international perspective." Besides, thirteen was an impressionable age, he said, and a trip to Mexico would help me with my accent. My father wanted me to speak Spanish like a native. Before his Aunt Mamie sent him to Roswell, he had picked up Spanish on the streets of El Paso and Juarez. As I fell asleep, I heard him over in the *cantina*, singing his version of *"La Cucaracha"* with some Mexican men.

When I'd first started learning Spanish back in seventh grade, he'd translated the lyrics, so I sang along silently, the words and the melody ringing in my ears.

> *La Cucaracha, la Cucaracha*
> *Ya no puede caminar*
> *Porque le falta, porque le falta,*
> *Marijuana que fumar.*

When he explained what the words meant, Father had staggered around, clutching his chest and acting silly. The cockroach smoked so much marijuana, he made himself all relaxed and couldn't walk to save his life. Watching him act like a clown in the circus, I laughed the way I did when he tickle-tortured me, except the laughing felt better because I could stop before I wet my pants.

HE HAD BEEN a better father when I was young. When I was five or six, he'd taken me down to the waterfront to fish. We sat on the wharf's creosoted timbers and let our feet swing above the water. He praised me for baiting my own hook, and he showed me how to tie on the red-and-white plastic bob. Sometimes, my mom and I met him for dinner, and he took us to Alioto's on Fishermen's Wharf. If we came early, he zipped me around Pier 44 in his jitney, and once, he took me down in a ship's cargo hold.

The other thing I liked about my father was that he told me things most grownups wouldn't, things my mother certainly wouldn't have told me, and that made me feel like an adult. Which is to say, trusted. When I asked him what marijuana was, he said poor Negroes smoked it. "Did you ever smoke it?" I asked. "Yes," he'd said. During the war, he'd smoked "reefer," which was a kind of cigarette, only stronger. After the war, he'd switched to Camels. That night in Orizaba, my father's smoke-deepened voice echoed along the corridors and through my open window; and, the next morning, Mother lamented that his singing had kept her awake.

"I slept fine," I said.

Mother had come in my room to keep from waking him, and she was folding my clothes and putting them in my suitcase. "He started acting up in Acapulco," she said. "I'm just so tired of it, I could scream."

Acapulco was the first corner of the triangle.

Father took me deep-sea fishing and we caught a sea turtle.

IN ACAPULCO, JUST as we were about to cross the blue-water line (the water close to land looked greenish because of the runoff from the hills), I looked down and saw a giant sea turtle swimming near the boat. The captain and two crew members used gaffs to haul the turtle on-board, and my father brought it back to the hotel in our Impala's big trunk. First, he threw it in the cashew-shaped pool, and when it began swimming, he took off his watch and jumped in fully clothed, straddling the poor creature and whooping like a cowboy. The bus boys at the restaurant helped him drag it out. The turtle was still alive, its arms and legs and head retracted in its shell, but Father said it wouldn't live long because it had swum in a chlorinated pool, and he convinced the restaurant's chef to kill it and make soup.

Turtle soup was a great delicacy, my father said, and I guess he was right because the guests in the hotel thanked him. When he asked if that wasn't about the best thing I'd ever tasted, I had to say, "It's fine. A lot better than scrambled eggs." Which was partly the truth. The turtle meat tasted as chewy as a gum eraser.

"When we get over to Vera Cruz," my father promised, "we'll catch a sailfish."

My mother reminded him she got seasick.

"You don't have to go," he said.

I actually liked it better when it was just Father and me.

IT WAS DUSK by the time we pulled into Vera Cruz. Father went into three or four American hotels and looked at the rooms. Finally, a block from the main drag, on a street named for Christopher Columbus, he found a Mexican tourist hotel, which was the kind of place he liked to stay. He went to the *oficina* to ask the room price, and my mother and I waited in the hot car.

"What's taking him so long?" I said.

"You know." She tipped a thumb to her lips and made a gulping sound.

My father's bitten nails hooked over the Impala's window. He opened my door. "*Vámonos!*"

"Does this place have a pool?" I said.

"That's the second time you've asked me that." My father cupped his hand to keep the breeze from blowing out his match. His eyes turned a hard, electric blue. "Don't make me have to teach you a lesson."

He didn't like repetitive questions from my mother or me.

"Is there a diving board?" I said.

"I don't know."

The hotel was a white, stucco building with a tile roof. I gathered up my art things and put them in my train case. My father opened the trunk and placed our suitcases on the pavement.

"Did you lock the back door?" he said.

"Yes." I had an Indian burn on my wrist from the day we went to the pyramid at Cholula. This time I went around the car and checked all the locks. Sealed up tight. Father didn't want our car to get stolen.

Although dusty and dinged from the gravel that spit out from the wheels of trucks, our Impala was the only new car in the parking lot. My father had bet on a horse named Round Table in the Santa Anita Derby, and with the money he made off the race, he bought this special model, which he called firecracker red. My mother thought he should have driven her '52 Chevy down, but he said, no, he wanted to show off the Impala to his friends. The car was evidence of what union organizing could do for the average working stiff. Without the union behind him, the working man was nothing but a tool and dupe of the capitalists.

Just before the trip to Mexico, we'd had his union boss, Harry Bridges, over to our house for dinner. He was the Australian labor organizer who headed the International Longshoremen's and Warehousemen's Union. The head of the FBI—J. Edgar Hoover— was trying to have my father's boss deported.

Soon after that, two men in gray suits paid a call. I had let them in the house, and when they asked to look around, I took them to the garage and showed them my new, three-speed Schwinn. My father said I had handled the situation well.

Just before we left San Francisco, I overheard my father tell my mom that Harry Bridges was trying to close down ports from Seattle to Acapulco. Because the FBI had tapped Bridges' phone, my father had volunteered to carry a message to the Mexican labor organizers. No one would suspect because my father was down here showing his family a good time.

In Acapulco and again in Mexico City, he'd met up with Fernando Lluch, a thin, suave, thirtyish man with tasseled Italian moccasins and an annoying habit of pinching my cheek. Señor Lluch took Father around to meet other communists, and he warned us to watch out for the *federales*. But my father wasn't afraid of the feds, theirs or ours. From under the front seat, he took the steel pipe he'd told me to use if the oil pan blew, and he held it like a walking stick, tapping hollowly on the red tile floor as he led the way to our rooms.

We passed the hotel's counter, where a man with his back to

us was sorting mail into letter-sized cubbyholes. My mother saw a restroom. "I'll join you in a minute," she said, putting down her suitcase and opening a door that said "*Damas.*" Just beyond the restroom, I saw a restaurant and *cantina.* It was getting dark. Several Mexican workers in straw hats had seated themselves at round wooden tables, and one had started shuffling cards. When the cards slapped down, my stomach skipped. If my mom and me were lucky, the card players would go home before my father joined them. My father was in some kind of hurry, though, because he'd gone off toward our room. Luckily, I could follow the tapping of his steel pipe.

I turned a corner and found myself in a completely different world, a magical garden with birds-of-paradise and red hibiscus and a gurgling fountain. In the fading sunlight, I saw a boy on the hotel's clay tennis court practicing his serve. His white shirt glowed. With high cheekbones and a sculpted jaw, he looked like a figure in an Orozco mural.

My father stood at the door of his room. "See that kid?"

"Oh, yeah. I guess." Of course, I saw him. He was the best looking boy I'd seen on the whole trip.

"He's rich," Father said. "Otherwise a kid his age would have a job."

"How old do you think he is?" I said.

"Fourteen or fifteen," my father said. "That kid's living on Easy Street."

That's what my dad said about my mother and me. We lived on Easy Street. Actually, we lived on Haight, across from Golden Gate Park.

The tennis court at the hotel in Vera Cruz is clay, Father says.

I wanted to talk to the boy, or just stand and watch the ball fly from his hand and his arm extend to reach the sweet spot in the sky, and then connect—twhack! The sound sent an electric thrill through my body. The boy dropped his racket and stared at me.

"Here's your room key," my father said, nodding to the room

next to theirs. "Change into your suit."

The key, like the one in *Treasure Island*—brass, with a big round end—sank into my palm, and I just knew we were in for an adventure.

My mother, a suitcase in one hand, train case in the other, clip-clopped toward us, her skirt swaying around her calves. "Will we eat here, Rex?"

"Yes." He handed me the key. "After she swims."

I STOOD BY the pool's ladder, too shocked to move. Acacia blossoms floated on the black water. The ladder into the deep end had turned all rusty, and there wasn't any shallow end. I had never seen a swimming pool that wasn't blue, and I was scared because the water looked thick and smelled like decaying leaves. It reminded me of *The Creature From the Black Lagoon.* In the eerie pink sunset, bubbles rose to the water's surface. The oily sheen reminded me of a Spirograph.

The hotel in Vera Cruz had a saltwater pool.

With his long pipe, my father pushed away the leaves and blossoms. "There," he said. "Jump in."

"The water looks yucky," I said.

"They take the water straight from the ocean," my father said. "It's cleaner than it looks."

"Rex," my mother said. "That water hasn't been changed in a year."

"No, Lorrie!" he said. "She wanted a place with a pool. She asked twice, which is against the rules. So, against my better judgment, I got her a pool." He turned, his jaw thrusting out. "Get in."

My mother looked at the sky, then over at the boy playing tennis. He was watching us and had his fingers hooked through the court's cyclone fence.

"Go on," Mother said. "It won't kill you."

I turned around and backed down the ladder. Inky water

swallowed my legs.

My father put his big hand on my head and pushed. "All the way in."

Gulping tears, I felt my feet slip on the ladder's steps. Salt stung my eyes, and when I surfaced, my hair was full of yellow blossoms. I dog-paddled to the ladder and looked up. My father had disappeared.

"Honestly! This just slays me. He can wipe his feet on me all he wants, but..." My mother held out a towel. "Take your shower before he comes back."

Flipping my hair over my face, I clawed to get the flowers out, and when I looked up, I saw a quick skitter through the bushes. I pointed. "What's that?"

"Oh, my god, it's a rat as big as a dog!" My mother shivered and hugged herself. "But, of course. It's a port, so they would be here." She draped the towel around my shoulders.

The first rule when we arrived at a hotel was that I was supposed to put my clothes away, but my closet didn't have hangers. With the towel over my shoulders, I ran past the tennis court to the office. My father was there, leaning on the counter and smoking a cigarette. He was asking about a fishing boat. At a pause in the conversation, I raised my hand. My father asked what I wanted, and I told him.

"I'm sorry." The manager, a thin, balding man with a quivering mustache, turned up his palms. "*No hay.*"

"*Porque?*" my father said.

"*Ladrones,*" the manager said. "People take hanger home."

My father asked if it was safe to leave his car in the parking lot, and the manager said, yes, but it would be better to have someone guard it. While they negotiated a price, I walked back to my room.

The boy on the tennis court spun his racket and smiled. "*Hola.*"

"*Hola.*" I waved my fingers. "*Cómo está usted?*"

"*Bien, y tú?*" He was using the familiar form. He dropped his racket, emptied his pockets of tennis balls, and came toward me. His eyes, the black of the pool, had double lashes, and he blinked them slowly, melting the chocolate of his eyes.

"*¿Cuántos años tienes?*" I said.

"*Quince,*" he said.

Fifteen. Not that much older than me.

"*¿Y que edad tiene tú?*"

The familiar form again. I wasn't good at it. Fourteen, I told him, fudging a year.

He plucked leaves from my hair, and then bent, took my hand, and raised it to his lips.

My heart thumped in my throat. I looked down the corridor to my room and said I had to go.

"*Hasta luego,*" he said.

He was planning on seeing me later. After it got dark, maybe he would come to my window and kiss me through the screen. If there was a screen. Otherwise, I would just lean out, like Juliet on her balcony.

I opened the door of my room. My mother was inside. She was folding her gross pink undies and putting them in a drawer.

"This isn't your room," I said.

"I'm going to stay with you tonight."

"Do you have to?" I said.

"We'll discuss it after dinner." She turned down the cover on one of the twin beds, lay on her back with her hands tucked under her head, and looked up at the ceiling. Silently, she pointed. A small lizard hung upside down. Its tongue flicked out, and I heard a sound like pop beads coming apart. Then she swung her legs off the bed and looked as if she'd made up her mind about something. "Hurry up! We need to eat right now."

My hair felt like taffy. That Mexican boy wouldn't kiss a girl this hideous. "I'm never going to get these leaves out."

"Take a shower and be quick about it."

I went in the bathroom. The shower was tile, with no shower curtain, so I kept my suit on. The shower stall had mold in the corners. "I hate this hotel," I said.

My mother opened the bathroom door.

I turned on the water. Cold water trickled out. I scrubbed with my fingertips, the way *Seventeen* said you should do, but the shampoo turned to mucilage. If I could just get the saltwater out of my hair, I could tape my bangs to my forehead, and maybe later, put my hair up in a bun so I'd look older.

"You've got more hair in your armpits," Mother said.

I clamped my elbows to my sides. "This stupid shampoo isn't working."

"They're probably on well water," Mother said. "Here, give me your suit. I'll rinse it."

"Get out of here," I screamed.

She backed away, and I leapt out of the shower and slammed the door. Then, I took off my suit and lifted my arm. How completely gross. By the end of the summer, I was going to look like those Mexican girls on the beach, dark hairy underarms and legs like the Missing Link.

PROPPED AGAINST THE headboard, Mother leafed through a *Life* magazine she'd brought from home. The room felt stuffy. A window opened on to the veranda, but it was closed. I pulled back the curtain.

"Don't open that." Mother checked her watch. "I don't want your father looking in."

The black phone between our two beds rang. Mother picked up the receiver. "What do you want?" She motioned for me to turn off the room's only light, and then she turned her back. In her pleading voice, said, "I haven't slept for a week, Rex, and it's ruining my health. Last night was the final straw! I can't take this anymore."

I didn't see what was so bad about last night. We'd been in Orizaba and it wasn't much different from any other night, except I'd met some kids my age. Oh, and it had been cooler because we were close to the volcano. Also, my room had closets with hangers. The room here in Vera Cruz felt like a closet, airless and dank. My mother raised a hand to shield her face, the way people did in confession, not wanting strangers to hear.

I slipped my hand under the curtain, turning the handle and inviting an inch of forbidden air into the room. My mother didn't know that before we went to the goat ranch in Hermosillo, through the rusty screen of our hotel, I had stayed up half the night kissing a boy who'd been diving in the pool. It was a high dive, too. And all the time I had been bobbing in the surf in Acapulco, with my mother napping in the shade of a giant umbrella, I had been kissing a boy underwater. On the lips. Before I got scared, I had let him put his fingers inside my suit and touch my breast.

The curtain fluttered. The boy on the tennis court toweled off, picked up the bucket of serving balls, and walked on tiptoe toward the veranda. Turned away from me, my mother sat on the bed, her forehead in her hand, her back hunched. I slipped my hand through the open window, crooking my finger for the boy to come closer. He crouched down, crept under the window, and turned his palm upside down against mine. His skin felt warm and soft. Then he let go of my hand and his mouth surrounded my middle finger, sucking. A delicious ripeness flowed through me, a peach, squeezing out its juice; he bit my knuckle.

Someone shouted, "Carlos!" Then he was gone, the bucket of balls left behind. Oh, if I could just get my mother out of the room. Tonight, he would come with *mariachis* strumming their small guitars. I wondered if he sang. It would be romantic if he could. The phone receiver clacked down. Mother's head dropped back, and she screamed silently at the ceiling. A fist thumped the wall. Quickly, I pulled the window closed, locked it, and dropped the curtain.

"Get away from that window in case he breaks the glass," Mother said.

Outside, Father kicked over the bucket of balls and cursed. I jumped back. While I was in the shower, he must have gone to the *cantina* for a pick-me-up.

He beat the door. "Lorrie! Lorrie! Open up! I'll be good." When no one answered, he said, "You stupid broad. If you don't open now, I'm going to have to teach you a lesson."

I crouched in the corner over my train case, pretending, in the dark, to want my colored pencils. I brought the back of my hand to my nose. Nutmeg and toast: That's what Carlos smelled like. I would never wash my finger again.

Mother sat on the sagging bed, leaned forward, and ran her fingers through her hair. In the heat, her curls had gone limp. She clicked on a lamp by her bed. The bare bulb drew bugs that circled with atomic fury.

"He'll be back," she said, batting the bugs from her lopsided face. "He's just going to get some liquid courage." She punched the pillow with her fist. "This is ridiculous. That pool stunt was the final straw."

I pulled back the curtain and saw my father stumbling toward the office. The *cantina* was down there.

"Do you think you could skip a meal?" Mother said.

"If it's scrambled eggs, sure," I said.

"Then put your clothes in your suitcase."

"Are we moving to another room?"

"No, we're going home."

"Do you have the car keys?"

"We're not taking the car." Mother's mouth was set in a firm line, the line that always crumpled when Father taught her a lesson. "We're going to fly."

For a minute, I thought of a magic carpet, and then I realized she was talking about a plane.

Never before had I seen my mother win an argument. Oh, she tried, but she always gave up. Father would say in a patient, teacherly voice, the same voice he used when he was telling me what to write down in my journal, "Why do you always have to learn the hard way?" To be fair, I had never seen him hit her. Father took her hand as if she were a little child and led her to their bedroom. Whatever he did to her was probably worse than what he did to me. Once he had gotten mad at me, lunged, grabbed my hair, and snapped it back until my neck cracked. I was down on my knees between his legs, begging him to stop. It was the first time I got all A's, and he claimed

I was too big for my britches. Getting one B satisfied him. I was smarter than my mother. It never took more than one lesson.

Mother beckoned me to the bed and pulled down the elastic front of her dress. "A woman should always have mad money in her bosom," she said. From the top of her corset, where two giant cones pushed her flesh together, Mother withdrew a tiny cotton sack, cinched with pink embroidery thread and held in place by a small, gold safety pin.

"Undo this for me," she said.

Touching her sweaty flesh, my fingers shook. The pin snapped sideways. I lifted out the little sack and handed it to her. Inside she had tucked a roll of American bills.

"The only problem I foresee is that the banks are closed. We won't be able to change money, but I'm sure they'll sell us a ticket at the airport."

"How do you know where the airport is?" I said.

"I don't, but the cab driver will. Last night, after your father went off to the bar, I went out and sat by the pool. The archaeologist came out to see the stars. That's how I know there's an airport in Vera Cruz. We can fly to Mexico City."

"Do you have enough money?"

"I think so." She stood and squeezed my chin. "As long as we're away from here, we'll be safe." Looking me in the eyes as if she wanted to tell me something important, and with the ruined half of her face gathered by the scar's bad stitching, she finally settled on, "You're a beautiful young woman. It killed me today to watch him push you underwater."

"It wasn't so bad." My voice came out in a squeak.

"No, Janet. It was bad. I've worried for a long time this was coming." Then, she strode across the room, opened the window, climbed on a chair, and swung her legs over the sill. I handed out the suitcases and boosted myself across. Mother threw the room key back on the table and pushed the window shut.

The spiky fronds of maguey plants cut my hands. Mother, flattening herself against the side of the hotel and dragging her suitcase, made for the *Avenida Cristóbal Colón*. When we turned the corner, I saw the curved, concrete roof of the *cantina*. It projected out like the prow of a ship, and beneath it, a half-wall encircled a table where five men sat playing cards. Above their heads flashed a strip of pink neon: "*Cabeza de Vaca*." Head of cow. A pink glow reflected off the white of my father's shirt. I expected him to feel my eyes on his back, but he didn't, and I felt sad because I was leaving, and he didn't have a chance to say goodbye. Then we were on the avenue where traffic and taxis whizzed past. My mother stepped forward and waved her white handkerchief. A taxi stopped and we got in. "Tell the driver to take us to the airport," Mother said.

"*Al aeropuerto*," I said. That was easy. Soon my Spanish would be as good as Father's. Meanwhile, this was like being in the middle of a Nancy Drew or Hardy Boys' mystery, with my mother and me threatened by dangerous *bandidos*.

The lights of the occasional passing car threw a momentary glow across the road, illuminating a *campesino* pedaling home on a rickety bike or pulling a cart of firewood. When the road turned to gravel, I didn't see any other cars. Maybe the taxi driver was going to kidnap us and take my mother's money. Maybe we'd be stranded and hope my father would figure out where we'd gone. Maybe he'd miss us. I felt a flutter of hunger and a confusing twist in my stomach. I would never see Carlos again.

At last, far from the city the taxi pulled into a parking lot. We unloaded our luggage. My eyes could barely make out the single-engine crop-dusters along the edges of a narrow runway. The planes looked like toys. From the double doors of a brightly lit Quonset hut, half a dozen Mexican cowboys reeled out, bellowing songs into the night.

Mother stood there, a suitcase in each hand. She squared her shoulders. "Tell the driver to wait."

"Let me think." Was "wait" *quedar* or *quitar*? I didn't want to tell him to leave by mistake.

"I speak English." The stocky young man with a silver crucifix around his neck closed the taxi's trunk. "Better I come with you."

The moment we stepped into the metal building, the drunk men outside bumped one another in their hurry to follow us. The Quonset hut smelled of oil and diesel fuel, and in the back of it, four dimly lit work-bays held pieces of disassembled engines. Propellers leaned against the walls. Toward the front was the snack bar's long counter and men sitting on wooden stools. When I looked their way, they shifted their hips and spread their knees. I slipped behind Mother and listened to the taxi driver ask the bartender when the next flight left.

The man's smile exposed a silver tooth. He turned to a calendar like the ones on the lockers at my dad's work. "*Mañana.*"

"Aren't there any flights tonight?" my mother said.

"Runway no have lights," the driver said. "If you want, buy ticket now, go tomorrow."

"Okay, okay, let me think." Mother looked up in her head for a moment, and then her eyes made a circle of the room. Like book-ends, a Coke machine and a cigarette machine stood at either end of a grease-stained leather couch. "What time is the first flight?"

The driver asked the bartender, and the man said noon. If the plane didn't break down, the driver translated.

"All right." She started to take money from her purse. She looked at the couch. "We can sit over there."

"You wait?" the taxi driver said incredulously. He looked at me.

Mother looked at me, too. "I guess you're right. It would be better to go back."

"Maybe we should stay here," I said. "We can sleep sitting up."

"Lady..." The taxi driver folded his arms. "I no wait all night."

I grabbed Mother's arm. "Mom! We'll be fine here."

Mother shook her head. "Don't worry. We can come back in the morning if he's still bad."

I couldn't form a picture of tomorrow in my mind. The plan, speeding fast in one direction, toward safety, was now rewinding back towards Father. I began to pray for one thing: That he hadn't discovered we'd ever left.

The driver loaded our suitcases in the trunk. "I sorry," he said. "I not know."

I slumped down on my seat, and when the driver pulled into the circle drive and a pink slash of neon cut across the back seat, I ducked down onto the floor and buried my head, the nuclear attack drill.

"Get up from there," Mother said. "Act like a big girl."

The driver let us off at the corner. Mother dragged the suitcases to the protection of the undergrowth and waited to keep them from being stolen, while I crept between the magueys and the wall. Across the stucco, the moon threw a wash of blue. Twenty identical windows were evenly spaced out. All but one was dark. My father was humming, and I could hear the sound of his unhurried pee. Our room was next door. I pushed open our window. My mother dragged the suitcases across the rocks. I put my finger to my lips. The bathroom light went out.

Mother whispered, "Give me a boost."

I laced my fingers but her foot burst through.

"Kneel down, then."

I dropped to my knees and let her stand on my back. A piece of glass embedded itself in the heel of my hand. Mother was half way through, legs outside kicking, head and arms inside.

"Put your hands down on the floor," I whispered. "Do a somersault."

"I'm too old," Mother said.

I pushed. Something ripped. Then she was in. I heaved the suitcases inside and pulled myself through the window.

In Vera Cruz, mother and I took long naps and slept through dinner. Father thought we had gone out to eat by ourselves.

Five minutes later, a knock came at the door. Mother looked at me. "Yes?" she said.

"*Señora* Stone," a man said, "open the door."

"Just a minute," she said. "I'll be right there." Mother's dress was hiked up. She smoothed it down. "Turn on a light," she whispered, and I did. Mother opened the door. It was the manager, his narrow mustache twitching, his bow-tie askew.

"*Toda la noche*, your husband drink," the man said, "and he come back to bar this minute."

"I'm sorry," Mother said. "He can be difficult."

"He say friend of Pancho Villa. You know what? Pancho Villa, he die in 1917."

"I didn't know that," Mother said.

"I not want your husband make trouble." The manager wiped his brow and looked over his shoulder. "I must close office. Go home."

I came to the door. "Sometimes I can calm him down."

The room threw a triangle of light onto the veranda. Coming toward us was Father, his white hair flying back, shirttail out, belt unbuckled. Metal clinked in his pockets.

"It's my lucky night." Grinning, he held a circle of silver, like a moon, between his thumb and forefinger. "I see you've met my old lady, Raul." He slapped the manager's shoulder. "But if she won't sleep with you, don't blame me. She's harder to fuck than a knothole, and drier too."

Mother never cried—Father liked it too much, and she didn't like to give him the satisfaction—but she was crying now. The left side of her mouth twisted like her handkerchief, while the right side remained frozen.

"Hey, honey," Father called from the darkness, "give your old man a hand with his key."

By his tone, I knew he meant me. His words didn't slur, so I couldn't tell how far gone he was. I prayed this was a beer drunk. Mescal made him mean. Any delay and he would start acting up. Pushing past the manager, I took the key and with my father propped on one stiff arm against the wall, his hot, sour breath in my face, I used my nail to find the tiny crescent where the key went in. Then, I stepped into the room and let my father pass.

He tossed coins on his bed and went into the bathroom. The faucets squeaked. His belt buckle dropped on the floor. "Turn the light on," he called. "I don't want to bark my shins."

I turned on the light.

"Try to get him to bed," Mother whispered from the doorway. She took the key to our room from her pocket, placing it urgently in my hand. "Let yourself in when you're done, but whatever happens, don't give him your room key. I don't think he'll harm you, but be cautious."

I put the key in my pocket. I didn't want the manager looking in. My father's key was still in the lock. I took it out and closed the door softly so Father wouldn't think about going back to the *cantina*. Then, I turned on the night light by the bed. The coins were larger and heavier than silver dollars. I scooped them up and put them on the dresser. Counting his winnings, I stood with my back half turned, catching the open slice of the bathroom door in my side vision. My father had taught me how to approach a mean dog. Stay calm inside, give the dog time to growl or challenge, but never take a step back. I put the coins in stacks of five.

In the dribble of water from the shower, my father sang.

La Cucaracha, la cucaracha
Ya no quiere caminar
Porque le falta, porque le falta
Marijuana que fumar.

He'd told me the lyrics were *no puede caminar*, not *no quiere caminar*. There was a big difference between the cockroach not being able to walk and not wanting to. I remembered the first time he sang me that song, how fun he could sometimes be. Maybe the shower would sober him up.

When the water shut off, I heard a towel sandpaper bare skin. He came out with it tucked around his waist, a pack of Camels in his hand, one lit and dragging down the corner of his mouth. His legs straddled the corner of the bed, and where the towel spread, I could see that thing in the middle like a pink, rolled-up sock. "Pe-nis." The word made me cringe, thinking of Mrs. Roberts, my seventh grade teacher, with a flip chart and her long pointer, saying "penis" and "vagina" and "testes" and "uterus." The word "penis" sounded foreign and ugly, but the way he was sitting, I could not help but look at his.

"How many coins are there?" my father said.

"Fifty eight." I picked up a coin.

"You know what they are?" he said.

"Silver *pesos?*"

"Nope. Guess again."

He liked to play this game of superior knowledge. That he was playing it now showed he was getting himself back in a good mood. Still, it seemed as if I had stepped into a battle my parents were fighting, and nobody had bothered to explain the rules.

"You're not scared to be in here with your old man, are you?"

"I'm not scared." Twisting a chair around so that my back was to him, I sat near the dresser and arranged the coins by the year they were minted.

"What kind of coins are these?" I asked.

"Mexican silver dollars," he said. "Navaho Indians use them for jewelry. The last time I saw any, I was in *Ciudad Juárez*, thirteen, your age, and a friend took me to see Pancho Villa. He gave me one. I'll show you when we get home."

He was still drunk.

"Okay," I said.

"Count out thirty and take them to your mother." He caught the ash in his cupped hand.

I counted out loud. One, two, three.

Father has a coin that Pancho Villa gave him.

I counted the coins all over again by twos and then by threes. Sitting on the corner of the bed, he was an arm's reach from me, and if I tried to run, he'd grab my arm and jerk it up behind my back, the way he did when we watched wrestling on TV.

He stubbed out his cigarette in an ashtray and brushed off his hands. "You remember last year's vacation when I took you to the FBI headquarters?"

"Yes, sir," I said.

"Can you name the Top Ten violent crimes?"

My mind could not make these sudden leaps—following him would lead to some trick—but the picture of a yellow poster board came into my mind.

"Murder. Arson. Armed robbery. Assault and battery. Felony theft. Kidnapping. Blackmail. Um, killing a police officer. No. That's murder. Uh, interstate flight. Narcotics."

"You've got nine," he said, holding up nine fingers. "What's the tenth?"

"I don't remember."

"Here's a clue." He stuck up his middle finger, the wave he made to women drivers when they braked on curves.

I got up from my chair. "I'm a little sleepy. Are we going fishing tomorrow?"

"Give up?" he said.

I was tired of this game.

"Need another clue?" he said.

"No." I put my hands in my pockets, trying to remember which key was his and which was mine.

"Come over and give your old dad a night-night kiss."

I looked at the door. Like the cockroach, I wanted to run, but couldn't. He half-stood, grabbed my shoulders and pulled my lips toward his. His towel fell on the floor.

In the shadowed light, his face reminded me of last summer's trip, how we'd been on our way back from the nation's Capitol and stopped at his cousin's place in Sioux City, and how, after a rain, Father had taken me out at midnight, on a secret mission, how we had crept across the unmowed grass, and how, in the slanted beams of flashlights, night-crawlers had arched from the earth, their segmented bodies thick with damp, how they had been undulating and waving in the blades of grass, and how some had gotten crushed beneath my knees as I worked to grab and tug them from the ground.

I made a fist and socked my father's stomach as hard as I could. "Daddy! No!"

Father grunted and fell back in bed. I staggered and groped behind me for the chair. I leaned on it. Sweat had formed in the small of my back, and I knew if I sat, my body would stick to the chair and be glued there forever.

"Fair enough." Father pulled back the sheet and got in bed. His sunburned arm reached for the light. "Don't forget the silver for your mother, and if she asks, tell her I didn't lay a hand on you."

Breathing hard and wiping my lips with the back of my arm, I scooped the coins from the dresser.

Inside my room, the lights were out. The moon, coming through the window, cut checkerboard squares on the floor. My mother had left a nightgown on my pillow. I went into the bathroom, stacked the coins on the sink, and scrubbed my face. With tweezers, I picked out the glass embedded in my palm. Mother's train case sat on the back of the toilet. I found the first-aid kit under her brush-rollers. With the Mercurochrome's wand, I treated my wounds, and then I went to bed. The cool sheets made me shiver.

Mother rolled over. "Did he go to sleep?"

"Yes," I said.

"What did you say to him?"

"I listened to him talk about his Pancho Villa coin."

"He always gets the last word, doesn't he?" She reached across the divide between our beds.

I turned my back and curled up. My shoulders shook and my knees jerked. To control myself, I hugged my pillow.

"Do you have a fever?" Mother said.

"No," I said.

"He didn't touch you, did he?"

"He didn't lay a hand on me."

And I would make sure he never did.

My palm smarted. The glass was still in there. My body ached from holding itself together.

In the night, while Mother snored and tossed fitfully in her sleep, Carlos crept to the window. His breath, like the breath of the Gulf, heaving and sighing gently on the sand, came to me in murmurs. "Psst. Psst. Psst." And as for the rest, Mother would not leave Vera Cruz, there would be no airplane ride, and Father would sulk until we gave him back the silver. One coin he let me keep. Cold and hard and heavy, it covers my palm, a souvenir of that trip.

The Journey
ALMOST PARADISE

———○———

JAMMED IN THE back of a Datsun pickup between bags of rice and farmers with live chickens, I was kind of wishing I had never come on this trip to Thailand. In Bangkok, Thais had actually walked backwards to prolong their view of my face, and when my cousin Nico and I stopped in a temple for a cheap massage, the masseuse refused to touch my back, even though I don't have a birthmark there. Now, Nico was taking me to a backpackers' resort down by the Cambodian border. A woman moved her feet to keep from touching mine, and with a tight mouth, whipped angrily at the humid air with a paper fan. Her little girl, squirming and tugging her mother's dress, kept looking at me. Nico was supposed to be running interference so this shit didn't happen, but his eyes were closed and his head was jerking back and forth like one of those dashboard bobble-dolls. I elbowed him.

"Geez, Walter." He rubbed his arm and looked around.

I nodded to the kid. "She's staring."

"Can you blame her?"

"Come on, Nico. Don't mess with my head."

"What am I supposed to do?"

"Say something."

He touched his cheek and pulled down his left eye. "Your makeup's running."

I swiped my cheek. Flesh-colored gunk came off on my hand.

"Does it look bad?" I said.

"You look like…" He studied my face. *Ugly* was on the tip of his tongue. "…like, I don't know. Worse than usual."

The Thai lady was giving me the evil eye. She lifted her daughter over her lap and put the girl next to the tailgate, which the driver had fastened with baling wire. It was dangerous for the kid to sit there. I leaned forward and held out my hand, trying to communicate telepathically that I wasn't some monster.

Nico made his hands into claws. "Stop staring, you little ankle-biter, or the boogie-man will get you."

The girl let out a wail, and the mom covered her daughter's face with the fan.

"Thanks a lot," I said.

Nico sat back, arms folded, shoulders shaking. "They probably think you're possessed."

"Explain it's a birthmark," I said.

"I only know a hundred words of Thai. Pussy. Suck my…"

"Don't be a jerk."

"Then stop whining."

I cracked my knuckles. I was not cut out to be a tourist. I had thought so in Bangkok, but now I knew for sure. Once again, my mom had pressured me into becoming a human guinea pig, and this experiment wasn't turning out any better than the one before, when she'd arranged all my surgeries.

The truck stopped by some wooden stores with corrugated metal roofs. While Nico went inside, I saw a street vendor and bought a straw hat. A moment later, Nico handed me a six-pack of water. I put the bottles in my backpack and saw my SmartCover and makeup brush. I took them out.

Nico looked around at the country people in their sarongs and baggy trousers. "Don't do that here."

"Why not?" I said.

"Because I said so."

"All right, but I'd look better if I could fix my face."

"Do it when we find a restroom."

I screwed the top back on the SmartCover and put it in an outside pouch. In my pocket, I had this Acquacolor spray stuff I'd snuck through airport security, and I was bummed it wasn't working. It was supposed to be humidity proof. Put my normal makeup on, their rep said, and the spray would hold it in place like a mask. Some people with birthmarks use the same makeup, year after year; but me, I'm a sucker for promises, and when a new product says it'll make you have skin like a baby's ass, I want to believe it.

Nico saw the straw hat looped around my wrist.

"Yeah?" I said.

"I guess it's good to have a souvenir."

"Want one?"

"No thanks." He threw his duffel bag over a shoulder. He wasn't carrying any more weight than I was, but he looked like he had a safe on his back.

"That was a brutal ride," I said, catching up to him.

"It'll be worth it," Nico said. "The place we're going is paradise."

"Bangkok was a shithole."

"Besides the people, the trash, and the food, what didn't you like?"

"Pollution," I said.

Heading for a long wooden pier, we passed a man pushing a wheelbarrow full of tiny, silver fish, and when we got to the waterfront, the air smelled like anchovies and rotten eggs. The tide had gone out. Beneath the slimy posts, blue-green mud bubbled like a fart machine.

I put a hand over my nose. "This place stinks."

"Do you have to make a negative comment about everything?"

"Fine," I said, "I'll keep my opinions to myself."

"Don't piss me off, Walter."

"You promised Mom you'd look out for me."

"I thought you wanted to get out of your rut."

"It's not a rut," I said.

"Could have fooled me." After shifting his duffel to his other shoulder, he lengthened his stride.

I hurried to catch him before he found a way to ditch me. When we were kids, he'd run down an alley or duck into the rectory, and then I wouldn't see him until my mom called his mom and got him in trouble. We had spent five days in Bangkok, and though he hadn't told me in so many words, I had the feeling that being a tour guide was harder than he'd expected.

Nico had zero experience in the travel industry, but that didn't matter because he was going to start small and build his business, the way I had built mine. After he showed me around Thailand, he could legitimately call himself a "travel escort." His mom, my Aunt Hildy, came up with the travel escort idea from some program she saw on the Travel Channel. Hildy, my mom's identical twin, had laid out cash for a money belt and a vest with twenty pockets. The two of them together had thrown the full force of their prayers into Nico latching onto a career he could settle into, the way I'd settled into mine.

At first, Nico had put up a good resistance. He had pretty much been a failure at everything he'd tried, but even he recognized he should move out of Nordstrom's mail room before they laid him off for stealing. When he suggested I come along, I rearranged my life to help him. For the hundred bucks a day I was paying him to show me around, I expected to be treated right.

Back in Chicago I didn't do much walking. The pier felt like it was a mile long, and I was out of breath. Beyond the fishing boats tied up where the water got deep, I saw the gentle swells of an oily sea, and on the horizon, a landmass that looked like the head of an elephant.

"What's that?" I called.

Nico stopped. "Koh Chang."

"You should translate the name. If you know it, that is."

Nico rolled his eyes. "It means 'Elephant Island.'"

"You ought to say it's shaped like one."

"That's obvious," he said.

Clouds swept over the island, blowing toward us. Back in Chicago, thick gray clouds like that would mean a tornado.

"Maybe we should stay on the mainland," I said.

"You're always so cautious," Nico said.

"*Fareng! Fareng!*" screamed a high-pitched voice.

I turned. A long-haired Thai in a flowered shirt was waving. Broad-shouldered and barefoot, he had breasts that bobbed as he ran.

"Here comes Lady-Man," Nico said.

"What a strange looking person," I said.

"Look who's talking." Nico opened his arms and embraced the person.

"Busy day," the person said, puffing for breath. "I suppose to meeted you, but I late." He dipped his chin and finger-combed his bangs to swing across the scar that ran diagonally from eye to jaw. Through the curtain of his hair, I could see one bright eye and a droopy eyelid. As I looked from his breasts to his face, I wondered if he was a she, or she a he, and what pronoun I should use for him-her.

The person looked at me. "What happen you?"

"He was born that way," Nico said. "When we were kids, it was worse."

"It's worse now," I said. "Darker."

"Why you no have fix?" the Lady-Man person said.

"He did."

If there was one thing I hated more than people who stared, it was people who asked questions. Nico's expression begged me not to get upset.

"I had eleven surgeries," I said.

Lady-Man whistled.

"He makes it sound worse than it was," Nico said.

"Like you would know," I said.

At one time, a port-wine birthmark had covered the left half of my face, from forehead to chin, but doctors put these water balloons under my skin to stretch it out, so they could remove the purple stuff. This started when I was nine months old, and it was supposed to be better than skin grafts. There wouldn't be any leg hair sprouting from my forehead when I went through puberty.

Every six to nine months I'd have another operation, with the only long break the time my mom held off long enough for me to have my First Communion; but a couple months after that, I sensed her gearing up for another "treatment." I threw a total fit. Just like my Lab—she pisses herself when she thinks she's going to the vet's—I wet the bed. Then, I went on a hunger strike. Mom started a novena, hoping the Virgin Mary would step in. Now this is sort of sad. I won the battle. My dad couldn't take the drama. He moved back to St. Louis, and my mom and us kids didn't have health insurance until she went back to work. The doctors never did operate on my cheek and eye, and as I grew older, the port-wine skin wrinkled up like a turkey's wattle. SmartCover gets stuck in the creases. The part I hate most is the blood blisters around my eye. If they were zits, which they're not, I'd be tempted to pop them, just to get the skin to lay flat.

Back when I was eight or nine, my mom and Aunt Hildy decided I needed a father figure. That was Nico's dad. When he took us to Cubs' games, people would stare and ask if Nico and I were twins. We were more identical than our mothers. Nico was cute and always hopping up and down, sticking his mitt in the air, while I kept my head down, recorded stats on our scorecard, and tried to make myself invisible. I didn't like going out in public, especially with Nico, because right away people would think, poor kid—the poor kid being me—if it weren't for that birthmark, he might have looked like the other boy. The same thing had been happening in Thailand. Fishermen, squatting on the pier and repairing their nets, looked from my face to Nico's and back again.

"He your brother?" Lady-Man asked.

"First cousin," Nico said, pressing his index and middle finger together. "Our mothers are twins."

"He like women?" Lady-Man said.

I hadn't come here for a hookup.

"If you weren't so self-conscious," Nico said, "you could get one."

"Women aren't Slurpies," I said.

"There are women on the island," Nico said. "Full body massage, if you know what I mean."

"I know what you mean," I said.

Lady-Man smiled at me. "I give you good price."

I didn't like to hurt a person's feelings. "How do we get to the island?"

Lady-Man looked at the sky, frowned, and checked his watch. "Boat come soon."

The three of us walking side-by-side made the pier sway. Or maybe it was me. I needed to get back into *Tae kwon do*. Like most everything in my life, I had given it up because there wasn't any payback for the effort expended. I hadn't suddenly become the most popular kid in *Tae kwon do* school.

Nico threw his duffel down in front of one of the shacks that sold beer, bananas, and plastic trinkets. Shielded by the hut from the eyes of fishermen who had put down their nets to stare, I was glad to take the load off. The shack had a bar counter and two stools, exactly like the ones in my dad's kitchen. Retired, living off his bus driver's pension, he had turned into a big Cardinals' fan, which made it hard to relate to him; and when I told him he owed me a favor for leaving me all those years ago, he volunteered, sort of, to stay at my place and look after my vending machine route. My sister took my dog Trixie, so I didn't have to board her at the vet's.

Lady-Man put two shot glasses on the counter. "Whiskey?"

"Orange soda," I said.

"Set me up." Nico began drumming his fingers.

Ever since we were kids, he'd played this little game. By the rhythm, I was supposed to guess the song.

Lady-Man put a binder on the counter. "You want look resort picture?"

"Might as well." I flipped the binder open. Someone had written in careful block letters, WELCOME TO PARADISE COTTAGE. RESORT OF GOOD SPIRIT. Polaroids of tourists sitting at picnic tables, playing volleyball, and lounging on the beach had been stuck into black photo-corners.

"Is 'Paradise Cottage' the name of the place?" I said.

"Yeah," Nico said.

"How many times have you been there?"

"Koh Chang?" Nico said. "Five or six times, but I usually stay at a different resort."

Lady-Man wrinkled his or her nose. "Paradise not best place, but have good spirit."

"I can read," I said.

"Most tourists avoid Paradise like the plague," Nico said.

"Beach, him no good," Lady-Man said.

"He doesn't care about the beach." Nico cocked his head in my direction. "And he doesn't like people he doesn't know."

"Not much people at Paradise," Lady-Man said.

Back in Bangkok, when Nico told me the place we were going to was paradise, I didn't realize he meant literally. I thought he was referring to a place like Tahiti, where Gauguin painted all those bare-breasted women. But Nico was one to take "paradise" in all kinds of different directions, mostly mocking. After high school, he'd played in this garage band of Catholic-school dropouts. He called the band "Paradise Lost," after the Milton poem that made him flunk senior year.

One way Nico and I are different is he thinks there's no point in exerting himself. He says, pretty soon, we'll all be dead, whereas I believe in an afterlife. On the flight over I'd thought, worst case, if we crashed I'd wake up in heaven where God the Father separates us from our bodies, and we live as purely spiritual beings. The hope that this was what God had in mind kept me attending Mass long after everyone in our family—with the exception of my Polish grandma, my mom, and Aunt Hildy—had given up on the Church. My sister, who has no excuse because she is just a house-wife with nothing to do but look after my two bratty nephews, only goes to Mass on Christmas and Easter. She might as well not bother. Religion is not like term insurance. Me, I try to live my faith, but not be unduly rigid about avoiding what the priests used to call "the occasion of sin." I do a little Internet porn. You can't go through life and never step in a puddle. On account of my birthmark, I had missed out on a lot of things guys my age take for granted. Nico filled me in, but half the time I thought he was making stuff up because I couldn't see any self-respecting woman doing the things he said.

Nico sipped his whiskey. His fingers drummed. The tempo sped up. "Can you guess what it is?" he said.

I smashed my fist down on his hand. "You know that annoys me."

"You crushed 'The Star Spangled Banner.'" He shook his fingers, swiveled around, and held his shot glass up like a monocle. "Walter, you need some excitement in your life."

Not this again. "My life's fine," I said.

"Your life's boring."

"I have my routines."

"Stocking vending machines?"

"Is there anything wrong with that?"

"I'm just trying to be helpful, okay?"

Back home, everyone was always trying to be helpful. They'd been helpful about my face. Now they were being helpful about my life. A few years ago, they didn't like that I had an early morning paper route. It was a huge route with lots of apartments, and I was done by nine; but to my mom, it looked like I spent my time playing video games and hanging out at The Cubby Bear. The one in Wrigleyville's close to my mom's place, and a few times a week, I stop in for a meal.

Back then, Mom was always pushing me to get what she called a real job and have a social life. So I bought this candy route off a buddy of mine. It only ran me $7,600, and now I have thirty-six machines. Snickers. Milk Duds. I can put whatever into them. Teachers used to say I had a lot of math ability, and maybe I do, because I have this system where I keep track of which candies sell out quickest. In Rogers Park, Butterfingers go fast. I don't know why. Maybe there's a Butterfingers' junkie in the neighborhood. In the bars around Wrigley, they go for the salty snacks—Fritos and Beer Nuts. Fans who sit in the right-field bleachers come out of the game dehydrated. I imagine my customers approaching the candy machine, feeling around in their pockets and counting out the coins. They're shadowy figures, but their hands are real—to me, at least. I hear the change fall and see their fingers lift the plastic door. Every so often, I squirt the door with Windex, but the plastic is hard to clean. There's an oily residue from all the fingers that have indirectly touched mine. Anyways, that's how my mind works. It makes these weird associations. My shrink says it's because I was traumatized by the surgery, but I never told him there was one good thing about the hospital: people, even women, touched me. I could be lying on a gurney, floating on my Demerol cloud, and nurses would stroke my hand and run their fingers through my hair.

Before going to Koh Chang, I didn't know I had never been happy, not even for one minute. I didn't know what happiness meant. Nico was the one person who understood me, the only one who could get inside the bubble I'd constructed around myself. And he was right about one thing. I was missing out on life.

PARADISE COTTAGES LOOKED just like the pictures, except the sky wasn't blue, and mildew had turned the palm fronds on the roofs all black. Lady-Man showed us to a bungalow. It was made of bamboo, sort of like the stick house in "The Three Little Pigs." Sticks of bamboo held open the shutters, and the windows didn't have screens. Two white, gauze nets hung from the rafters. Nico started checking them for holes.

"Are you sure these places are safe?" I said.

"This is what you find at all the resorts," Nico said. "That's why they cost ten bucks a night."

"What if there's a *tsunami*?"

"The *tsunami* hit the other side of the country."

Okay, so it was on the other side of the country. But still. I threw my duffel on one of the rubber mattresses. A mirror hung on the door. I took out my makeup kit. Something bit me. I slapped my arm.

Nico tossed me a green plastic bottle. "Put on some DEET."

I pulled my shirt away from my body and rubbed DEET on my arms.

"Your face, too," he said.

I sniffed the bottle. "No way. This stuff smells like fire starter."

"Did you take your pills this morning?"

"Of course," I said.

"Then you're probably okay."

"I don't want to come down with malaria."

"Walter, I told you it's okay."

Nico was stripping off his clothes as if he couldn't wait to go for a swim, but even through the window, I could see the sky darken. I changed into trunks, took my new hat, and joined him on the veranda. There was a quadrangle of Bermuda grass, and on three sides, bungalows like ours. On the fourth side, facing the ocean, three rows of palm trees were spaced out like bowling pins.

"Smells like rain," I said.

Nico did a long-jump onto the grass. "Monsoon won't start for another two weeks."

Stepping off the porch, I followed Nico down a trail to the beach. "I wouldn't want to get stuck here in a storm."

"Give it a rest," Nico said.

"I was merely offering an observation."

At the beach, I shaded my eyes and squinted. A mudflat stretched the length of three football fields to a graveyard of white, twisted bones. The coral reef. Nico pulled two beach chairs together. I adjusted the back of mine, rubbed my legs with SPF-65, took off my shoes, and put on a long-sleeved shirt. The straw hat shaded my face.

"You look like a coolie in that thing," Nico said.

"I don't need skin cancer."

"Did anyone ever tell you you're a hypochondriac?"

Sweat trickled down my ribs. I sat up. "I think I'll go for a walk."

"Do that." Nico pulled a towel over his face. Through it, he said, "And don't freak out if I'm not here when you get back."

"Where'll you be?" I said.

"Somewhere you're not," he said.

I took a couple of steps. Grainy, orange pebbles crunched under my feet. I put on my shoes.

"You could come with me," I said.

"No thanks," he said. "I need some space."

"That's why I'm going for a walk," I said. "You're not the most patient tour guide in the world."

Nico pulled the towel off his face and looked at me. "The first time I came over here, I didn't have anyone holding my hand."

"Wait'll you get some of those old fogies from church."

"I wouldn't take them here."

"Where would you take them?"

"Up to Chiang Rai. Maybe to Kanchanaburi and 'Bridge Over the River Kwai.' It's kind of touristy, but still nice."

"Why didn't we go there?"

"You said you wanted to get away," he said. "You don't like it when people stare, so I thought what could be more perfect than Lonely Beach?"

"Is that its actual name?"

"Yes," he said.

I looked down the long stretch of gravel. Lonely Beach was deserted.

"You could have taken me someplace better."

"Good times are to be had, Walter."

"Another thing. I didn't expect the humidity."

"We're on the equator." Nico put the towel over his face. "Besides, it's not much worse than Chicago in August."

"Yes, it is." I turned my back and started walking. Every step left me short-winded. To get out to deep water was a twenty-minute walk through brown mud, and, besides I wasn't a big fan of the ocean. I don't like getting saltwater up my nose. Lake Michigan's water was clear and fresh, and when the weather was humid, like now, I could go up to the beach in Rogers Park and have a swim.

On Sundays Mexican families came from their hot apartments to cool off. Fat grandmas with ponytails and swimsuits under their tee shirts. Mothers, not quite as fat as my mom, and little kids with skin as brown as the people's over here. No one paid attention to me, and I pretended I was part of the group, roasting a weenie over the fire or popping a jalapeño in my mouth, shooting the breeze with the young, single women with cherry lipstick, halter tops, and firm boobs.

The heat sapped my energy, and I returned to the bungalow, picked up my baseball cap, and threw the straw hat on my mattress, and got my towel and a bar of soap. I found Nico playing solitaire at one of a dozen picnic tables in the main building. The wide breezeway and block walls reminded me of the rest stops on I-80.

"I need to clean up," I said.

"I'll show you the facilities."

Nico walked me to a door that had a stick-figure drawing of a man. Inside, he pointed to a turquoise toilet. "There you go."

"At least, it's not one of those squat things," I said.

"And there's your water." He pointed to a big ceramic vase, like the kind my mom grows her *ficus* in, only bigger. From a rusty nail hung a dipper.

The old bucket flush. "I don't have to take a dump," I said.

"That's the shower," he said.

"No way."

"Soap up and give yourself a sponge bath."

I walked over to the vase. Larvae squirmed on the surface.

"The water's not clean," I said.

"This is as clean as it gets."

"I'll just wash my pits." I stripped off my shirt.

"You should wash your face," he said. "I can run get your makeup."

"I don't want you rummaging in my things," I said.

"You can be such a prick." He closed the door behind him.

After I finished washing off, my skin felt good. A lot cooler. I didn't feel like putting on my face. I peeked out. Lady-Man was serving a bowl of soup to a bare-chested white guy with matted, Rastafarian braids and a tan so deep it looked like he'd gone shirtless his whole life. I'd kill to have skin like that. I came out and shut the door behind me.

The man's blue eyes locked on my face. He spit out his soup. "Shite, Mate. You've come a gutser!"

"What's that supposed to mean?" I said.

"Some bloke bloody walloped you." He touched his eye.

"Fuck off," I said.

He held up both hands. "No offense, Mate. I was just mucking about."

"Muck off, then."

Raising his eyebrows, he saluted.

I passed behind him. Rarely, if ever, do I say anything. I don't think well on my feet, and besides, telling someone to stop staring just makes them embarrassed. Myself, I'm the same way when I see some geek in a wheelchair. I always feel guilty, like, Should I be watching out the corner of my eye, or look away?

In the bungalow, I hung my towel on the door. Nico must have gone down to the beach, I figured, so I walked out to the sand. The folding chairs were empty. The sky was grayer than it had been. I felt a drop of rain. Thinking I should apologize to the Australian dude, I went back to the main building, but the guy with the matted braids had left.

Pots banged in the kitchen. I followed the sound and saw Lady-Man up to his elbows in suds.

"Have you seen my cousin?"

Lady-Man looked around. "Him not here?"

"No."

Lady-Man frowned. "Him go other island side."

"He left me here alone?"

"You not alone." Lady-Man picked up a towel and wiped his forearms.

I wished Lady-Man would give it a rest. "Did he say when he'd be back?"

"Him not say."

So much for my tour guide.

"You hungry?" Lady-Man said.

"Not yet." A gust of wind blew through the breezeway. It was a lot cooler here than in the bungalow. I could amuse myself.

On one of the walls, tourists had written on a white-board. "Mark, meet me at the Unicorn in Bali." "Kendra, get me one of Mr. Loh's tee-shirts before you leave." On and on. There were messages in other languages I couldn't read and dates as far back as 2005. It seemed like the whole world had passed through this place at one time or another. On a saggy couch, someone had left a *People* magazine. Sitting, I put my feet up on a coffee table and flipped the pages. There was Jennifer Anniston at last year's Academy Awards. The caption talked about her satin dress. It was almost too dark to see the picture. I brought the magazine closer. Her tits and belly-button showed. Even her snatch. I spread the magazine over my lap, put my arms behind my head, and closed my eyes. At home, it must be two or three o'clock in the morning, the time the adult channels start running the good stuff.

The pounding of a two-stroke engine sounded like a headboard slamming against a wall. I looked around. Out behind the breezeway, Lady-Man stood over a generator. Three bare bulbs came on, sixty-watters, but not enough light to read by. Seriously bored, I opened the drawer in the coffee table. Red Diamond playing cards with bent corners. I dealt seven.

On the ward after my surgeries, when other kids worked puzzles and stood at easels painting flower pictures, Nico and I played Old Maid and War. He never won at cards. I usually did pretty well. I could picture the cards, and more important, remembered which cards were still in the pile. Compared to playing against another person, Solitaire required zero skill, but I couldn't concentrate. The generator hurt my eardrums.

I poked my head in the kitchen. Lady-Man was dicing onions.

"Does that thing have to stay on?"

"I need for light," Lady-Man said. "Cook dinner."

"Can you make me some fried rice?" I said.

"Sit down," he said. "I bring."

A family of tall, blond Scandinavians seated themselves: husband, wife in a long, see-through skirt with bikini panties hiked up her ass, and a toddler with the kind of curls artists who paint churches put on angels. The woman looked at me, smiled, and tousled her child's hair. My mom had never looked at me like that. Even when I was a kid, her expression was half-way between migraine and exasperation. Lately, she'd been saying I was the reason she'd put on so much weight, but I wasn't, because Aunt Hildy had gained weight, too, and she blamed Nico. He could have gone to college, she thought, but he didn't apply himself in high school. If she'd asked me, I would have told her he still wasn't applying himself.

After dinner, Lady-Man brought a bowl of lychee fruit and said he wasn't going to charge me. I had a beer with the dessert, and thought about Trixie and how, the moment I set up a TV tray to eat my dinner, she'd put her muzzle on my lap. Right now, she'd be lying next to the radiator in my sis's front hall, waiting for me to come home.

It started to rain. I didn't want to get trapped, so I went back to the bungalow, spread my sheet, folded my pants for a pillow, and lay under my net, reading a mystery by flashlight. The battery gave out. Far off, I heard thunder.

The door creaked.

"Nico?" I said.

"It me," a woman said.

"You're in the wrong place," I said.

Feet padded toward me. The light was dim, but a woman in a sarong knelt beside me. Lightning flashed. Hair fell over breasts. I saw brown nipples.

I had a ticking clock inside, halfway between my stomach and throat. I tried not to breathe. I couldn't. "You should go."

I smelled breath mint. Lady-Man's face was next to mine.

"You not like way I look," he said.

"What?" I said.

Lady-Man's hand came through the mosquito net. He pulled my hand from beneath my head and placed it on the knotted scar that ran from his temple, across one eye, and down to his chin.

"Can I talk you?" Lady-Man said.

"What about?" I said.

"Face."

I didn't want to talk about my face.

Lady-Man slapped his arm. "Mosquito."

"Get under the other net then."

Lady-Man scuttled around the foot of my bed. The net over Nico's bed shimmered as Lady-Man crawled in. He/she scooted the mattress closer.

"Don't get any big ideas," I said.

"You no think I pretty."

"Not because of your face," I said.

Lady-Man propped his head on his hand. He lifted one breast. "You no like?"

"Your boobs are fine."

"I take pill," he said. "Expensive."

"I don't like guys," I said. "Or guys pretending to be girls."

"But I girl," Lady-Man said.

"Okay, okay."

"You think bad?"

"It's against my religion."

"Here, lot of men like me."

"Really?" I said.

"Dress like woman. Wear lipstick. Fix eyes."

"That's weird," I said.

A mosquito zinged. It was right next to my ear. It had found a hole in my net, or maybe it had been there all day, waiting. Buckets of bee-bees dumped on the roof. I threw off the mosquito net. "Let's sit on the porch and watch the storm," I said, grabbing a shirt from my duffel bag. I tossed it to Lady-Man and told him to put it on. The bungalow felt like a steam bath, and as we maneuvered Nico's mattress through the door, I was glad to feel the wind.

Lady-Man slipped the shirt over his head. The shirt hung to mid-thigh. Hands over his head like a temple dancer, he did a little jig. I laughed. Lady-Man smiled to himself. I sat. Behind me, the bamboo posts sawed and swayed. Water sheeted off the roof, and through it I could see the tide had come in, a black shadow sucking the waves back toward the ocean. The island felt like a sailboat, buffeted and capable of overturning if the wind hit it right. The storm was awesome—a combination rock concert and car wash. The lawn became a lake.

"Sit here." I patted the mattress. "But no touching."

Lady-Man plopped down, hands around his knees.

I told him about the time Nico and I jumped in the Chicago River at Montrose and someone called the fire department to haul us out.

"Chicago, big city?" Lady-Man said.

"Same as Bangkok," I said. "Nine million people."

Lady-Man shifted position and sat cross-legged, arranging his sarong to cover his legs. "Nico tell you, I not always work here?"

"Where'd you work?" I said.

"Patpong."

"I know Patpong," I said. "We walked through the Night Market." Nico had purchased a bong and some jade necklaces for our moms.

"What did you sell?" I said.

"I work club," Lady-Man said.

"What'd you do, cook?"

"Before pimp cutted me, I work prostitute."

I swallowed. Nico and I had a couple drinks at the "Super Pussy." Women sat in our laps. At least, I thought they were women. Lightning flashed. Like ballerinas, palm trees bent toward the sea and touched the foam.

"In week," Lady-Man said, "I have sex change operation."

I drew my knees up to my chest. "That's going to hurt."

"I not care."

"You must be desperate."

"When I woman, I be happy."

I wondered about that. Catching happiness was like catching a mosquito. You could hear it buzzing right by your ear, but it always got away.

"I don't think I've ever been happy," I said.

"Really?" Lady-Man said.

"I don't think so."

Lady-Man hugged his knees. "Patpong make me happy."

"Why?" I said.

"I never alone. Exciting life."

NICO SHOOK MY shoulder. "Wake up. It's almost noon."

"I'm in the middle of a dream." The mosquito net felt like a woman's hair. A dark-haired woman with pointy brown tits sat astride me. I felt all sticky.

While Nico dry-shaved in the mirror, I hopped up and changed my shorts. He asked why his mattress was outside, and I said I'd been watching the storm. He raised his eyebrows and smirked. That look sort of made me mad. I wondered if he'd set me up. He, of all people, ought to know better. Outside, the sky was still gray, but the rain had slacked off. Lady-Man had splashed across the spongy grass a few hours before.

"You know how you used to say St. Jerome was full of shit?" I said.

"I can't handle a theological discussion right now," Nico said.

"I think Jerome might have been onto something."

We went over to the eating area and sat on opposite sides of a picnic table. Nico picked up a salt shaker and poured salt in his hand, dipped a finger in it, and touched the finger to his tongue.

"Jerome said you could lose your virginity by just thinking about it," I said.

"Walter, I hate to disillusion you, but nobody loses their virginity by having a thought."

"But a thought is like a dream!" I said. "You know how you wake up and it feels like you're still in the world of the dream? Maybe that's what Jerome was getting at."

"Can you shut up?" Nico said.

Lady-Man, in a skirt and embroidered blouse, came to take our order. She had on red lipstick and a gold chain. SmartCover hid her scar.

"Boss man call on short wave," she said. "Monsoon come early."

"That's good for you," I said. "The Lady," as she liked to be called, would have her operation. The makeup did her a whole lot more good than it had ever done me. She looked pretty.

"I don't think I can eat," Nico said.

"Had too much to drink?"

"Mekong whiskey," he said.

The Lady raised an eyebrow. "Rice soak up alcohol."

"Bring it," Nico said.

I ordered tea and toast. The Lady, swinging her hips, retreated to the kitchen.

"Where'd you go last night?" I said.

"Down the road to the Porn Shack." He drummed his fingers. "Hope you don't mind, I snagged a couple thousand *baht* from your wallet."

"You went through my things?" I said.

"I'm good for it."

"That's not the point."

His mouth twisted. He looked out to sea.

"It might have been closer to five thousand."

Real money. "Is this how you treat clients?"

"You're not a real client," he said.

"Aren't I writing a testimonial for your web page?"

"Oh, that." He rolled his eyes.

"I see," I said.

He shrugged. I was annoyed with him, but not as annoyed as I might have been on any other day.

The Lady plopped a bowl of rice down. "Two hour. You musted

go off island."

She slid my toast across the table.

"We just got here," I said.

The Lady held up two fingers and glanced at me from the curtain of her hair. "Not much time."

"Maybe you could take us somewhere," I said.

"Me, many thing do, but I show." The Lady brought a map. The island was green, with a dome of mountain in the middle. Her finger ran around the island's perimeter. She had painted her nails. "You like waterfall?" she said.

"It's too far," Nico said.

"Not big one. Close by." She waved the rag she used to wipe tables. "Follow road uphill. Ten minutes."

"I really don't feel all that great." Nico excused himself and went to the men's room.

The Lady put down her rag and hurried over.

"Sorry I talk too much," she whispered.

"I talked too much, too."

She put her hands on her hips, batted her eyes, and brushed her hair away from her face. "What you think?"

"Looks good," I said.

"You want back?" she said.

"Keep it," I said.

Water gurgled in the men's room. The Lady jerked her head in that direction. "I make tea."

A moment later, a tea kettle shrieked. The Lady returned with a pot.

Nico looked pale. He sat down and unwrapped his chopsticks. "I got into this poker game," he said.

"Did you lose?" I said.

"I knew you were going to make me feel guilty."

"I'm glad you had fun," I said. "I had an interesting night, too."

"I should have stayed here."

"I'm glad you didn't." The wind picked up, and rain blew into the breezeway. "Want me to run over and get our ponchos?"

"There's no point." He leaned back and groaned. "You'll just bitch if you get wet."

"I won't bitch," I said. "I tell you, I'm in the best mood of my life."

Nico rolled his eyes. "Sure, you are."

He couldn't tell I was in a good mood. Amazing.

"Let's find the waterfall," I said.

THE ROAD HAD turned into an orange river. Rain came down like diagonal knives. Nico carried his shoes. My feet had always been tender, except for the years I'd done *Tae kwon do*, when all our workouts, including breaking boards, were done barefoot.

My sneaker got sucked into a puddle and stayed behind. I backtracked, and when I dug around to find my shoe, my arm sank up to my shoulder.

"Hey," Nico shouted, motioning me to come over. I hopped on one foot. He pointed to a drainage culvert. Water gushed from it. On the other side of the road, he discovered a stream and a trail that led into an orchard of red, hairy fruit that looked like Christmas ornaments.

"It must be up there." I pointed to the mountain.

"I think it's someone's farm," he said.

"We're not going to hurt anything."

"It's trespassing."

I put my shoe back on and started walking up the trail, but Nico grabbed my arm. I took a swing, and my left hand grazed his cheek. He put his hand to his face and looked surprised. I laughed. He swung at me and I blocked it with my forearm. He tossed his shoes into the weeds, and when he came at me, both hands up so that I was looking at his eyes through his fists, I laughed because it was such a classic Marquess of Queensberry pose. I had my hands up too, but my palms were flat, and I jabbed him in the chest with my right. He fell back and gasped. As I shot my leg toward his jaw, I felt my foot go out from under me, and then I fell in the mud, and he threw himself on top of me.

I grabbed his shoulders, flipped him onto his back, and put my hand on his forehead. Mud swallowed his head. I felt his arms around my waist and backed up, trying to shake him off. He flung himself out of the hole and head-butted my gut.

"You always get your way!" he screamed.

I sat in the road trying to catch my breath. In an hour, I'd think of something I should have said. Nico had a picture of me in his mind. Whiner. Hypochondriac. Even if the birthmark vanished, he'd still see purple on my face.

"I could've killed you!" I said.

"Your mom always says what an angry person you are."

"She never told me that."

"Yeah?" he said. "Well, everybody knows it."

I didn't. An angry person?

Nico ran his fingers through his hair. "Geez, I'll never get this mud off."

"Let's find the waterfall," I said.

At the orchard's far end, the jungle began. A rocky path, slick with leaves, wound uphill. I tripped on the roots of a giant gum tree. Liana hung from its branches, and I grabbed the vine to keep my footing. Light dimmed. Pink and orange hibiscus flashed like neon. The trees pulsed with twirps, chirrs, and whistles. Nico cupped his ear, then raced ahead.

Certain things about Nico I didn't understand. For one, I thought he loved me like a brother. For two, he was jealous. Of me.

When I caught up, I found him staring at a veil of water that plunged into a charcoal pool and rose up in mist. "This place is paradise," he said.

"Almost," I said.

Nico gave me a disgusted look, then clambered down boulders and belly-flopped into the water. He dog-paddled then flipped over, his arms and legs outstretched.

"Move out of the way!" I shouted, ready to cannonball. "I'm coming in."

"Get your own damn swimming hole," he said.

Below him I saw another pool, six foot deep, the stones mag-nified below the surface. I slid down the bank, splashed in, and scooped up handfuls of fresh water. I took off my shoes and put them on a rock. Paddling, barefoot, I could not touch bottom. When I lay back, water filled my ears. The trees rose to a small circle. From the halo of sky, rain fell. Drops patted my face, and I floated.

KEY WEST

————o————

IN FLOWERED SHORTS and a halter top, Lana Buskirk sat in baggage claim and filed furiously at her nails. The luggage wheels of arriving passengers set up an unbearable din and reminded her of the whiny children on the plane. Horns honked. Gusts of Gulf air blew through the revolving door. As college kids on spring break filed past, shedding their parkas and popping open cell phones, she grew more and more annoyed. To save money, she'd taken the early flight from Indy and put Todd on the later one, so he could talk his advisor into letting him off academic probation.

A gym bag on his shoulder, big feet slapping the floor, Todd shuffled towards her. As tall as his father, with that same straight posture that made him a natural leader, he could do anything he wanted to in life, if she could just convince him to marshal his resources. She didn't have much to brag about—no money, no husband, and no personal life to speak of—but she'd done a good job raising her boy. Not a good job. An outstanding job. He stopped to pull a sweatshirt over his head; his face emerged from the fleece. Days-old whiskers. Hair that blotted up grease like a paper towel under bacon.

"Pulling all-nighters?" she said.

"My little Mommy." He patted her head. "New hair."

Oh yes, the bangs she absolutely hated. Right after he'd called to tell her about his insomnia—Was it her fault he hadn't slept in three weeks? She hoped not!—three parallel lines had appeared on her forehead. Worry was counterproductive, her hairdresser said, squatting to make sure he'd cut the bangs straight. But he didn't have kids, so what did he know?

Todd tossed her the sweatshirt. "Carry this, will you?"

She caught it. "Can't you?"

"My bag's heavy."

Good. Books. She turned the sweatshirt right side out. It was the red, "IU Kokomo" sweatshirt she'd given him at Christmas. He'd spilled a drink down the front. "We'll have to get you some spot remover."

"They won't let me carry it on the plane."

"Okay, well, then we'll find a laundromat."

Outside, a taxi line snaked down the sidewalk. The airport must be pretty far from Key West: either that, or they didn't have many taxis.

"Look at the palm trees and bougainvillea!" Lana said. "Are those real?" The place was an arboretum. She blinked at the glare and dug in her purse for sunglasses. "This is a totally different sun down here," she said.

"Yeah," he said. "Intense. I'm going to have to get new shades."

"What happened to your other ones?"

A taxi honked.

Todd pointed. "I think that's for us."

AT THE BED-AND-BREAKFAST, where pastel, cinder-block buildings surrounded a shady courtyard, Lana gave her credit card to a woman with four chins. Church Lady, Lana thought, like the gossipy old hags, wearing their flowered dresses and sitting out by the clothesline to smoke their cigarettes. Brown Jug Corner. If she hadn't moved to Indianapolis, they'd still be calling her "that Buskirk girl." But she'd shown them. She'd made something of herself. "For $225, the room better be nice," Lana said.

"You're lucky to have a room at all." The woman dangled a key.

"If you don't want it, I have a wait list."

"Are rooms always this expensive?"

"On spring break they are."

Feeling anxious, the way she always did when she felt cheated, Lana marched down a wooden gangway to the farthest room. When she opened the door, she saw a picture of dogs playing poker: a St. Bernard with reading glasses raked in his chips. An English Bulldog and a Bull mastiff growled, and a half-dead Greyhound hung his head. So much for the B & B concept. What happened to the Victorian pillows? Cotton batting spilled from the seams of a faded bedspread.

"Look at that, would you?" Lana said. "This place is a dump."

Todd dropped his duffel bag. "Where's my bed?"

"Here." She patted the king-sized mattress.

"Don't they have a room with twins?"

"You heard what she said."

"I didn't come down here to sleep with my mother." He charged past her and slammed the bathroom door.

She followed him, listened, and heard nothing. Hopefully, he was not upset. She raised her hand to knock, but looked at the clenched fingers squeezing her thumb and decided, best not.

"Let's not make a fuss," Lana said. "We shared a tent on camping trips."

"When I was ten."

"Okay, okay. As long as you're in there, why don't you take a shower and wash your hair?"

"Don't tell me what to do," he said.

Oh crap. He was in one of his moods. A moment later, she heard the spatter of water on a plastic curtain. Once he cleaned up, he'd feel better.

Changing into a bikini, she turned sideways to the mirror and felt the tight muscles of her abdomen. Look at the perfect arch of those ribs; no stretch-marks. All the stretching had taken place inside, her instinct to comfort and protect at odds with what the parenting books said: Boys needed boundaries, discipline, a push into assuming the responsibilities of men.

Water pipes hammered. Todd had finished his shower.

"My advisor is giving me massive shit," Todd said, his voice muffled.

"Have you told him you can't sleep?"

"Yes."

"Well?"

"He sent me to student health."

"And?"

"They said not to drink so much coffee."

"But you hate coffee. You never drink it."

"I got behind, and then I couldn't sleep, so I started drinking coffee to get through finals."

"Why couldn't you sleep?" she said.

"I couldn't stop thinking."

"It's not good to think too much, honey. You gotta just keep putting one foot in front of the other."

Hangers rattled as Lana hung her clothes; the closet stank of mildew. Before Todd called, she had been thinking about a fall cruise to Bermuda with her girlfriends, but now that was totally out of the question.

She supposed she should be grateful Todd was such a good kid, worth the time and effort. And the worry. God, if she could just get him past this speed bump and see him walk across the stage at graduation, she could get on with her life. In the bathroom she heard the toilet flush.

"Are you decent?" he called.

Lana threw a tee-shirt over her head. "Ready to rock and roll."

He burst through the door. "Let's go work on our tans."

"I guess you can study after dinner."

Bending down to look in the dresser mirror, he spit on his fingers and roughed up his hair. "Are you kidding?"

"This place has Internet access," she said.

"I didn't bring a computer."

"But, Todd, our agreement was..."

"I'll do better next term. Or maybe I'll take a little break."

"No breaks," Lana said. "You better be done by June."

Bare-chested, with a gut that spilled over his pants, Todd began rummaging in his duffel bag.

Lana, a personal trainer, grabbed his love handles. He looked like a casserole. "What's this?" she said.

"Hands off." He pushed her away.

"Okay, then," she said. "After lunch we're definitely getting some exercise. You need to look good when you go for interviews."

He paused, shoulders sagging, his things strewn across the bed. "Mom, please. I don't even like accounting."

"You want to bag groceries at Dominick's the rest of your life?"

"No, but I might change majors."

Lana grabbed her hair and screamed. "Four years of tuition. That's all you get."

"Don't threaten me." Todd opened the screen and strode down the walkway. Planks squeaked under his weight.

Let him cool off. She needed to cool off, too. One of her friends had a kid in his sixth year of college. No way. She took out polish and sat on a chair, finishing her nails. Todd came back.

"Guess what?" he said.

"I don't feel like playing twenty questions." She held up her nails and blew them dry.

"Allison's here."

"Allison Konicki?"

He nodded. "She came down with some girlfriends. I invited her to lunch. Is that okay?"

"Are we going Dutch?"

"Is money all you think about?" he said.

"No," she said, "but it's an issue."

THE RESTAURANT WAS a swank place with outdoor tables shaded by a grape arbor. Tourists strolled by, looking through the lattice at people eating lunch. Lana would have been just as happy with a turkey wrap from the take-out place they'd passed, but oh no, Allison had to choose this place, a sit-down lunch with a lot of Mediterranean this and Tuscan that. Of course, she had worked five years in marketing before coming back to school to "retool," and she was used to spending money like it was going out of style.

Allison stood on tiptoe and gave Todd a hug. The big pockets of her loose Bermudas looked like they were hiding extra inches on her thighs. Todd had always said he didn't mind her weight, but Lana did.

For a couple of years, Lana thought she was going to have to put up with Allison as a daughter-in-law; but then on New Year's Day, when Allison realized Todd had no plans to give her a ring, the snooty bitch broke it off. Todd had practically been living at her condo—very comfy, with a wide-screen TV and margarita-maker. Allison was a gourmet cook, and several times Lana had driven over to Kokomo for Sunday brunch. She would have been happy to go more often if it weren't for the floating cat hair in Allison's apartment and the cat-box smell.

Todd beckoned the waiter and ordered a beer, but Lana nixed it and asked for two iced teas.

"Watch your calories," she said.

Allison ordered a tuna salad.

Todd, glowering, studied the menu. "I'll have a hamburger," he said.

"Todd, you should have a salad," Lana said. "Your big meal's at dinner."

"Oh, all right." He turned to the waiter. "Make it a Greek."

After taking a sip of tea and wrinkling his nose, Todd leaned towards Allison. "What's the vet think about Garfield?"

"He has a cyst on his spine," Allison said.

Lana frowned. It sounded like Todd was current on Allison's life, but how could that be?

Turning to Lana, Todd said, "Garfield has been dragging his hind legs."

"Buy the animal a treadmill," Lana said. "I've always said it was obese. Any cat that has to lean against the wall every three steps..."

"The vet thinks I should put him down," Allison said.

"Why don't you let me take her?" Todd said. "At least on weekends."

"You're not in a position to assume responsibility for an animal," Lana said.

"I've been looking at dogs," he said. "There's a Lab at the animal shelter."

Allison smiled. "I always suspected you were a dog person."

"A dog would help me structure my time."

"But you can barely take care of yourself!" Lana said.

"I'd have to walk it in the morning. That would give me a reason to get out of bed."

Lana rolled her eyes. Who needed a reason to get out of bed? You set the alarm. You brushed your teeth. You started your day. And at the end of it, you came home and fell asleep. That's why she hadn't been all that sympathetic when Todd said he needed to get out of Kokomo. Coming home to Indy didn't suit him. Okay, she could get that the gray skies dragged him down, but a dog wouldn't help. If he needed structure, he could increase his hours at Dominick's.

The waiter brought their lunches. Fruit flies hovered above the bananas in her salad.

Lana batted the air. "Allison, what are you going to do when you graduate?"

"Look for a job."

"Where?"

"I've narrowed it down to Chicago or St. Louis."

"See, Todd? She has a P-L-A-N."

Todd picked at his salad. "I should have ordered a burger," he said. "All this green stuff makes me feel like a bovine."

"It's good for you," Lana said.

Todd spread his fingers on the table. They were long and thin;

blond tufts covered the backs of his hands. What a tow-headed angel he'd been.

Allison cocked her head. "How did you do in Ad Pol?"

Todd laced his fingers. "I pulled it up to a D."

"Really?" Allison stared at him.

"I got killed on the final. He expected us to know all kinds of stuff that wasn't in the book."

"All you had to do was go to class," Allison said.

"I slept through it."

"You mean you didn't set your alarm?" Lana said.

"I set my alarm," Todd said. "I just didn't wake up. It was an eight o'clock."

Lana looked from one to the other. She thought Todd said he'd been having trouble sleeping.

Allison's eyes were down. She finished her salad and motioned to the waiter to clear her plate. "Take mine, too," Todd said.

Lana exhaled. What a waste of money.

When no one spoke, she said, "Let me tell you what's happening in my life." She made several boxing jabs across the table, then stretched out an arm to show the improvement in her muscle definition. "I have a new job." She had moved from the Indianapolis Bally's, a total pit where customers didn't even bother to wipe off the equipment, to the NIFS gym, Indy's best. "You know, where Greg Louganis, the diving champion, trained?" It was a great facility. They'd paid her to become certified in Boxing Aerobics. Lana punched Todd's arm playfully.

"I'd forgotten what a character your mom is," Allison said.

The waiter brought the bill. "I'll get it," Allison said.

"How about we split?" Lana said.

Allison looked at Todd. "Are you going to contribute?"

"I didn't stop at the cash machine," he said.

"No surprise." Allison took out a pen, looked up at the trellis, and calculated the bill. "Your share comes to $36."

"Really?" Lana said.

"Unless you want me to pay for him." Allison handed over the paper. "Check my math."

"I trust you." Lana signed, hoping the credit card company would let her go over her limit. If she didn't get her mind off money, she was going to ruin the trip. She pulled out a map of the attractions. Some looked pretty cheap. "Todd, what say we walk over to the aquarium?"

"See?" Allison said.

"See what?" Lana said.

"First, the tea. Then the salad. Now, the plan for the afternoon."

"What's wrong with a plan?" Lana said.

"Nothing," Allison said, "but maybe Todd wants to make his own plan."

Todd's chin bobbed as if pulled by a string. "That's what I've been feeling."

"F...f...feeling?" Lana sputtered. "A feeling is 'I'm angry' or 'I'm sick of my job.'"

"My therapist says Todd is not to blame for the person he's become," Allison said.

"What are you, Freud? Todd's a fine person. There's nothing wrong with him." Lana threw down her napkin and excused herself.

In the little girls' room, she splashed water on her face and hoped Allison would take the hint. Am-scray. But when she returned, Allison was still there.

THE WHITE, STUCCOED building had a false front and stair-step roof, like the saloons in Westerns. Could this place, with its fake shark mounted on metal poles, possibly be the aquarium? Jammed on the street corner between other tourists, Lana noticed the shoelaces of Todd's sneakers had come undone. He could trip.

"Tie your shoes," she said.

"Yes, Todd, be a good boy and tie your shoes," Allison mimicked.

Todd bent and tied them. "That make you happy?"

"Overjoyed." Lana lowered her voice. "Why is she tagging along?"
"I asked her to," he said.

Allison bought two tickets and pushed Todd through the turn-stile. Lana bought her own and followed. Inside the cavernous, vaulted aquarium, she saw that Todd and Allison had stopped next to a crystal ball that dispensed jawbreakers. Todd held his hands under the chute. Pure sugar, Lana thought. His face would break out, and he'd be back on those expensive antibiotics. But okay, he could get them from student health. Forcing herself to relax, Lana looked up at the birds soaring in the rafters. She guessed Allison did have a valid point, sort of. Todd was twenty-one. He could vote. He could drink. Other kids his age made their own decisions; maybe in six months or a year, he'd be ready.

She watched them stroll over to an enormous indoor pool that occupied the center of the building. She followed and stood some distance away. Shadows slithered along the pool's turquoise bottom. There was an aroma of salt and kelp that reminded her of Todd's adolescent sheets. Todd didn't have his arm on Allison's shoulder or his hand down her shorts; and Allison wasn't staring up at him with that look of hero-worship that so quickly morphed into contempt. If they didn't fall back in lust, things might be okay.

Parallel arcades ran the length of the pool. Arches hinted at more displays. She ducked into the shadows, eager to learn more about the underwater world. Ear cocked, standing sideways to a column, Lana peered out. Todd and Allison had walked halfway around the pool, but they spotted her and began to laugh. Her neck prickled, her face grew warm, and she moved further back into the darkness. Tanks of fish confronted her, a wall of bright, blue windows that reminded her of her fish tanks at home. She tapped the glass. Tetras flashed by. Quick as rioters disappearing into stores, they popped into jagged coral grottoes. Floating among the anemone was the little figure of a scuba diver. From his mask rose a thread of silver bubbles. The little guy's fists were up, and he had a knife strapped to his scuba belt. She should check to make sure they hadn't run off without her. Lana turned and bumped Todd's chest.

"Where's Allison?" she said, pressing two fingers against her carotid artery.

"Gone to meet friends," he said.

"Whew!" Lana said. "What did you decide about the cat?"

"She'll probably put him down."

"Thank God," Lana said. "Are you really going to get a dog?"

"I don't know if my landlady would allow it."

"Well, find out. And think about the cost of dog food."

"Mom, please." He grabbed her shoulders and spun her around to face the aquarium. "Look. Jedi Knights."

Fish had been his only pets. Squatting down, he cupped his hands and put his nose against the glass. When he was six, his father sent a Christmas present, a box of *Star Wars* figures. Then, everything had been about *Star Wars*—his books, his artwork, his little action men. Jedi Knights. That's what he called the darting tetras, she remembered.

"There's Obi Wan and Luke Skywalker," Todd said, "living their little fishy lives, oblivious to suffering."

"Fish don't suffer," Lana said.

Todd straightened up, sniffed, and turned away. "She's the one person who truly gets me."

"What? I don't get you?" The shriek of an amplifier drove pencils of pain through her ears. A tornado siren? Alarmed, she looked back toward the pool. People were lining up around the perimeter.

"Come on, Todd," she said. "There's a show."

She found an opening and grabbed his hand, giving him her place at the rail. She hoped he would say, no, you stand in front so you can see, but he didn't. In many ways, he was still a child.

An announcer in rubber hip boots splashed through the water. Talking into a body mike, he said sharks weren't as dangerous as they seemed. Great whites rarely attacked humans. "Nurse sharks are sweet as pussy cats," he said. Sure, they were, Lana thought. Until they bit. He bent over and picked up a nurse shark with gray, elephant skin. The fins were wings, all except the one on top, a rudder. The announcer splashed through the water, making a circuit of the pool and holding the shark for children to pet. Then, returning to the middle where everyone could see, he stuck out his tongue and brought the shark to his puckered lips.

Women shrieked. Lana covered her eyes.

"I can't stand this," she said.

"It's cruel to contain them," Todd said. "They'd be happier in the sea."

"I don't think sharks have feelings."

"Maybe I'm a shark," he said.

"You have a brain and you can think with it," she said. "Theirs are the size of walnuts."

BACK AT THE ROOM and desperate to work off neck tension, Lana unlocked the door. "I'll change into tennies," she said. "They have bikes at this place. We can go for a spin."

"I'm supposed to meet some guys," he said.

"Where?"

"At the beach."

He dumped his duffel bag on the bed. "Damn. I forgot to pack my flip-flops."

"The sand'll burn your feet."

He unzipped a side pocket. A smile broke over his face. "No worries." He held up the flip-flops and slapped the soles.

"It'd be good for you to have a cardiovascular workout."

"I'm saving myself for beach volleyball."

"Be back in time for dinner."

"As usual, you're three steps ahead of me. Try to relax and give yourself some down time." He kissed her forehead, grabbed a towel, and headed out the door.

Lana followed him to the patio where the roots of a Banyan shot up between the glass breakfast tables. Next to the office, she saw an ice dispenser and Coke machine. Todd dropped in quarters and reached for a can.

"I'm just saying, I don't want to eat alone," Lana said.

"Me neither," Todd said. "I guess it depends on what the guys have planned."

"Remember when you were little?" Lana said. "I told you, I can handle anything. Shoplifting or cutting school or fights. I have only one rule. You must always tell me the truth."

"I tell you the truth."

"If you want to be with Allison…"

He smirked. "She's hanging with her friends."

"Tell me if this makes sense." She counted on her fingers. "You don't want to study. You don't want to catch up on sleep. You're going out drinking."

"I'll sleep in tomorrow."

"Tomorrow, we're going kayaking."

"It better not be early."

"Ten thirty's hardly the crack of dawn."

"I don't know if I'll be in the mood."

"Fine, Todd, but if you're not doing what you said you wanted to do, why am I taking days off when I can't afford it?"

Todd looked up, as if the answer were tattooed on his forehead. "Because I'm the perfect son?"

Surely, he was joking. Yes, of course, he was. She returned to the room to think. It would cost a hundred bucks to change flights, but that would cost less than four more nights at the fleabag inn. She called the desk and told the clerk they'd had a change of plans. They were leaving tomorrow. After she'd called the airline and booked evening flights, she looked at the clothes he'd left on the bed: his sweats, a nasty jock strap, his wallet! She opened it. There was a picture of Allison's out-of-focus face, head tilted, hands holding a tiny satin pillow beneath her chin.

Lana reached for her phone. Todd's voice mail answered. "Come back by six o'clock," she said. "Be here or else. I need to tell you about a change of plans."

Lana waited. Silence on the line. He wasn't picking up.

She packed her suitcase and rode to the beach to find him.

Holding the high handlebars of the B & B's old, fat-tire Schwinn, she searched for his pale body among the oily sunbathers, basting themselves and brushing off sand. It would be easier to find him on foot. She locked the bike to an overflowing trash can. After jogging from one end of the beach to the other, she paused to watch a game of volleyball and the ribbons of clouds across the horizon. As the sun went down, the beach emptied.

Not knowing what else to do, she rode back to the B & B, showered, changed into a dress, and took out the brochure for the kayak trip. Pictures showed tourists paddling through a mangrove swamp. The way things were going, reaching into the water for starfish and spiny urchins promised to be the highlight of her vacation, and Lana didn't want to miss it. The brochure said to be on time: They didn't wait for stragglers.

Hungry, but wanting to give Todd's wallet back to him, she walked to Duval Street. It was a mob scene. Crowded into an alley by a rowdy gang of drunks, she heard someone behind her and turned to see a tall, thin blond pulling down the front of his swim trunks and taking a whiz. "Todd!"

A stranger turned, giving her a look of happy stupor.

"If your mother saw you urinating in public," Lana said, "she'd die of shame."

"What she doesn't know won't hurt her." He gave himself a shake.

She walked down the street like a blind woman, scraping her arm on brick, her gut too empty for hunger.

THE NEXT MORNING when she stared down through the top of a glass breakfast table, Lana saw that someone had made an effort to level the table's feet with matchbooks. One came from "The Green Parrot," a bar she'd checked every hour until midnight. Todd had not come home. She peeled paper from her muffin, four hundred calories and loaded with fat. She'd work it off kayaking. The Banyan that shaded the patio looked like something out of

Swiss Family Robinson, but its vertical branches, rising up fifty feet to the canopy, made her feel caged. She checked her watch. It was ten o'clock. If she was going to make that kayak trip, she'd better get going.

The patio gate swung open. Todd, in baggy shorts and a Polo shirt, grabbed Banyan roots as handholds and groaned with every step. Walking straight to the ice machine, he filled a bucket and motioned her to follow him.

"I'd almost given you up for lost," she said.

The backs of his legs had turned flamingo-pink.

In the room, Todd pulled off his shirt and straddled a chair. "Could you ice my back?"

"You have fifteen minutes to get your shit together," she said. "Then, we're going kayaking. It's the one thing I want to do on this trip, and by golly, I'm going to do it."

"Who's stopping you?" he said.

She glanced at the clock. No reason to panic. The ice shrank in her hand, blisters rose up, and his body gave off a sweet and salty smell that, fleetingly, she associated with the aquarium. Twenty minutes, yet.

He lifted his head from his arms. "Yesterday was a major bummer. I lost my wallet on the beach, and now I'll have to get new ID. The guys I was with—we were playing beach volleyball—shirts and skins. If I'd been one of the shirts, this wouldn't have happened."

Basketball was shirts and skins. Lana looked at his round eyes. "Don't lie to me."

"Don't you trust me?" He lifted his eyebrows.

Now, she recognized the smell. "You were with Allison."

"Oh, Allison, sure. I bumped into her and her girl friends, but she was mad at me. I probably shouldn't tell you this, but me and my buddies ended up at a strip joint."

"Without your wallet?" She opened her purse and tossed it to him.

He caught it with both hands. "See? I'm not trying to deceive you. I said right when I came in, I'd lost it."

"You hooked up with Allison."

"I told you. I was with some guys."

"Do you think I was born yesterday?" she said.

Todd yanked out the drawer of the nightstand and grabbed a Gideon Bible. "Do I have to swear on this?"

"Swear," she said.

He held the book and scratched the gold inlay with his thumbnail. Then he pushed away the chair and flung himself diagonally across the bed.

"Are you going to give her a ring?" Lana said.

"Don't be dense. I needed to relieve the pressure."

"The pressure of what?"

"School."

A fly was buzzing somewhere in the room. Lana looked around and didn't see it, but she could hear it, throwing the full weight of its body against the windows. "You failed more than just one class."

He grabbed a pillow and covered his head. He had failed them all. Was probably kicked out of accounting. He'd come down here, on her dime, to lick his wounds, and he'd known from the start that Allison would be here, too.

Lana's nose itched, and she rubbed her finger back and forth. There must be something growing down here, some plant or allergen with spores drifting through the jalousie windows.

It was 10:19. "Todd?" She picked up her purse.

He kicked off his flip-flops. They dropped on the floor.

"Todd?" she repeated.

"You're not going to pry it out of me," he mumbled.

"What?" she said.

"A confession."

She blinked and sucked in her breath.

"Of course not," she said.

"You have to get used to it."

"Used to what?"

"I'm not your ideal little boy."

"I never said you had to be."

"Yes. You. Did. It's how you measure success."

Lana pressed her fingers to her eyelids. She listened to the silence and looked around for the fly. A big, fat one, it sat on the alarm clock rubbing its feelers. It looked satisfied, as if it had somehow made everything happen in this room that had happened: her, standing paralyzed; Todd, sunburnt, sprawled across the bed. Poor trapped fly.

Todd blew his nose on the sheet. "Don't you have someplace to be?"

She looked at the clock. It was 10:21.

"As a matter of fact, I do." She held the door open. "We're taking a plane back tonight. Pack your stuff."

"But I didn't sleep last night," he said.

"We have to vacate the room by eleven."

"What am I supposed to do, sit on the patio and twiddle my thumbs?"

"I don't know," she said, closing the screen softly. "I'm sure you'll come up with a plan."

PROUD TO BE AN AMERICAN

———o———

THE MOON SHINING like a searchlight on the cornfields made Billy Rippelmeyer proud to be an American. Steering one-handed, air streaming through his fingers and bugs stinging his outstretched palm, he wished his boss, sacked out in the back, would climb forward into the shotgun seat. Mile markers flicked past, and the white line of the county road got sucked beneath the wheels of the panel truck. In a pool of darkness far ahead, red lights flashed. Billy pulled up behind a school bus. Kids in hoodies scrambled across a culvert and disappeared into a wall of corn. Looked like a detasseling crew out before dawn. He had started detasseling in seventh grade, getting his dose of the American work ethic. Now, he was getting his second dose. Truck stop coffee. Twelve hour days. After just six weeks, remodeling mall stores was getting old. There had to be a way he could get from the life he had now to some other life he couldn't quite imagine.

At Easton Town Center north of Columbus, he drove past the skeleton of a new anchor store. A tower-crane swung a load of I-beams onto the top deck. He had no idea how these steel monsters went together, but one of these days the economy would pick up, and construction was definitely a path to a better future. Back in Macomb, miners couldn't get work but two or three months a year, and Pella had laid off its third shift. His uncle, a plumber, made out okay, but couldn't justify a gofer.

Billy found the mall's service entrance and killed the engine. "Hey, wake up." Billy looked back.

His boss, Tom Jovanovich, wormed out of the sleeping bag. His eyes looked bloodshot. He needed a shave.

"Did you get any rest?" Billy said.

"A little," Tom said.

"At least, one of us did."

"You got twenty years on me, kid." After sitting up, Tom pulled on his socks.

"Throw me my pills, will you?"

"Sure." Tom tossed Billy a paper bag.

Billy popped the lid on his antibiotics and swallowed a pill with the last of his coffee. Fatigue sat on him like the lead apron the dentist had thrown across his chest back in Davenport. Billy had worked for days in agony, milkshakes sending waves of pain through his jaw, heartbeats drumming in his ears, until Tom had finally asked what was wrong. An afternoon at the dentist's had set them back time-wise and taken a chunk of change out of Billy's paycheck. Luckily, the Foot Locker in Davenport wasn't one of the big stores, but even so, they'd had to rush to get it wrapped up and move on to this one, three states away.

Grabbing the clipboard from the glove box, Billy hopped out and walked over to the mall's service entrance. A security guard let him in. The service corridor had the usual windowless block walls and gunmetal-gray doors. The Foot Locker was back by the theater. "Shit," Billy said to no one in particular. This was gonna be one, long carry. He unlocked the service door and, inside the space, found shoe boxes, register tape, pizza cartons, and the odd sneaker. At least the fuckers had left trash bags. He snapped one off.

Tom's last helper got tired of picking up the garbage and left Tom in the lurch. Leastwise, that's how Tom told it. The deal was this: Tom paid Billy by the hour. Cash, of course. A week ago, Billy had asked for a raise. Thing was, there were a lot more ways Billy was costing Tom money, ways Billy hadn't even considered. The first week, Billy had called out the wrong dimensions and wasted a whole sheet of slat-wall. Then, there were the groceries—the gallons of milk, the jars of peanut butter, the jumbo Cocoa Puffs.

"You're eating me out of house and home," Tom said. "Plus, teaching you cuts into my productivity. Understand?"

"I guess," Billy said. He came away from that conversation feeling like a liability, like maybe he should be paying Tom instead of the other way around. He guessed he was lucky to work for eight bucks an hour, no benefits.

"We'll talk about a raise after you develop a skill-set," Tom had promised.

Tom's skill-set was pretty high. He was an actual architect with A.I.A. after his name. The initials stood for American Institute of Architects. Tom hadn't started at a junior college. He'd gone straight from high school to the University of Illinois. And not just undergraduate. He had a master's degree. He'd worked at an office in the Loop. He'd taken a licensing exam that lasted three days. There was a lot of book-learning before you ever got to that step, he'd explained. "Oh," Billy said, not sure if those were the skills Tom meant. Billy was the kind of person who learned better when he wasn't slumped in a classroom chair.

The first store they'd remodeled, Billy had learned something new every day. He had never used a laser level or installed a drop-ceiling. He'd never even heard of slat-wall, the grooved, Formica-covered sheets that came twenty feet long and were a bitch to carry. Now, he'd learned everything there was to learn, and the time-line for the build-out at this Easton store sounded like it was going to be another grueling push. Sighing, Billy threw the bags of garbage in the corner.

When Billy returned to the truck, Tom stood at the side-mirror. Like the former Illinois governor, Blagojevich, who was prideful about his thick, dark hair, Tom was never far from his lime-green comb. Much as Billy admired Tom and wanted to be like him— have his own van and helper to boss around—the comb was just one of the things Billy found annoying. Tom was full of himself.

Trying to decide what to bring in first, Billy looked in the van. Tools and supplies sat on the top shelves, and on the bottom shelf sat plastic crates that held Tom's espresso machine, his burr grinder, the Breville juicer, the Coleman cooler, and the George Foreman grill. All his gadgets and gizmos. They, too, had begun to annoy Billy.

After giving one final pass with his comb, Tom said, "Let's get a move on," as if Billy were some kind of slacker, which he wasn't. He was just tired and he was burping up antibiotics.

Billy grabbed the sleeping bag and punched it into the stuff sack. "I'll get this out of the way." He closed his eyes and stood a minute, trying to moisten his eyes.

"Wake up!" Tom said.

"Say, listen …" Billy said.

"How's the tooth?"

Billy probed with his tongue. Pain shot up to his eye socket, and he blinked back tears. "All right," he said.

"Good," Tom said.

"Are we going to put in a full day?"

"We have to."

"Maybe could go to the Extended Stay and take half-an-hour's nap."

"Check-in's not till four."

Billy pulled at his overall straps. "I been wearing these since yesterday, and I could use a shower."

"Can't it wait?" Tom said.

Billy wasn't stupid. He could tell when something was a question and when it wasn't.

Tom slung a nail apron over his shoulder and picked up drywall buckets. Tools clanked.

"What the hell, Billy!" Tom dropped the buckets. "Put the tools where they belong. Don't just throw them any old where."

"I was tired, okay?"

"That's no excuse."

"Not saying it was."

"Well, then, do it without me having to remind you."

The guy could be such a prick. But no sense getting all heated up. Just let it go, his dad would have said. Be grateful for the work. And, he supposed he should be more like his dad. Humble. Never a mean word unless it had to do with politics, and then, oh boy, did his dad have opinions about the mess the country had got itself into.

Tom headed toward the service entrance. Billy unlocked the trailer and took out panels for the enclosure. Spray-painted blue, each flakeboard panel had a Foot Locker logo. "For brand recognition," Tom said. The panels cut into Billy's shoulder and bounced with each step. When he'd carried the panels all the way down the service hall, he kicked open the back door and grunted for Tom to unlock the front entrance. Tom raised the metal grille. Billy dropped the panels to make the maximum amount of racket. He didn't like feeling all sullen, but he couldn't help it. His tooth hurt, he was tired from the drive, and he wanted a shower.

"Let's get the store closed off ASAP," Tom said. "I want the 'Tommy Horse' out of sight before those union dudes take their coffee break. You start the demo, and I'll deal with the enclosure."

"Whatever you say, boss." Billy unwrapped a lemon drop. The food court wasn't open yet.

"C'mon," Tom said. "Your tooth put us a day behind schedule."

"Excuse me for living," Billy said.

Tom looked up. "Don't cop an attitude."

Billy thought of the dentist's bill. Four hundred bucks for a root canal. He couldn't afford to get himself fired. He'd told the dentist just to pull the tooth, but Tom had insisted the guy fix it if he could. Somewhere on the road, Billy would have to hunt up another dentist to finish the job. Either that or wait till he got back to Macomb.

Three more trips and he had all the sections of the enclosure stacked out front, beyond the display windows. Tom had better get his butt in gear if he wanted to keep those union guys from coming around. Assembling the panels was the easiest thing they'd do all day. No heavy lifting. No laser-leveling. All Tom had to do was set the panels upright and tap in the hinge pins. Instead, Tom was leaning against the wall.

Hand over his cell phone, he made a circle with his finger and pointed to the back door. "Give me some privacy, Billy. I'm on the line with my lawyer."

If Tom wasn't on the line with his lawyer, he was on the line with Foot Locker corporate or the mall managers. While Billy worked, Tom talked on the phone.

It wasn't like that in agriculture. The farmer worked as hard as the hired hand. It was a point of pride almost, and even on the long days of getting in the corn, the seventy-year-old dudes kept pushing until all that was left was rabbits chopped to pieces in the fields.

Billy went back to the trailer for the panel-saw and the Tommy Horses, the invention Tom hoped to patent. Made of plywood and as easy to assemble as a cardboard box, the Tommy Horse popped open, its legs spread at a 45 degree angle. The invention was the best sawhorse Billy had ever seen. Tom might be a slave-driver, but he was a genuine inventor, like Thomas Alva Edison. Once when Billy was little, he had read a book about Edison. One of those Easy Readers. Whenever the inventor came up with an idea, the book showed a light bulb over his head. Edison had been an average student. Then, all of a sudden, he'd become rich and famous.

Back in the store, Billy unfolded the sawhorses and dropped in the T-shaped pieces that locked the plywood ends together. Made from a 2x4 screwed to a six-inch-wide piece of plywood, the "locking piece," as Tom called it, was what distinguished the Tommy Horse from other prefab sawhorses. Tom had filed a method patent on the idea.

"Done!" Tom closed his phone. "If you ever invent something…"

"That'll be the day," Billy said.

" …remember this. Before you get the patent, you gotta be like a nun." Knock-kneed, Tom clamped one hand over his mouth and the other over his crotch.

"Don't be grabbing yourself or people'll think you're a homo,"

Billy said.

"You think I'm joking."

"Are you a homo? Because if you are, it's okay. Just as long as you don't..."

Tom rolled his eyes and gave his hair a swipe with the comb. "You are so dumb. I'm trying to educate you."

"Sorry," Billy said. "What were you going to say?"

Tom looked over his shoulder and took a deep breath. "If you ever get an idea for an invention, you've got to be absolutely close-mouthed before the patent's filed, but when you start marketing the product, you've got to put yourself out there and be a whore."

Billy felt like saying he was a whore anyway, so what was the difference. But he ought to be grateful. Tips like these were something they didn't teach in school.

"I'm about to pass out from hunger," Billy said.

"I thought you said eating hurt your tooth," Tom said.

"The medicine's not sitting well on an empty stomach."

"There's o.j. and coffee cake in the cooler," Tom said.

"I'll go get it."

"Don't stress about the enclosure," Tom said. "Since you're heading back to the truck, you can take out the trash."

Can take out the trash? Billy thought. "We don't have a dumpster yet," he said.

"It'll be here this afternoon."

Contractors were territorial about their dumpsters, and if they caught him throwing in Foot Locker crapola, the mall managers would slap a big fine on Tom. This had happened up at Woodfield Mall. Tom hadn't even docked Billy's pay. Tom meant well, Billy told himself, but he was sick of people meaning well and screwing him. He slung the bags of trash over his shoulder. "What do you want me to do with these, then?"

"See if the new store has a container," Tom said. "Don't call attention to yourself, or we'll have the union on us like a rash."

Unions didn't believe in the American way of life, not the way Libertarians did.

IRON-WORKERS IN orange vests crisscrossed the steel skeleton of the new anchor store. On the second level carpenters in yellow hardhats assembled steel-stud walls.

The parking lot was empty. The dumpster corral, surrounded by a cyclone fence and camouflaged by canvas, sat out in the open. No one seemed to be looking his way. Head down, four bags over his shoulder, he made his move.

After high school, Billy had taken out a student loan and enrolled at Macomb Community College. Along with his drafting class and one on computer-aided design, he had been forced to take English 100. His advisor told him he had to pass with a grade of C or better if he wanted to transfer.

During their stop in Davenport his forwarded mail had finally caught up. Tom had been cooking spaghetti with pine nuts and this green sauce that looked like fresh alfalfa, while Billy sat at the counter and opened his grades. With the grade slip shaking in his hand, Billy tried to tell Tom why the D he'd earned in English was unfair.

The teacher had told him to write a term paper on a topic he felt passionate about, so Billy wrote about the Trilateral Commission, a super secret club made up of top people from formerly communist countries, plus leaders from the socialist countries in Europe. Once a year, they met in Geneva to set food prices. Putin, who had once headed up the KGB, was engineering a plot to keep food prices artificially low. As payback for the collapse of the Soviet Union, Putin wanted to crush the American family farmer and bring America to its knees. George Bush senior was a member of the Trilateral Commission. Very few people knew that, but Billy's dad subscribed to a newsletter for family farmers, and the newsletter had a lot stuff that didn't make it into the *Macomb Eagle*. According to his dad, the last decent agricultural subsidy had been back when Eisenhower was President. You couldn't question Ike's loyalty. He was as American as it gets.

"Don't believe everything you read," Tom had said, a smirk on his face, so Billy knew he was not being taken seriously. Sitting in the dentist's waiting room, Billy had brought up the Trilateral Commission again. Tom put up his hand. "Listen, Billy, I know you're sincere, but I can't listen to any more of this drivel. Give it a rest." What Billy's father said was true. No one cared about the little guy.

The deep-deep-deep of the dumpster truck backing into the corral made Billy look up. The truck emptied the two fifteen-yard containers. That was costing someone money. The truck left. Billy jogged over, opened the gate, and stomped his bags to make the contents less identifiable. He threw them in. Soon, his garbage would be covered with construction debris.

Hurrying to make his escape, he closed the gate.

"Hey, guy. What are you doing?" a man's voice called.

Billy froze.

A young carpenter, hustling toward the corral, was holding the head of his hammer to keep it from bouncing against his leg. At least it wasn't a guy in a tie and white shirt or a security guard. All the same, best not to engage the enemy.

"I'm working around the other side." Billy tipped his head in a circle, indicating the far end of the mall. These guys were like ants. They'd send out scouts until they found a grain of sugar.

Introducing himself as Rick, the carpenter said, "You ever think about going union?"

"Nah," Billy said, turning to go. "I'm a self-employed contractor." Not true, but that's what Tom told him to say. The carpenter was gaining on him.

"Looks to me like you're a carpenter working for an hourly wage without benefits," he heard the voice behind him say. "Do you have medical insurance?"

Billy turned. He hated lying, but there'd be hell to pay if he didn't. Matchsticks in the outlets. Air let out of the van's tires.

"I'm co-owner of the company," Billy said.

"You don't look much older than me."

"Yeah, well." Billy was eighteen-and-a-half, but because of his dimples, people always pegged him for younger. This guy, with an

Adam's apple pointy as an elbow, looked like he'd come from the work crew of a high-school project house.

That was how Billy had learned to frame and trim, building a house under his shop teacher's supervision. Then, he'd had friends to hang out with. At three o'clock, they'd knock off for the day, spend half an hour sweeping up, and drive up Coal Road to Argyle Lake, stripping off their sweaty tee shirts and diving from the bank into cold, green water. He missed the splash fights and the way his body felt—tired, but not exhausted. Plus, he had buddies who knew what he was all about. He wanted to talk to this carpenter, but he was afraid.

"Shouldn't you be getting back?" Billy said.

"I'm on break," the young carpenter said.

"I don't take breaks," said Billy.

"You should. Half hour, morning and afternoon, plus a forty-five minute lunch break. It's in our contract. The rest of the crew went to grab a soda, but I seen you out here and said, that's a farm boy. You got a slow walk, like you made too many trips to the milking barn."

"We don't have cows in Illinois," Billy said.

"That where you're from?" the carpenter said.

"Listen, I have work to do."

"You got to rest your body. Leastwise, that's what they're always telling me. I'm always go, go, go. Guess that's from Dad."

"We must have the same dad," Billy said.

His eyes on a '95 Ford Bronco in the parking lot, Billy started walking back. His dad Russ drove a Bronco, but its rocker panels had rusted out, and a new car cost more than a mobile home. Russ said the job remodeling mall boutiques sounded like a fine thing. After losing the farm, Russ had filed for bankruptcy, and he wanted Billy to do anything but farm. Billy didn't tell his dad, but he had never wanted to be a farmer, worrying about the price the elevator would give him for beans, or arguing with the bank about a loan. Anyways, he wasn't sure he could do the math.

After the farm got auctioned off, Russ had not been able to

help Billy with tuition. Russ said nobody gave him money to go to school, so he didn't see why Billy couldn't work and go part time. Lately, Billy had been thinking about his dad a lot. Russ had moved into town and fallen back on his trade as a soft shoe farrier. Billy's mom worked in a grocery store. Giving him a kiss goodbye, she'd said, "Don't think we don't love you." But, then, of course, that's what he did think. Neither of his parents were especially warm people. They were grudge-carriers.

TOM BROUGHT LUNCH from McDonald's. Sitting on the Tommy Horse, Billy listened to his boss wonder aloud whom he should approach at Home Depot. Maybe Lowe's would be interested. If either one of the big stores nibbled, he would have to gear up to produce in volume; but, by and by, the Tommy Horse business would run itself.

"If this thing goes," Tom said, "I'll set up a factory in Nogales."

"I thought everything came from China," Billy said, wiping his chin with the back of his hand.

"I thought about China, but shipping's prohibitive."

"How long's it going to take for the patents to come through?"

"Depends."

"On what?"

"On if the idea is in the public domain, my lawyer says. If every Tom, Dick, and Harry knew about the Tommy Horse, I couldn't prove it was my idea." Tom whipped out his comb. "C'mon. We gotta get going. We're about ready to start cutting."

While Tom had been erecting the enclosure, Billy had popped off the old slat-wall with his pry-bar and chiseled down the blobs of mastic. Boutique stores had to remodel every five years. It was part of their lease.

After swallowing another pill with the last of his shake, Billy wadded his aluminum wrapper and gestured at the gutted store. "What about all this?"

"The boutiques?" Tom said.

"Yeah."

Tom put away his comb and buckled on his nail apron. "We've only got one more on this contract."

"But that's two weeks." Billy tried to judge whether the pounding in his throat was making his voice sound funny. "When's the next contract start?"

"There isn't going to be one," Tom said.

"Did somebody low-ball you?"

"Not exactly," Tom said.

Maybe the Trilateral Commission had a hand in this.

"You made it sound like you'd need me another year," Billy said.

Tom looked away and shrugged. "Yeah, well."

"You just don't want to do it anymore," Billy said.

Tom raised his eyebrows. "You're probably right."

"Did you decide not to put in a bid?"

"No, I could still do it."

"Then, what?" Billy said.

"It's a trade-off."

"For making a go of the invention."

Tom nodded. "That's part of it. Once this patent goes through, I'm going to need to put on the full court press."

"And you can't be traveling."

"No, I can't."

Billy looked at the gutted space. Sealed off from the mall, the store was dark, illuminated only by a single drop-light hanging from the ceiling struts. Before lunch, he hadn't noticed the smell of popcorn. Now, he did. It must be coming from the theater.

"What if you handled the design," Billy said, "and I did the build-out? At least to start with."

Tom spread the legs of the laser level and bent over, his eye to the ocular. "You'd need a partner."

Maybe Rick, Billy thought. "Where would I find somebody?"

"I don't know. You'd have to sell yourself to Foot Locker."

"You could talk to them."

"I don't think so," Tom said, straightening up.

Basically, Tom was telling him his job was going to end. While Tom was out glad-handing it with home improvement stores, Billy would be back in Macomb shoveling asphalt on a highway crew.

"I wish I'd known," Billy said.

"Did you take your medicine at lunch?"

"Yeah," Billy said.

"Remember. You've got to take all the pills," Tom said. "Don't stop just because you're feeling better."

"I won't," Billy said.

"Go get the respirators from the truck, and cut the light on your way out, will you?" Tom said. "I want to shoot a level."

When Billy returned with the respirators, he threw them on the rolling tool chest. He didn't feel like suffocating behind the rubber mask. He knew he should, but something inside him didn't like the way they felt. He popped a lemon drop and probed the temporary cap.

Tom held out his chalk box. Billy grabbed the hook. The taut, blue string snapped horizontally across the wall. The one thing he'd learned was you had to have a continuous level-line around the store, or you were in deep doo-doo when it came time to hang the slat-wall. Considering how he'd busted his butt, it wasn't much of a take-home lesson.

Tom called out the dimensions, and Billy made hash marks, then tied a bandanna around his nose before lifting the slat-wall onto the panel saw's aluminum rack. He squeezed the saw's trigger. The blade zipped through the slat-wall and threw out a cloud of dust. For the past week and a half, the formaldehyde in the glue had been bothering him. He coughed and pounded his chest.

"Humor me and put on a respirator," Tom said. "I don't want you getting emphysema."

"You should wear one, too," Billy said.

"Okay, if you say so." Tom smiled and held out a hand. Billy tossed him the mask. After adjusting the strap, Tom pumped fresh adhesive on the wall and hoisted the slat-wall onto his knee. "Pick up your end," he said. Together, they lined up the bottom of the panel with the chalk line. Billy felt the mastic squish.

The fumes came right through the mask. He started coughing. Particulate cartridges didn't do shit for solvents. He ripped off the mask and headed for the door.

"Hey," Tom said, pushing the mask up on his forehead. "Wait till the adhesive grabs."

Billy came back. Palms flat, he pushed. His cough started up.

"I'm going to buy you some Robitussin," Tom said. "Get some air. And, while you're out, steal me a piece of dimension lumber from the dumpster," Tom said.

"Why?"

Tom let go of the slat-wall and stood back. One end began to dip, and he rushed toward it, guiding it back to level.

"The patent attorney wants me to send him a photo of the Tommy Horse, and I want to show him a fresh 2x6 on top."

"I thought I wasn't supposed to call attention to myself."

"A big lummox like you inevitably calls attention to himself."

Billy put his hands on his hips. He stared at the gouges in the concrete wall where his chisel had hit. Stones had fallen out and left deep dimples. "Is that why you hired me, for my size?"

"I didn't hire you for your brains," Tom said, turning and pressing his back against the slat-wall. He flipped open his phone.

With the toe of his boot, Billy made a circle on the floor. He unbuckled his nail apron and let it drop. He touched his tongue to his tooth. A sharp pencil drove into his eyeball. He had to stop doing that.

"Why don't you take five," Tom said, "and don't forget the 2x6, long's you're out there."

IN THE CORRAL Billy climbed into the dumpster to retrieve the dimension lumber. He knocked off dried concrete and hoisted himself back over the side, disgusted by the rotten smell.

A voice called, "Want a Coke?"

Billy turned and saw the apprentice holding two Big Gulps.

"I knew you'd come," Rick said, "so I quick drove over to Seven-Eleven."

"Sorry for stealing the lumber," Billy said.

"I don't care," Rick said. "The scrap's on its way to a landfill."

Looking at the new construction, Billy saw two iron-workers, feet dangling off a girder, opening their lunch pails.

"You work with a buddy?" Billy said.

"He's over there having a cigarette," Rick said, motioning with his drink.

"How long you been on this job?"

"Two months." Rick pulled out his wallet and passed Billy his scaffold card, which entitled him to erect and work on scaffold any-where in the United States. "The card's a meal ticket," he said. "If you wanted to join the union, why, we'd be glad to have you."

Billy felt like he was sitting with one of the Jehovah's Witnesses who used to come by the farm. "Did someone send you out here to recruit me?" he said.

Rick smiled and shrugged. "Sort of." The Brotherhood wanted all working carpenters to earn a decent wage, and the only way to do that was to organize. And train. The Brotherhood would give him training better than any college.

"What do you learn?"

"Right now I'm learning to build a sawhorse," Rick said. "They tell me if I can build a sawhorse, I can frame a roof."

Billy looked at Rick's prominent Adam's apple and at his sin-cere grin.

"Next time they ask you to build a sawhorse, do it like this," Billy said, picking up a scrap of cardboard. The one thing he'd been good at was drafting. He sketched the pieces of the Tommy Horse.

"You can make this out of five-eighths ply."

"It looks flimsy," Rick said.

"It'll hold my weight, no problem."

"Where'd you come up with the design?"

"I invented it," Billy said.

"You invented it?"

"Yeah," Billy said. "I filed a patent. I'm marketing it through Home Depot."

"What about Walmart?" Rick said.

"Them, too."

"Is it going to be made out of steel, or what?"

"No, plywood. With a 2x6 on top." Billy held up the scrap of lumber. "This here's the key that holds the legs together."

"I'll show it to my apprenticeship teacher," Rick said. "They're always looking for ideas."

"Do that," Billy said.

"Could you autograph this?" Rick held out the drawing.

Billy looked at the sketch and signed in neat block print. William Dwight Rippelmeyer, Inventor and Architect, A.I.A. His full name, with the initials beside it, looked important. He closed his eyes and, along with the sunshine, felt the importance of himself sink in.

TEŞEKKÜR

---○---

I FELT LIKE an old, gray rug, discardable and as invisible to myself as to my two traveling companions. My granddaughter Jennifer had worn a long skirt and spaghetti-strap top, and our guide Mehmet, who hadn't even broken a sweat, watched her pin up her hair. The heat was killing me. The camera strap chafed my neck. But yes, fortunately or unfortunately, I was still here. I held up the guidebook to shade my face and squinted into a thousand broken mirrors of the sea.

"Traveling sure takes it out of you," I said.

"I can go for a while longer." Jennifer took a chug of water.

Sure, she could run a marathon, but not me. My hip ached something fierce and my ankles felt wobbly from the cobblestones. "Jen, honey, Grandma's feet are just a skosh tired."

"Oh, Grandma," Jennifer said. "You'll perk up. This culture is so fascinating, I don't want to skip anything."

Mehmet spat in the weeds. "This last stop on coast."

"Good," I said.

"Next, we go Saklikent Gorge," Mehmet said.

"Not more walking!" I said.

"We stop for tea." Thin mustache twitching, Mehmet was not a man who liked to be challenged, but I was of an age where I truly didn't care.

"What's at this gorge place?" I said.

171

"Famous butterfly and Hidden City," he said. "Must see."

"Is Hidden City another crumbling ruin?" I said.

"I think," he said. "Last time I there, water high. I no go in."

Turkey's Anatolian coast was just one rock-ruin after another. "Maybe we could…"

"We go see ruins here, and then we drive to next place and you rest. If water high, Hidden City stay hidden. Okay?" Drawing his eyebrows together in a scowl, he looked at Jennifer and then at me.

A rocky path led down the embankment to the ruins of a Lycian necropolis. Burial chambers. If I made it down the hill, I might never make it up.

"Shall we?" Jennifer said.

"I think I'll save myself for Hidden City," I said.

Mehmet looked at Jennifer's scoop-neck blouse. "We go, then?"

"Is that okay, Grandma?"

"You're a grownup," I said.

From all the walking we'd done that morning, my stockings had slipped down around my ankles. After opening the car door, I sat sideways, and, one leg at a time, pulled the stockings above my knees. I've always been fit, and the thick, elasticized nylons made me feel ninety, not seventy-three. I'd sprained my ankle a year ago, and it ached something fierce. By the time I stood up, Jennifer and Mehmet had reached the tombs. A few of the burial vaults were still intact, the stone roofs shaped like Wisconsin barns.

With the hot wind off the ocean came the smell of salt. Mica glinted off granite boulders. It was a beautiful spot, really; and if I'd been here with my husband, I might have ventured down, leaning on his arm for support. As it was, I felt a bit like a third wheel, an observer of the white heat that blazed from Mehmet's eyes. Even looking down through my bifocals, I understood why he'd want to hide behind reflective lenses. In my day, we would have called that leering. Yes, Mehmet was definitely ogling my granddaughter, a girl who, my son said, greatly resembled me.

Jennifer had tanned up. Her shoulders were bare. I made a fist and looked at the skin on the back of my hand. Age spots. The sun wasn't doing me any favors, and this was the third day I'd been out in it. I might as well have been on the trip by myself, but then that was my life right now. The decades had backed me right up against the precipice, and every experience that might have been shared, I was forced to do alone. I missed the warmth in my husband's eyes and knowing a nap did not necessarily mean sleep. I missed the unspoken.

Mehmet had taken us to Ephesus—*Efes* on the Turkish map—where Paul of Tarsus had preached a sermon that caused a riot in the Coliseum. I thought I'd seen my fill of Roman columns, but no. Mehmet insisted we stop at Pergamom and, after that, Artemis's obliterated temple. Yesterday, in Kekova, Mehmet found a coffee shop for me to wait in while he and Jennifer hiked to the top of an old Ottoman fort; and at Aperlae, he'd sent me down a paved road while he steered Jennifer toward a goat path, half-obscured by crumbling walls. I had paid for this trip, so I guess, in a sense, I owned it, but it was not the same dynamic with a third person.

Back when my husband was still working in this part of the world, Jennifer had come for a month-long visit. Wanting some time alone with her, I had hired Bedouins to take just the two of us to the old Nabatean city of Petra. Jennifer had been nine. Camping in the desert under a million stars, then coming upon Petra with its pink stone and giant columns had hooked us both on adventure travel. Grandma's Number One Adventure, she'd called that trip. The camels. The stratified rock. The discovery of a place that had been discovered, then rediscovered, and now, was being overrun.

I was glad we'd done the trip when we did. Jennifer and I had been equally matched, with me still able to keep up. I hated the things my body could no longer do.

SITTING IN THE back seat of Mehmet's car, eyes seared by the sun, I leaned on Jennifer's shoulder and closed my eyes. I woke to see an open valley filled with fruit trees. Picking apricots, an army of women in long-sleeved blouses and harem pants stood on wobbly ladders. Jennifer had brought long-sleeved blouses, but that morning said she couldn't see wearing anything but sun-tops in this heat. Now that we were underway again, she complained about the cold.

Mehmet fiddled with the air. "That okay for you?"

"Oh, it's much better." Jennifer looked at me.

"I'm fine."

Jennifer hugged herself and, smiling, glanced out the window. "I feel like I've learned so much about Turkish culture in the past two days."

"Yeah," I said. And a lot about Turkish men.

The car, dragging a balloon of dust, bumped across a riverbed and crawled up an embankment onto a gravel road.

Mehmet flipped down the visor and looked at us in the mirror. "Secular Islam die out."

"Don't bet on it," I said. "If the fundamentalists try to make Turkey an Islamic state, the military will step in."

Jennifer glanced at Mehmet, frowned at me, and put a finger to her lips.

She'd gone to grad school in Middle Eastern Studies. Now, she was waiting to see how she'd done on the Foreign Service exam. But book-learning wasn't the same as living here, absorbing the facts-on-the-ground. It had been quite some time since I'd lived in the Middle East—Somalia and Beirut, back when it was still known as the "Paris of the Middle East," and Tunisia, before Muammar Gaddafi. Turkey had been on my bucket list for a long time.

"You see news this morning?" Mehmet said.

"No," I said.

"Bomb blast near Grand Bazaar."

"What?" Jennifer leaned forward.

"Last night."

"Who did it?"

"Kurd." His eyes flashed.

"I wouldn't jump to conclusions," Jennifer said.

"Kurd do bad thing. Always."

Jennifer tapped Mehmet's shoulder. "Are you Wahhabi?"

"Yes! Sure!" Mehmet said.

"Ah," she said. "Erdogan supporter. Was anyone injured?"

"Six kill," he said.

Jennifer leaned towards me. "I hope trouble doesn't start here."

"It would be a shame," I said. In the last couple years, I had almost stopped caring about this part of the world, a region that had once seemed as complex and interesting as its beautiful, patterned rugs. Somalia, for instance: the land of *hees* and *mansos*, where "combat" meant combat poetry. Like threads of a spider's net, oral verse connected the clans, and if a dispute arose, the most eloquent poets would duke it out on the battlefield of words. And the Kurds. They had a beautiful language, which Turkey had tried with all its might to suppress. On one of his many trips to Ankara, my husband Tom had befriended a dissident Kurdish poet, and a single line from one of his poems had stayed in my memory. "Lying beneath the stars, I listened to the bark of lambs..." The bark of lambs. It had seemed so perfect. The rest of the poem had faded away, one of life's ephemera.

"I wonder why you think the Kurds would bomb the market," I said.

"Wreck economy," he said. "Bring down government."

The hand of memory pressed my chest. My husband had been stationed in Somalia in '69. I thought of Siad Barre and his coup. Italian tanks rolled down the streets of Mogadishu, and the ungreased tank guns shrieked as they panned back and forth across the street. We burned papers in an old oil barrel our cook used to singe the pin-feathers off chickens, and then our driver took five of us—me on my husband's lap—down the coast road to Kenya. Even with Tom's arms around me, I had never felt so physically vulnerable in my life.

It scared me thinking about the bomb blast in Istanbul. There would be a curfew, no doubt, and I wondered if we would have trouble getting from the airport to our hotel. It wasn't near the

Grand Bazaar, but near the Hagia Sophia, which had once been a Byzantine church and might well turn into a target because of the tourists.

"Maybe we should go back to Istanbul," I said.

"It would cost money to change our flight," Jennifer said.

It might be worth it. "Where are we, exactly?" I looked through the space between the headrests, hoping to see a road sign.

A shirtless, shoeless boy jumped off a pile of rocks and planted himself on the hump between the ruts. In one hand, he held a cardboard sign, and he stabbed the air with his finger.

"*Chukumu yala!*" Mehmet looked in the rear-view mirror. "Why, every time I come here, he do this?" The engine revved.

"Does what?" I said.

"Block road."

The car sped forward. The wheels chattered. I grabbed the armrest on the door. My head bumped the ceiling. As the car hurtled toward the boy, I could read the letters on his sign. BESAS. Surely, the boy with his "I dare you" look would jump aside. A small boy with skinny arms. Barefoot. Brown shorts. The child pulled the sign to his chest and froze.

"Look out!" I screamed.

Jennifer peered around the passenger's headrest. "Oh!" she said. Leaning forward, she touched Mehmet's shoulder. "Stop right now. You're scaring us."

Mehmet slammed on the brakes. The sedan fishtailed, and the back end swung around ninety degrees. I felt a thump under the wheels. Dust enveloped the car.

"Did you...?" I said.

"I not hit," Mehmet said. "Only bad road."

"We should get out and make sure." Jennifer unbuckled her seatbelt.

"Wait!" I put my hand on her arm.

The dust settled. I turned around. Through the back window, I saw the gouges our tires had cut. Mehmet had swerved into a driveway. A grape arbor and low tables hid a whitewashed house.

The boy stood at an open door, shouting and gesturing. A pregnant woman in a white headscarf and long apron marched briskly toward us. Drying her hands on a towel, she motioned for Mehmet to roll down the window.

Mehmet laughed. "I teach he lesson." Opening the car door, Mehmet picked up something from the ground. Then he backed away from the house, leaving the two in a dust cloud. "He not do again."

A hand on my breast, I said, "I about had a heart attack."

"I was imagining all sorts of wild outcomes," Jennifer said.

I looked at Mehmet's eyes in the rear-view mirror. Unrepentant.

"Why isn't that boy in school?" I said.

"Must work," Mehmet said.

"What sort of work?" Jennifer said.

"Stop cars." Mehmet's head jerked sideways. "That place to eat." He handed back the cardboard sign. "*Besas*. Mean 'appetizer.'"

"I thought it meant 'kisses,'" I said, "but I guess that was last year's trip."

"I think Spanish is *beso*," Jennifer said.

"Yeah, maybe."

"How's your ankle?" Jennifer said.

"It's holding up."

Last year, Jennifer hadn't been able to break away from her master's thesis, so I'd decided to travel with a group—couples, mostly, and other widows. Mexico had been a disappointment. The sinking cathedral and floating gardens. A quick look at a Rivera mural. The Pyramid of the Sun. Getting off the bus, I'd sprained my ankle and finished the trip on crutches.

"Is the gorge rocky?" I said.

Jennifer laughed. "Everything's rocky."

"I'm glad we're down to the last ruin."

Mehmet looked like I'd said Kurds were the best thing since sliced bread.

"What? You no like ruins?"

"After a while," I said, "one ruin starts looking like all the rest."

"Hidden City not same as other." He pulled into a parking lot and stopped the car. "You see. Nature place."

"Where exactly are we?" I said.

"Taurus mountain," he said.

Taurus, the Bull. Tom was Taurus, not that I particularly believed in the signs of the zodiac. I opened my door. "Ah," I said, refreshed by the breeze. "This is more like it."

The Taurus mountains loomed up at the parking lot's far end. The rock was gray, with patches of pink, and I could not be sure if the color came from stone or from lichen. This was a geologic wonder—the V-shaped cleft of a mountain split down the middle by the earth's upheaval. Already in shadow, the right face of the gorge rose straight up, like a loaf of pumpernickel lopped in half by a knife. To the left of the gorge, in sunlight still, though I could see a shadow advancing up the wall, stood the higher and less steep half. I couldn't help but think of the Pied Piper of Hamlin and the way the cliff opened and all the children disappeared.

Jennifer spun around. "This is off the beaten path for sure."

"Local place," Mehmet said. "You first tourist I take."

I do believe Mehmet would have run that little boy over. It made me not like our guide. Until then, I had thought him overly attentive, but now I thought him sadistic. I reached back in the car for my bag.

"If I give you my money," I said, "is it safe to leave my purse in the trunk?"

"Maybe better, you keep," he said. "And bring camera."

Jennifer hugged herself. "Smell the air, Grandma. Listen to the music of the river. Are we in the real world, or in a place fantastical?"

"The real world." There was only one world, unfortunately, the world of putting one foot in front of another. I hoped we wouldn't have to switchback up a grade or tackle another steep descent.

WE CROSSED A bridge, and below us, the water being flushed from the mountains made me nearly deaf. Then, the bridge turned

into a wooden walkway. One person wide, the walkway canti-
levered out from the canyon's wall. Through the knotholes and
cracks, I looked down at the roiling water. Strung from a clothesline above our heads, a red Turkish flag with its crescent moon
and five-pointed star flapped in the breeze. Mehmet stopped.
"Moon star," he shouted. "*Ay Yildiz*."

I nodded that I had heard him. "How much further?"

"Near," he said. "And flat all way."

He started off and Jennifer hurried after him.

Families passed, going in the opposite direction, and the
rhythms of their different strides made the walkway dip and sway.
Pricks of pain shot through my ankle.

The gorge widened. Built out over the river were two tea shops,
one with reclining pillows and low tables, and the other with
wooden chairs. I wondered if this was where Mehmet wanted to
stop for tea. Hoping so, I decided to catch my breath. Mehmet,
without looking back, continued his forced march past the little
cafés. The walkway ended, and he hopped down onto the bank
of the river. Continuing his long strides, he leaned forward and
hooked his thumbs into the back pockets of his jeans. Jennifer ran
to catch up. They spoke a moment. She gave me a roundhouse wave.
If I didn't try to complete this last stop on our itinerary, I would not
be the cool, adventuresome grandma. I would be a burden, and she
wouldn't want to go on another trip.

I stepped down onto the sandy bank, and saw, not far ahead, a
wooden bookcase divided into cubbyholes, like the old post office
boxes in the hotels of my youth. In each cubby was tucked a pair
of plastic shoes. It looked like we were supposed to rent them
and wade the river. Mehmet and Jennifer sat on a tilted bench.
Kneeling on the ground, an old Turk in a red fez had begun fitting
the shoes. The wind blew a strand of hair across Jennifer's mouth.
Mehmet brushed it back.

"Hey!" I said, coming up to them.

Jennifer offered her place. I looked down at her shoes. They
were like Mary Janes. Through clear plastic, I could see red toenails.

"These shoes feel kind of tight," she said.

"Better if tight," Mehmet said, "or you walk out of shoes. Then I must carry you."

"Don't be fresh," I said.

Mehmet motioned for me to sit back down. "I joke, Madame. If I carry she, I fall down, too."

"Where is this Hidden City?" I said.

"That way." He waved toward the canyon.

"More walking?" I said. "I mean, it was a mile to here already."

"I can take pictures," Jennifer said. She had one of those tiny cameras that hooked up to her computer.

I patted my Nikon. "I prefer slides."

Jennifer looked up. "It's not going to be light much longer."

"Must hurry," Mehmet said. Carefully, he began folding the hem of his pants, creasing each fold with his nails in a gesture that reminded me of a child folding a paper airplane. At one moment, he could run down a child, and in the next, be the boy himself, worried about ruining his precious pants. Jennifer tied the Indian fabric of her skirt between her legs and waded in. A wave bounced against her back, soaking the fabric. Her thong undies showed through. Mehmet looked up, tugged the folded hems of his trousers above his knees, splashed through the water and took her hand.

"Watch out," he said. "You slip."

Jennifer wobbled like a tightrope walker. "It's freezing."

"Remember this is Turkey!" The waterfall sucked my words into the vacuum of its roar. I turned to the man in the fez. His wool sport coat was a size too large and of a color that was neither brown nor gray, more like the rags Turks used when they mopped floors. He knelt and pointed at my shoes.

"Size 9." I held up nine fingers.

He looked at my hands. His eyes were a startling greenish brown and flecked with yellow, his eyelashes as long as a child's. The bench shifted, creaking like a long-closed door. "Oh!" I said, steadying myself. He untied my shoelaces and matched the soles with a pair of clear plastic slippers. He left on my support hose. It wouldn't hurt to get those wet. My ankle would thank me. As I fastened the straps of my slippers, I looked into the breast pocket of his sport coat and saw a roll of Turkish lira. I wondered what I should tip and wished Mehmet had not left me stranded. I took out a fifty lira note, and the man shook his head no, flattened his palm and traced three hundred on it. I gave him that, and he examined the bills front and back, then nodded for me to go.

Across the channel, Jennifer and Mehmet waited on the gravel bank. Just beyond them, a shallow creek led back into a side canyon. The water surging through the channel before me spilled from crevices in the cliff to my left. They were like jets in a fun park, but where the springs joined at the bottom, a milky plume fanned out.

Two men, their shirts open and shorts turned up, headed back in my direction. I waited to see how they crossed. Before plunging into the current, they slid down the gravel embankment on Jennifer's side and walked along the opposite canyon wall, putting one hand against the rock for balance. Ten giant steps, like the kind we used to take in "Mother May I," and then they were over and climbing the bank to surrender their shoes. Ten steps. I could do it.

I put the strap of my purse over one shoulder, the camera strap over the other, and wished that I could leave them in the old man's care. It probably wasn't safe. His sunken jaws and gray whiskers made him look like the poorest of the poor, someone whose existence was so precarious that working for this shoe concession was the best he could do.

When I stepped in the water, a volt of ice raced up my right leg and exploded in a fireball against my heart. Cubes of ice caught in my throat. The current dragged my right leg sideways. Rocks moved. My feet slipped, and to keep my balance, I stepped out into the flow with my left foot. Water up to the hips. A lunge forward. The effort to stay upright. My thighs burned. I started to sit down.

Mehmet's hand, fleshy and damp, grabbed mine. One step at a time, he pulled me to the other side, scrambled up the loose rock, turned, and wrestled me from the water. Dry land.

I staggered to a boulder.

"Sit," Jennifer said.

"Don't worry, I will." My heart pounded like a fist.

"Mehmet didn't think you should cross." Jennifer took the straps from around my neck. She kissed the top of my head, and my cheeks winched up.

"This hard part," Mehmet said. "Please, Madame, you catch breath. Is famous place. Must see."

"We'll go back," Jennifer said.

"No, we've made it this far," I said.

Mehmet looked over his shoulder.

"Are the ruins just wonderful?" I said. "Am I going to see the Parthenon if I walk back there?"

He frowned. "That Greek place."

How careless of me. No love lost between the Turks and Greeks.

"I meant Ephesus," I said.

"No, not like," he said.

Jennifer bent over, hands on her knees. "Listen, Grandma. Why don't Mehmet and I see if the walking gets easier. If it does, we'll come back for you, and if not, you stay put till we return. Does that sound like a plan?"

These are your choices, children. "Sure. Go ahead."

Looking down at me, Mehmet said, "I think butterfly more special thing about this place."

"Okay," I said. "I'll sit here and see if I see a butterfly."

"Good," Jennifer said, bending down to give me a hug.

Mehmet took off his river shoes. In bare feet, he started down the canyon.

I swiveled around. They vanished around a bend. The boulder I sat on came to a point, so it was kind of like sitting on the apex of a teeter-totter. The gouging in my rear made my foot tingle. My leg went to sleep. Shadows soon began to cover the canyon floor. The pools of violet water looked shallow. I forced myself to stand. Rocks dug into my soles. I took three steps. "Ow! Ow! Ow!" Enough. Though I clapped my arms and hugged myself, my teeth chattered. If I stood here much longer, I'd get hypothermia.

Two Turkish families passed me. The were on their way out. The men, with small children on their shoulders, waded through the rushing water, followed by their wives, women who delicately lifted their heavy skirts and made the crossing look easy. The pain of walking on the rocks would be limited to a dozen steps. I would do what the two men had done earlier, work my way down the canyon wall, then make a dash across the channel.

COLD SHOCKED MY ankles. The water deepened and the current sucked my feet. With a hand against the canyon wall and my eye on the old Turk kneeling in front of the wooden cubby, I pushed into the current. The cold turned my feet wooden. My shoes slipped on the stones, but I could not feel the stones themselves. My purse and camera swung in opposite directions like dual pendulums of a manic clock. I gasped and looked downriver. If I fell, it would be a quick trip. Somewhere down there, the channel would widen, and I could just float until I saw a sandy riverbank. It was the stones. The stones were killing me. I lifted my camera and purse, holding them above my head. I sank down and the water rose to my breasts. In rainbows of spray, the old man appeared. He took my hand and pulled me from my crouch, then dragged me toward the shore. Standing in foot-deep water, I couldn't move. The old Turk scrambled up the bank and leaned toward me, holding out his palms. I put my hands in his, and he pulled me to dry land.

"It's the shoes." Seated on the bench, I hiccupped tears. "The soles are like paper."

Nodding, he knelt on one knee. His red fez covered his gray, clipped eyebrows. He undid the buckles of the hateful slippers.

"Oh, God, it feels so good to get those off!" I said.

He balanced my right foot on his thigh and, with a dirty towel, wiped my leg from the knee to the ankle. The towel, and his fingers squeezing, did not so much move down my leg as caress it, squeeze it as if shifting all the muscle-ache and tiredness right down through the weary arch of my foot and across the rock-bruised soles. He discarded the towel, reached under the hem of my skirt, and found the rolled top of my stocking. He slipped it down my leg. The tips of his fingers touched my skin. His lips compressed. He closed his eyes. I gripped the splintered bench. His fingers clasped the sides of my feet. With my stockings off, he separated my toes and examined them one by one. I wiped my eyes in gratitude. His hands had warmed my feet.

He reached back for my shoes, loosened the laces, and pulled up the tongues. The hollow bunion holes and comforting arch supports made me smile. He sprang up from his squat, and with a furtive gesture, pushed my stockings into the pocket of his pants.

"You want those?" I said.

He nodded, and then flapping his arms, pointed to the tea shop.

"All right." Warm tea would feel good and Jennifer would be none that wiser that her hypothermic grandmother had almost drowned.

I stood, and the old man kissed the back of my hand.

"Thank you," I said.

"*Teşekkür*," he said, his eyes sparkling. "Tea and sugar."

WALKING TOWARD THE tea shop, I felt the planks flex and vault me forward as if I were bouncing on a trampoline. Giddy with relief, I stopped at the first table. A waiter brought apple tea in a glass cup, two cubes of sugar, and a tiny spoon.

"*Teşekkür*," I said.

He smiled and looked in my eyes. I stretched my legs and leaned back. When he turned to go, I called after him, "*Teşekkür!*"

"*Teşekkür ederim.*" He turned, smiled, and bounced down the steps to the kitchen on the other side of the river.

Learning to speak the language was what I had always loved about being in a new posting: the small niceties of life that signaled our common humanity.

Warmed by the tea, I watched Jennifer and Mehmet slog back through the water. Wet from the waist down, Jennifer sat on the bench, and the old man knelt before her. With the same towel, he wiped her feet. The shoe-man's fingers slid down each of Jennifer's toes. Jennifer looked up at Mehmet, who spoke sharply, then swatted the old man with the back of his hand. The man in the fez threw the towel to Mehmet and hobbled away.

Mehmet wiped Jennifer's feet and placed her shoes on the ground. While she put them on, he rolled down his pants, slipped on his sandals, looked over, and saw me on the tea platform. He tapped Jennifer on the shoulder. She looked over and frowned. A moment later they stood by my table.

"That long walk," Mehmet said. "I tired."

"It was a hard walk, Grandma," Jennifer said. "You wouldn't have liked it."

I waited for them to ask how I'd crossed the river, to be surprised or to compliment me on making it back alive. Nothing. But then, of course not. They were young.

Mehmet turned. At the next restaurant, low Turkish couches were covered with faded, brick-red rugs; silver tables shimmered in the raking light. "We take tea there."

"Why not here?" I said.

"Ottoman couch." He picked up my tea cup, and when the little spoon dropped, he snapped his fingers for the waiter. With me on one couch and Jennifer and Mehmet on the other, our guide leaned back, sighed, and dipped his hand in the river. "Look," he said.

Above, caves dotted the sheer rock wall. I stretched my legs.

"Your legs are bruised!" Jennifer reached down and touched a purple welt. "Did you fall?"

"Certainly not! I'm not helpless."

"We walked a mile into the canyon and never saw a single butterfly or ruins either."

"I think call 'Hidden City' 'cause big rock fall down," Mehmet said.

"A natural ruin," I said. "Like me."

Mehmet threw back his head and, with a hand on his stomach, laughed as if I had said something funny, when in truth, I was just stating a fact. Jennifer smiled and finger-combed her ponytail. These young people could not yet fathom the difference between old, when you could still do things, and the old I was now, when I had to be careful what I attempted.

The waiter arrived with tea. Steam rose from the glasses. At the distant opening of the canyon, a fireball of light hovered above the water, and I thought of the River Styx, the underground stream into which all life disappeared. Mehmet spread his arms and lounged against the pillows, his ankle near Jennifer's. As if accidentally, Jennifer let her foot graze his.

"Sorry. I can move feet if in your way."

"They're not in my way," Jennifer said.

The footsie dance. "I'd like another tea," I said.

Mehmet shouted to the waiter.

The tea appeared before me. "*Teşekkür,*" I said.

Mehmet said, "Good speak."

"Turkish is a beautiful language," I said. "Like poetry."

I looked up. Clinging to the sheer rock wall were shrubs with dark green leaves and white blossoms. The flowers stirred. Like paper torn in squares, a cloud of butterflies floated above our heads. Blown by the breeze, the butterflies drifted away. I sipped my tea. Far down the canyon a persimmon sun hung above an indigo stream, and I settled back into my pillow.

TWO TRAINS IN MANMAD

———○———

HER HUSBAND HAD been after her to stop teaching and spend more time at home, but Leslie Flynn—Coach Flynn, for whom winning was everything—told him to bugger off. She would do what she had to do, no problem, but basketball season was here.

Blowing a whistle, she signaled the end of scrimmage. This year's Cougars were tough; the girls could run their opponents into the ground. As they raced down the court and bent to touch the suicide lines, the screech of rubber soles on the maple floor reminded her of the way she'd peeled out of the driveway that morning, eager to escape, but worried about leaving her mother-in-law behind. Mother Gokhale had lost her husband, and now, it was Leslie's job to help the old woman make a new life in Ontario.

The minute hand on the scoreboard clock hit 6:00 P.M., and Leslie made a T with her hands. Girls headed for the shower. Balls slammed the floor and the gym echoed behind her as she stepped, head down, hood up, into the darkness and freezing rain and ran for her car. She threw her gym bag on the seat. The car smelled of cumin and coriander, spices she'd picked up on lunch break. Impatient for the defroster to clear the windshield, she vowed to consolidate the daily "to do" lists. This was not India. Canadian winter was sweeping across the plains from Regina, where her mom, also a new widow, reported a record snowfall; and tomorrow, the weather was due to hit Detroit then blast through London, a whistle-stop on the way to Toronto.

When she turned into the *cul-de-sac* of brick ranch houses, she saw her neighbor draping Christmas lights across the hedge that divided their properties. Lashed down to his frozen lawn stood an inflated, plastic Santa. Leslie waved and opened the garage door. The car's headlights flashed across two sawhorses and an old canoe. They had not had the canoe in the water for three years. Summer heat had opened its seams, and Ashok, her husband, had started to re-caulk them. A tennis ball hung from the ceiling and touched her windshield. She stopped. That was his solution, not finishing the project but suspending a stupid green ball from a string and making her feel like a bitch for suggesting he put the canoe away until he had time to do a proper job. One day, her foot would slip, and she would ram the bloody thing.

Head resting on the wheel, she sat for a moment, knowing she should go in and deal with the newest project he'd begun, his mother's relocation.

LESLIE LET HERSELF in by the back door. Through a beaded curtain that divided the mudroom from the kitchen, she saw a tiny woman in a gray sari. Standing barefoot on the counter, her ankle bracelets jingling, Mother Gokhale was reaching for the highest shelf.

"What on earth?" Leslie wrapped her hands around the old woman's waist and sailed her to the floor.

"Put me down!" Mother Gokhale said.

"I did."

"You do not always have to worry about me."

"Ashok would kill me if you fell."

"Can you take down the crock pot?"

Leslie heard her throat let out an involuntary eek. "There's already a lot of stuff on the counter."

The old woman looked from the shelf to the counter and back again. Inevitably, the crock pot joined the old *karahi* deep fryer with its disgusting brown rim, a rice steamer, a copper saucepan for making *ghee*, a mortar and pestle, a pressure cooker, and, a teapot in which Mother Gokhale steeped her Darjeeling. With a night in the kitchen, Leslie thought, she could rearrange her cabinets and make room for all this junk. "Why don't you let me cook dinner?" she said.

Mother Gokhale jiggled her head from side to side in the gesture that looked like "no," but sometimes meant "yes." "All done already."

Leslie looked at the stove. Six pots with lids. Another luke-warm *thali* dinner.

"Maybe we could save it."

"It is better eaten tonight."

Question settled, Leslie thought. Win some, lose some; but at home, she had not been winning very many. Mother Gokhale arranged the pleats that tightened the sari around her hips. Scars, like the ivory combs above her ears, fanned up from her bare mid-riff. She turned away, lifted a lid, and stirred whatever was in the pan. Leslie liked Indian food, but not every night, and she worried about the ingredients that had recently gone into her cupboards. Fifteen years ago, the last time her mother-in-law came to Canada, the house had been infested with mealie bugs for a year. Back then, Leslie had decided that long school vacations were a boon: better to go to India than have India descend on them.

"Leslie, where is the strainer?" Mother Gokhale said.

"Move, please. I'll get it." On hands and knees, she searched in the back of the Lazy Susan. "Here it is!" Leslie waved the colander. "When you're done, please put it back. In Canada, we try to keep a tidy kitchen."

"That's your problem, Leslie."

"I didn't know I had a problem."

Mother Gokhale did not reply. Leslie waited, then in a voice of false cheer, said, "So, did you venture out?"

"Too cold."

Somewhere in Garrard Street's East-Asian ghetto there had to be long underwear you could put under a sari. Maybe her daughter, who had picked up Mother Gokhale at the airport, could find something.

"Sheela said she's organizing a get-together."

"Sunday, I will be free," Mother Gokhale said.

"I don't think she can pull it off that soon."

It would have been good for Mother Gokhale to see her granddaughter, but Toronto was an hour's drive away, and the 405 treacherous in snow.

"I'd take you, but I need to get stuff organized around here," Leslie said.

Her head bobbing in silent conversation, Mother Gokhale took a cleaver from the drawer. A tinsmith in Poona had made it from a scrap of Bessemer steel, and the blade never dulled. Head bent, braid swinging like a rope, she began sawing away at an onion.

"Please, don't cut on the Formica!" Leslie said.

"How shall I cut then?"

"Use this." Leslie pulled out a breadboard. "When you're done, wash it so it doesn't stink."

As if waiting at a bus stop in the rain, Mother Gokhale shivered, her shoulders rippling under the sari's gauze. Her cheeks were sucked in, her skin a bluish gray. Leslie folded her arms and leaned back against the counter. Ashok had promised to make an appointment with a cardiologist; he was worried about the impact of so many life-changes on his mother's health, and Leslie worried, too. Long-married couples often died within months of each other. Her own mother was in that situation, a sudden round of doctors' visits that revealed nothing but heartache. Leslie admired Ashok for trying to ease his mother's burden. When Mother Gokhale had agreed to relocate, he had flown back to sell the family property. Even now, the old, walled compound with its spacious courtyard was being demolished by barefoot laborers in loincloths.

But that was all he'd done. Before Mother Gokhale moved in, Leslie had emptied Sheela's dressers and closets and repainted the bedroom; she'd sent a box of their old Bollywood movies to a store in Toronto that converted them to DVDs, and, hoping to have a welcome party, she'd contacted a number of Indian women from the Health Sciences Center. Unfortunately, like her husband, his colleagues were busy; this time of year, all the hotshot Indian researchers, women included, were cranking out proposals for next year's funding cycle.

Leslie looked at the bead curtain. "I should bring in the spice."

"I have enough."

"Then why'd you tell Ashok you needed it?"

Mother Gokhale held up her hands. "I told Ashok, if you were too busy, it could wait."

"He didn't tell me."

Mother Gokhale smiled. "He is a man. Men forget."

"Not a man who expects the house to run like a German train."

Leslie caught her breath and listened. Ashok always seemed to be within earshot when she mumbled some snide little comment to herself. This was a character trait she had picked up from her mother, and despised. Ashok was, by nature, a man of extreme moral rectitude and candor, as harsh on himself as with others, but he was never careless with his speech. If he said something, he meant it. She'd have to find a way to deal with her mother-in-law's requests without letting the anger spill out at either of them, and that was hard because lately, her moods had ricocheted worse than ever.

Feeling chilled, she picked up her gym bag. "I should get out of these clothes."

Mother Gokhale turned. "Did you know I did not have an arranged marriage?"

"Ashok might have mentioned it."

"Choosing my own husband was unheard of in my day. I wanted to be modern. That is why, when Ashok said you would be his wife, I thought, 'Good boy. He is not stuck in the old way.' And when I found out a child had been conceived before the wedding, before I had properly met you, I felt very angry at my son for taking advantage. If such a thing had happened to me, I would have been cast out of the family."

"That's India for you."

"Yes, but in my country, women form close friendships. If I had not had the help of friends, I don't know how I would have managed this last year."

Pancreatic cancer was a terrible way to go. Ashok's father had suffered.

"I understand," Leslie said.

"Do you? When you came for visits, I made you welcome in my home. Now that I am here, we stand talking like strangers. What is wrong, Leslie?"

"I've had a long day."

"Every day is a long day."

"Today was an especially long one. I've had hot flashes."

Mother Gokhale reached out.

Leslie flinched as if a drop of oil had spattered on her wrist. "Don't touch me," she said. "I'm sweaty."

Mother Gokhale looked her up and down. "Perhaps a shower would refresh you."

"That's exactly what I had in mind."

AT THE TOP of the stairs, Leslie found a basket of laundry. She carried it to the bedroom, dumped clothes on the dresser, and began pairing Ashok's socks. Oh yes, he was such a good boy. After she'd told him she was pregnant, he'd deserted her and run off to India, seeking his mother's forgiveness. For three weeks, she'd waited without so much as a phone call. She'd never been able to pry out of him what had happened on that trip because, as he said, he liked to keep his own counsel. Now she knew. She swept his socks into a drawer.

The mindless task made her feel better. At the end of the day, she needed her down time, a couple hours watching the tube while she puttered with dinner. As it was, she felt like sticking her elbows out and pushing everyone away. Even Sheela. It was good to have her daughter living in Toronto. No more cars pulling in at three in the morning. No more emergency trips to the cash machine. Now, though, there was Mother Gokhale. It wasn't so much the tasks that got Leslie down as the wear-and-tear of a new dependent. After dropping her clothes in the hamper, she turned on the shower. Water flooded her face.

What was wrong now had been wrong in the beginning. She had married Ashok out of necessity. She'd been desperate for a ring and quite good at turning on the tears, not that she'd had any control. They had flowed out, along with the fear and rage that something so unexpected and life-altering had happened. Until her pregnancy, she'd thought of Ashok as a place-keeper, the older, patient boyfriend she went back to between other men. Those were the days of big desire—grinding, glorious sex. But marriage to Ashok had not fit any mold she'd envisioned. If she'd married at all, it should have been to some guy who worked on an oil rig in Alberta, or maybe a park ranger from Algonquin. She liked outdoorsy men. Ashok was such a brain.

He had been in med school when they met, and continued without missing a beat while she struggled through her first year of teaching. He was a tender father—no objection to pinning diapers or shaking up the Similac. "It's easier than chem lab," he'd said. Only by sheer willpower was she able to tough it out until he earned his MD. Then a lawyer told her she could get a better financial settlement if she waited three more years. By that time, Ashok had joined a hematology research team at London's Health Sciences Center, not a high-paying job, but one he loved. Flush with confidence about a steady income, he had taken out a mortgage to buy a home, and she'd held her breath, watching the principal diminish and figuring she could move out and buy a condo when Sheela left for university. Why had she hesitated to take the longed-for step that would put her in charge of her own life again? Chicken, she guessed.

And it was not that life was all bad. For years, Leslie told herself that friendship was as good as love; but, after nineteen years, she supposed it was not. That his work would consume all his energy, she never could have guessed. Nor that he would use his Blackberry to fit lovemaking into his schedule. She had tried so hard to love him that, now, even affection felt manufactured.

After toweling off, Leslie stepped into her closet. A dim bulb barely lit the double wardrobe. Ashok had replaced the 100-watter with an oven bulb, and the sad thing was, he probably didn't notice the difference. She groped through her blouses and felt a frill. Her old blue blouse. When she slipped her arms into the silk and felt the cool, soft fabric touch her skin, she shuddered with regret at the marriage that might have been.

IN THE DINING room, Mother Gokhale had seated herself in Leslie's place. Ashok had taken the armchair. For once, he'd come home early, but the purple circles under his eyes told her he'd had another rough day. Because his father's illness had called him back to India so often, he was behind on his proposal-writing. Director, now, he put in late nights with university bureaucrats and provincial legislators, and came home drained by interminable meetings. She felt an urge to lay her hand on his.

"Mother G., why don't you move down here?" Leslie patted the chair at the end opposite Ashok. "You'll have more leg room."

"Better to sit by the door," Mother Gokhale said.

So she could hop up and down like one of the servants back home.

"In that case ... " Leslie was not going to worry about it. She heaped rice on her plate and spooned up *sag paneer*. The rice felt cool to the touch. She went to the kitchen to use the microwave. While the plate warmed, she looked at the magnet on her refrigerator: *I have one nerve left, and you're standing on it.* The gray-haired lady with her finger in a socket looked like Leslie's mother. She could just hear her mom, hands akimbo. "You made your bed. Now lie in it." Her mom could always find a hurtful, edifying lesson in the deepest, darkest pile of shit. At least, Leslie thought, Mother Gokhale didn't get on her case for being unhappy, and she hoped the old woman would never guess. It was better to see if this thing could somehow work out, and if not, why then, Ashok had his mother to look after him.

Leslie returned to the table. "Dinner smells scrumptious."

Mother Gokhale spoke to Ashok in Marathi. Ashok spread out his hands on the table; his fingers opened and closed like scissors. In a low voice, glancing quickly at his mother, he let fly—the same staccato that often told Leslie she'd overstepped.

Fork midway to her mouth, she stopped eating. "Are you guys arguing?"

"Not arguing," Mother Gokhale said.

Ashok looked at his mother. "But Sheela wants to see you."

"Why don't you drive your mom to the city tomorrow?" Leslie said.

"I have to work."

"Silly me. I forgot."

"I don't expect him to interrupt his schedule."

"Of course not. How could he?" Leslie picked up her fork. She was hungry. Not hungry. Starving.

Ashok frowned. "My mother talked to Vasanp and Kunda today."

"How are they?"

"Getting rich."

Educated in the days when the Indian government sent their best students abroad, Ashok, his brother, and four sisters had scattered across the continents. Ashok was the eldest, and he had called first dibs on his mother. Vasanp, the baby, an endodontist in Orlando, wanted his mother to "come to him."

"It is thirty degrees in Florida," Mother Gokhale said.

"If you have a heart attack down there," Ashok said, "it will cost a fortune."

"I'm sure your mom's heart is fine," Leslie said. "She's been such a busy little beaver, she puts me to shame." Actually, it was good to have dinner appear magically on the table. There were black flecks in the peas—char floating up from the bottom of the pan—but the rest of dinner hit the spot. She did the boardinghouse reach for the basket of *naan*.

"I hope you will reconsider," Ashok said.

Mother Gokhale shook her head.

Leslie couldn't be sure if that was a "yes" or "no."

"Reconsider what?" she said.

"Her airline arrangements."

Leslie fanned herself with a napkin. The house felt like a sauna. The moment she left for school, the old woman must dart upstairs and crank the thermostat.

Mother Gokhale motioned to the buffet where a pile of leather-bound books served as a prop for a Gurkha East India cigar-box. "When I went through your father's library," Mother Gokhale said, "I found a memento."

"Father's cigars?" Ashok said.

"Leslie would never allow that."

Ashok picked up the cigar box and shook it. "What could it be?"

"Look inside."

He opened it. A smile broke over his face. Holding his necktie, he leaned toward Leslie and offered a two-inch, metal square. "It's a tintype of grandfather," he said. "Hold it by the edges."

Leslie took it. The man in the picture was young and wore a hat that reminded Leslie of a Shriners' fez. The tintype looked like a negative—dark skin, light eyes. The eyes were a marker for all the Brahmans of their caste. Supposedly, they had descended from Persian sailors.

It was amazing how everything associated with India seemed to come straight from myth. The weird, elephant-headed god Ganesh. The Taj Mahal. The *Kama Sutra*. When they were first together, Ashok had plumbed the Sanskrit manual for ideas, and, giggling at the book's illustrations, coaxed her through all sixty-four positions. That sure was a thing of the past.

"I don't know if you remember my father," Mother Gokhale said. "He was alive when you first brought Sheela."

"I remember," Leslie said. The old man, dressed in a high-necked, muslin shirt, his lips and teeth red-stained, sat all day in the shade of the courtyard's mango tree, hailing street urchins who ran to the nearby *paanwallah* for packets of betel leaf. A sitar player, collector of foreign stamps, and headmaster of a Normal School, he occupied his rickety bench, staring vacantly into space, his bony fingers gripping the armrests as he swayed and chewed, spitting cardamom and lime paste.

Straight out of *Passage To India*, Leslie thought, recalling her high school English teacher's insistence that this was one of the great works of literature. Not to a girl from Regina forced to read about a place she'd had no interest in ever seeing. But then, she'd found out there was such a place as India; it didn't just exist in books. Year after year, besides the amazing trips to Agra and the caves at Orissa, she had put up with the beggars, the spotted bananas, the market flies, and the pungent odor of excrement.

The putting-up-with-India began on their honeymoon. They had gone to a national park where they tried and failed to find tigers. Traveling with Sheela, who had just begun to crawl, they arrived in Manmad, the crossroads where the narrow- and wide-gauge rail lines met: Manmad, where the narrow tracks broke off abruptly the instant they were embraced by the wider ones. It was in Manmad that the marriage had begun to fall apart.

Leslie passed the tintype and Mother Gokhale wrapped it in a paper napkin.

"I would love some tea," Ashok said.

Mother Gokhale cleared the table.

"Could I have a spoon please?" Ashok called. "Oh. And some milk? I take two percent. Watching my belly, you know, although you have certainly spoiled me with these dinners." He laughed, and his mother laughed, too.

Leslie thought of their usual dinner—broiled fish, salad, and fresh fruit—and the battles she had fought over towels dropped on the bathroom floor. Her husband was reverting.

Ashok took off his glasses and rubbed his eyes. "What a day."

"Did you lose a patient?" Leslie said.

"In a manner of speaking." He picked up a small brass elephant spoon. "Mother has decided to go to Florida."

"That'll be a welcome change, come February."

"Not for a visit," Ashok said. "To live."

"What?"

"She's leaving a week from today."

"But she's only been here a fortnight."

"I changed my ticket," the old woman called from the kitchen. She returned with a tray of tea things.

Leslie pictured her fist pumping, Yes! Yes! But that was ungenerous. Like Sheela, Mother Gokhale was their glue. Despite her neediness, which Leslie was sure would pass, Mother G. had a way of creating moments for affection to creep in.

On her first trip to Poona, Leslie had been amazed at Mother Gokhale's warmth and thoughtfulness. Bounding up steep, rail-less, concrete stairs, sleeping mats on one shoulder, sheets under her arm, Mother Gokhale had prepared their sleeping places on the roof. In the lantern light, Leslie found a sprig of jasmine on her pillow. Smoke hung in the air. The night was hot and damp. Looking up through the cook-fire haze at the faintly gleaming stars, Leslie decided, I can do this. Stay married to this Indian. Of course, what choice did she have? None to speak of. She reached across the mat where Sheela slept, her tiny body curled beneath a sheet, and took Ashok's hand.

"I love you," she said, not entirely sincerely. It was more a wish.

"This thing will work out," he said. "Here, it is normal to have an arranged marriage. We are arranging it ourselves."

Now, Ashok sat like a question mark and tapped the elephant spoon slowly on his empty cup. It made a hollow ting.

"Basketball's not going to last much longer," Leslie said. "I can be home at five o'clock. Your mom and I can go to some movies, or—"

"I do not belong here." Mother Gokhale moved her head from side to side.

"You're not being fair," Leslie said. Life wasn't fair, of course. She could just hear her mom say that. No one got a hundred percent of what they wanted.

Mother Gokhale removed the top of the teapot and pulled out the tea ball, giving it several shakes. "I think the tea is ready."

"I'm off tea," Leslie said.

"Ashok? This is *ayurvedic*."

Ashok nodded.

Mother Gokhale poured. "Vasanp and Kunda are moving furniture to make a bedroom, although I told them, I am so small, I can sleep in one of their big closets. You know we Indians. All we need is our mat. We can unroll it in a corner of the room, and people will make a space for us."

Leslie pictured the closets in Vasanp's palatial digs. Kunda would give Mother Gokhale the care she deserved, the care Leslie didn't have time to give.

GETTING READY FOR bed, Leslie sniffed the air. Curry and cabbage. God, the smell had wafted all the way upstairs. She splashed cologne in her armpits and groped her way through the dark until she reached the bed. Ashok was under the covers, his back turned. She climbed in. The sheets sucked warmth from her body, and she cuddled against him.

"Well, that was unexpected." She put her hand around his waist.

He pushed it off. She ran her hand down his side. He had on his pajama bottoms. He normally slept in only the tops.

"Out here in the 'burbs, she's stuck," Leslie said. "No friends. No community."

She placed her hand on his leg.

"Not now." He removed it.

"Orlando has a big Indian community. There will be other old women to gossip with."

"About what?"

"Whatever old women gossip about," Leslie said.

"My mother does not tell tales out of school."

"What did she tell you?"

"Nothing."

"Then why are you mad at me?"

"I'm disappointed." He rolled over and folded his arms beneath his head.

She looked at the profile of his nose and lips and chin, the scallop where she had many times pressed her thumb. She wanted to do that now, to expose the corn-cob teeth that looked so jolly when he smiled. Once, he'd been into licking and biting. It had been a long time since they'd made love, but when he held her, she felt comforted.

"Your poor mom. I guess I didn't come home in the best of moods. I felt bad leaving her alone all day, all week actually, but it's like having a puppy. The instant I come in, she pounces."

"Turn out the light. I need to get some sleep." He rolled over and checked the alarm.

"We'll sort this out tomorrow," she said.

"I cannot imagine what made her decide to leave," he said.

"Maybe if you hadn't dumped the whole burden on me—"

"Is my mother a burden?"

"Did you come home early even once this week?"

"My mother has been made to feel unwelcome."

"Ashok, who stopped by Indian Spice and filled her shopping list? Who drove her to the post office so she could mail her bloody aerograms? You didn't. You came in and plunked yourself down at the dinner table and didn't lift a finger."

Ashok sighed. He kicked off the covers then unbuttoned his pajama tops and pitched them across the room.

"Please! Don't throw clothes on the floor."

"It's sweltering."

"Your mother turns up the heat."

"You're blaming my mother for that, too?"

"I'm not blaming her for anything. I'm just tired," Leslie said.

"Mother is trying to help. She says you treat her like a naughty child. The question I am asking myself is this. How can Leslie not see what great pain this is causing me? How is it you do not understand that I have waited my entire life to repay her kindness?"

"You're such a mama's boy."

Ashok threw his legs off the bed and padded over to the closet, taking out the Indian mat he used for yoga.

"What are you doing?" Leslie said.

"We Indians are the most portable people on earth," he said in a falsetto. "We only need our mat, and we can easily make ourselves at home."

The mat rustled.

"Ashok, don't be ridiculous."

He disappeared below the foot of the bed. God, this was so annoying. She scooted down and lay on her stomach. There he was on his stupid mat, an eighth-inch of bamboo, or whatever they made those things out of, separating him from the floor. Well, fine. If he thought he could sleep on a hard surface, let him. Propping her chin on her hands, she willed him to feel her stare. His breathing slowed. He began to snore. In the middle of an argument, sleep was his favorite defense; but she was more awake than ever, alert for a movement that would allow her to press on with her logic. Excuses, he would say. All right, so she'd been in a bad mood, but just because his mother had moved in, he couldn't expect Leslie to have a fake smile plastered on her face. And anyway, she couldn't stand her own mother for more than two seconds. It was hard for women to share a kitchen.

She looked down. His shoulders rose and fell. Maybe he was fake-sleeping.

"Ashok?" she whispered.

His leg jerked.

She leaned over and poked his back. "This is so stupid."

"I want a divorce," he said.

"What?"

"You heard me."

Light came through the blinds. She pulled the top sheet free and covered him. Ashok's bony ankles stuck out. His knees were drawn up and his hands were crossed on his chest. His pose reminded her of that time in Manmad, her so-called honeymoon.

God, Manmad again.

The narrow-gauge train had pulled in, discharged its passengers, and chugged away. The wide-gauge train had been delayed. How long would it be? "No telling," the stationmaster said, wagging his head. There was a saying: *A man could go mad waiting for a train in Manmad.* A woman, too. Thirty hours the wait had been, thirty hours with a baby. Tired of taking a turn at holding Sheela, Ashok put her down to crawl on the filthy floor. At dawn, ready to kill him and unable to tolerate the stench of ammonia from the WCs, Leslie stormed out of the first-class lounge to find fresh air.

The sky had turned from gray to pink. Looking down the spittle-stained platform, she saw hundreds of shapeless rags, stirring. It was like the start of a ballet, dancers writhing onstage. It was Dante's *Inferno*. Then, behind her, she felt the warmth of his body.

He lifted the hair from her ear and whispered. "We must learn to do this thing."

"I hate India," she said.

"Hate India if you wish," he said, "but please do not hate me."

Now, she looked down at him. Lifelines bisected the arches of his feet and his toes were dipped in pink. The house had cooled. He shivered. She went to the linen closet for a comforter. Hatred. Defiance. Regret. How fast the years had sped. There must have been a different track, one she had missed. Exhausted, she lay beside him on the wooden floor, as close as she dared. His body warmed the comforter and, finally, she slept.

FINDING PETER

————○————

IN PREVIOUS SUMMERS the break from teaching had never seemed long enough, but this summer felt like it would never end. Her blouse still damp, a bra chafing her skin, Anna Ringaard splashed through puddles on Prague's Charles Bridge, where a dozen sooty saints scowled down from the balustrades. Cowering and feeling like a mom who'd let go of a toddler's hand, she offered her missing-person's flyer to Czech street artists in dreadlocks and olive drab. Seeing her, they put up their hands, shook their heads, or responded with wan, dismissive smiles. Okay, so they were sick of her coming around. Her picture of Peter looked a little menacing, his eyes glowering out from under his mop of hair. He hadn't liked being photographed. No biggie. Art was more truthful. It spoke from the soul, her soul, at least. She had drawn him as she remembered him: a troubled young man.

Across the bridge in Lower Town, she caught a tram. Every day after lunch, she went to the station to wait for the Thalys, the international train. Unless her son was hitching, he'd have to be traveling by rail. Sometimes he did hitch, though. According to Peter's friends, the day after graduation he had left Boulder, hitched to Denver, and flown to Amsterdam. He'd sent her an email:

> Sorry to cut out without telling you. Don't worry, Mom. I'm not hitting the Red Light District. Ha! Ha! Sketching

tourists in squares. Looking for others of eastern European descent, same physiognomy. Lots of people in Holland look like you. Didn't realize how many blonds were in the world until I landed here. Plan to head south, then east. Finding my dark-haired clan. Peter

For a while, she'd tracked him by his ATM withdrawals. Then those had stopped, and she began to panic. A postcard from Florence had reassured her that he was still in the land of the living, though not anywhere he could be contacted.

Museums closed. Frescoes behind scaffold. Italians fun—*bella, bella Italia!*—but so far Amsterdam and Prague are where the action is. Peter

Standing on the platform, she looked at the big, round clock. Only minutes until the Thalys arrived. If Peter's money ran out, he'd come back here. Prague was the bean-bag chair where all young, cash-strapped travelers eventually landed. She could picture him, an easel bungee-corded to his backpack, stepping down and looking around.

The platform wasn't crowded today: five American college girls, assorted Germans with big suitcases, and two little girls traveling with their parents. It would be easy to spot him. A whistle blew. The train, chuffing and hissing, bucked to a stop. From behind the snack bar a young woman, early twenties, stepped out. A nest of hair was loosely pinned to her head, and she wore a diaphanous blouse and a long, brown skirt with three tiers of ruffles.

"Are you English-speaking?" she said.

"Yes," Anna said, standing on tiptoes. The tall girl blocked her view. "Excuse me. I'm looking for someone."

The girl moved aside. Disembarking passengers, none with Peter's slouch, spilled down the steps of the train.

"If you're leaving, you might have some spare change," the girl said, "or perhaps a phone card?"

"What?" Anna said.

The girl repeated her request.

"I'm not leaving," Anna said.

"I'm sorry to trouble you," the girl said.

"Oh, you're Dutch," Anna said, catching the accent. One of those nice Dutch girls with the wide lips and high cheeks, like the ones in Amsterdam. Anna had spent ten days there and not once visited the Rijksmuseum. She took out a flyer. "I'm looking for my son. I wonder if you've seen him."

The girl held the flyer in both hands. She looked from Anna's face to Peter's. Even when Anna had pushed Peter in his baby carriage, passersby had looked up, back, up, back. The difference in hair and eye color was the first thing people noticed. Anna could see the girl studying the S-curves of Peter's eyebrows and the intense dark eyes.

"Oh, he's a Peter!" the Dutch girl said. "My son is a Peter."

"Have you seen him?" Anna said.

The young girl looked up and frowned. "Maybe."

It was the first "maybe" Anna had heard. A man in uniform came toward them.

"I have to go," the girl said. She turned and started down the litter-filled subterranean passage that led to the station's exit.

Anna ran to keep up. "Where did you see him?"

The girl was outside already, heading toward the tram stop.

"Can I buy you a coffee? Or strudel?"

"I must get home." The girl looked over her shoulder. The uniformed man spoke into a walkie-talkie. "You can come with me if you wish," the girl said.

"I will!" Anna said. "Is that man following you?"

"Probably," the girl said. "I come here a lot."

"Me, too," Anna said.

They arrived at the tram stop. A tram rang its bell. "Hurry!" the girl said, looking over her shoulder. "We must take this one." She sprang on board.

Anna's way was blocked by an old Czech woman with heavy ankles and worn shoes. Anna pushed her aside and fingered her sweat-crumpled pass, trying to force it into the punch. Finally, it clicked. The penalties for riding without a ticket were stiff. She couldn't afford to get in trouble. The police were sick of seeing her at the station. The Dutch girl took Anna's hand.

"My goodness," Anna said, stepping around shopping bags in the aisle. "That was close."

"They chase you if you come often to the station," the girl said.

At first the police, who could barely speak English, had been sympathetic. Now, they treated Anna like some kind of nut case. She was a mother with a lost child. Under the circumstances, hysteria was normal. It had taken her a while to figure out that Peter had cashed his student loan check, not put it in his bank account. For all she knew, he could have been robbed and lying in some morgue.

In the back of the tram the Dutch girl found an empty seat.

"Sit." The girl motioned for Anna to slide in. Their hips touched, and Anna caught the sickeningly sweet smell of patchouli. The smell was familiar. In Amsterdam, Anna had passed out flyers in coffee houses that reeked of pot and patchouli; she had been shocked to see young mothers buy marijuana like bulk granola. In Prague—and Amsterdam, too, of course—the police told her drugs were rampant. But, perhaps the Dutch girl was merely covering up body odor. No one showered the way they did back home, and on the trams, there was always a sour, underarm smell. From frequent washings in the hostel's sink, Anna's white blouse smelled strongly of mildew.

The Dutch girl hadn't said so much as a peep.

"Have you really seen my son?" Anna said.

Jiggling in her seat, the girl said, "Yes, of course. I said that once, didn't I? Just give me a few minutes to think."

The tram sped away from Old Town and rumbled alongside the Vltava River, where a barge moved slowly through the languid, brown water. In the window, Anna caught a glimpse of her blue eyes, as blue-white as the overheated sky, and wondered when Peter had become so fixated on his looks.

THE FIRST HINT of trouble came when he started hanging out with the stud-wearing dope-smokers who gathered in the mini-park across from school. While her students worked at their easels, she had looked out the second-floor windows and seen him, big as life, a cigarette in his mouth. She still didn't know what kind.

Students at Centennial had to commit to the six Ps: they had to be prompt, polite, and prepared; they had to participate, have a positive mental attitude, and produce. Peter, despite his P-name, had never bought into the school rules, or the rules she tried to enforce at home. Listening to his iPod, he painted after dark, and turpentine fumes, supposedly odorless but toxic nonetheless, circulated in the heating ducts.

One morning, headachy, still in her bathrobe, Anna came into his room and asked him to open the windows. He put down his brush and came toward her. She thought he was going to give her a hug. Instead, he put his hands around her neck and stared at her throat, squeezing it softly.

"That's how a python kills," he said.

She backed out of the room and slept with a locked door, wishing her husband had not moved out and that she had not been so preoccupied with the paperwork of the divorce.

Something was wrong. The school psychologist recommended a therapist, the best in Boulder—Dr. Tanner, a specialist for troubled youth. Peter began seeing him, and a month later, Tanner invited Peter's parents to attend an appointment with their son. Peter's father had not been able to come, but then he had never really shown up for his son. More and more as the years progressed, it had become clear to Anna how much Peter had been her project and not her husband's. Later, she thought her husband's departure might have made Peter feel abandoned. But maybe not. Probably the demons had been there all along.

She and Peter had sat silently in the waiting room. Peter, circles under his eyes, examined his fingers; but when Tanner opened the door, Peter, allowing the doctor to grasp his hand and pull him into the office, had actually smiled. Tanner asked her to take a seat and get comfortable. She sat. The room was barely large enough for two office chairs plus Dr. Tanner's desk, piled with manila folders. A painting hung above it: a woman with orange eyes and a blue face crowded her pink-faced son out of the picture. Anna wondered if this was some sort of Rorschach test to see how teens felt about their mothers. If not, then Tanner had terrible taste in art.

Dr. Tanner had dressed in layers—wool slacks, vest, and sport coat—as if he were eager to present an image of rumpled authority despite the oppressive closeness of his office. She peeled off her black sweater and smoothed her electrified hair, wondering if she could ask him to turn down the heat. Through the doctor's trifocals, she could see his magnified eyes and she began to tremble.

"Peter?" Dr. Tanner said. "Would you like to start?"

Aside from his jiggling foot, Peter sat absolutely still, his arms crossed. The fluorescent light made his skin look jaundiced. He stared up at a corner of the room, his eyes bugged out like a lemur's. Now, Dr. Tanner would see what it was like at home: Peter clamming up, not telling her what was bothering him. Just like her ex.

"Yes, Peter," she said. "Please tell me what's wrong."

"You know," Peter said, "sometimes I don't feel like I belong here."

"Belong where?" she said, feeling a clutch in her throat.

"Boulder. All the outdoor types. The snowboarders. The guys who live for rock climbing. I'm suffocating."

"Where do you belong?" she said.

"I don't know," he said. "I want to travel. Maybe I'm a gypsy at heart."

"Excuse me, Peter." Dr. Tanner clicked his pen. "Do you mean a vagabond or a real gypsy?"

"I dunno," Peter said. "A real one, I guess."

Anna took a deep breath. Tread carefully, she thought.

Peter pushed back bangs that covered his eyes.

The dark hair, often greasy, the body hair on his chest, unlike anything she'd seen in her fair, Danish family—it was remotely possible some gypsy girl had deposited a little blanket-bundle on a church step. Over there in Czechoslovakia or Bulgaria or Romania or Hungary or wherever he came from.

"I suppose it's possible you could be Romany," she said.

"Now, we're making progress," Dr. Tanner said.

"I've never seen a single other person who looks like me." Peter touched his high cheekbones. "Sometimes, kids at school call me 'the Indian,' but I'm not, because American Indians don't have this much facial hair."

His beard had come in thick. He needed to shave twice a day, but didn't. "You're becoming a man," Anna said. "That's all."

"But what kind? I'm certainly not a jock."

"Most artists aren't," she said.

"Peter is having a hard time finding a mirror of himself." Dr. Tanner glanced over at the picture.

"I have no idea what you're talking about," Anna said.

"A mirror. You know, a mirror?" Dr. Tanner jotted a note to himself. He looked down at his scratch pad then raised his eyebrows. "When you look in the mirror, don't you see your ancestors?"

"Well, of course," she said. "I'm Danish, and proud of it."

Peter leaned forward, his hands on the chair arms as if he might spring to his feet. "But I'm not Danish! When I was a kid, my friends' parents were always saying stuff like, 'He looks like his mom or dad or my side of the family or yours.' I never heard that from you, not once."

"We know you look like someone," Anna said. "We just don't know who."

"So, Peter," Tanner said. "Can you say more about how you feel about being adopted?"

"I feel like I'm supposed to be grateful she rescued me from the trash heap."

"You don't have to feel grateful," Anna said, reaching for a kleenex. Honestly, he could be so self-dramatizing. "You were an adorable baby. I was thrilled."

Peter swiveled around to face her. "You wanted someone who'd look like you and be like you, but I'm not like you at all."

"Of course, you are," she said. "You're an artist, just like me."

"I wish you weren't an artist," Peter said. "I don't want my art to come from you."

"Thank you, Peter," Dr. Tanner said. "Let's give your mother time to process this information."

"I'm processing it all right," Anna said.

Tanner looked at her and raised his eyebrows. "All right, then." He turned to Peter. "I wonder if you could share more of what being adopted is like for you."

Peter sat back. He seemed more relaxed than she'd seen him in a long time: less sulky teenager, more man. He looked down at his stomach. "I have this hole inside."

"What kind of hole?" Dr. Tanner said.

"A hole." Peter held up his hands. The circle his fingers made was the size of a pie pan.

This new revelation about the hole was more than Anna could bear. Peter had no idea what it felt like to lose three babies, babies with heartbeats, whose turnings reminded her of miniature gymnasts. The last had died at eight and a half months, a blond-haired boy born covered with wax, a cord wrapped around his neck. She didn't even have a name for the pleasures of motherhood these deaths had denied her. And all that time, she'd thought, if I'd only been able to carry those babies to term, it would have been different. Peter wasn't totally unlike her, but a child with her genes might have had an easier adolescence. She wouldn't be sitting here trying to come up with answers to unanswerable questions.

"How are you feeling, Ms. Ringaard?" Dr. Tanner said.

None of your god-damned business, she thought. She was here to talk about Peter, not herself. "I feel fine," she said.

"Is our discussion giving you some empathy for your son?" Dr. Tanner said.

"Yes, of course," she said. "He feels a void."

Dr. Tanner glanced at Peter, then back at her, blinking and frowning as if puzzled. "You do understand, he's asking your permission to search for his birth mother."

Anna remembered how Peter's eyes looked: black, angry, watchful. Her face turned hot. "When he turns twenty-one, he can do what he wants. I wash my hands."

Looking back, she could hardly believe how blindsided she'd felt, or how stupid she'd been to react so negatively. If he'd just waited until he was out on his own, he could have brought whomever he wanted into his life, and she wouldn't have had to know about it. Not that finding his birth mother was even possible. His adoption had been private, handled by a lawyer who specialized in babies from former Soviet satellites. Peter's biological father and mother worked in a factory, that much she knew; but the most the lawyer could tell her about his ethnicity was that he was "of eastern European descent."

He had been four months old.

TWENTY MINUTES OUTSIDE the city, the girl stood up. "My stop."

"But you haven't told me anything specific," Anna said.

"I'm trying to remember." The girl moved to the tram's door.

Anna had never come this far from the center of Prague, but it would be an easy matter to cross the tracks and return. The girl was waiting. Sighing, Anna stepped onto the platform, introduced herself, and offered her hand.

The girl shook it. "I'm Neeltje."

"Neeltje," Anna said. "It's hard to say."

"Not if you're Dutch," Neeltje said. "We learn the 'cghh' sound as babies." She looked across the tracks at a white, concrete apartment building where fire had scorched a balcony. Windows were boarded up. She pointed. "That's it."

"Where are we?" Anna said.

"Home," Neeltje said. "The Soviets built this."

Neeltje led the way through a tunnel beneath the tracks. It reeked of urine. Graffiti covered the walls. Coming up the stairs, Anna took a deep breath. Above ground, steppingstones led through dry, knee-high grass. Like the trees that lined the roads in France, a lone, blotchy-barked, plane tree with a thick trunk and low, horizontal branches stood sentinel. As she walked beneath it, Anna noticed how much the leaves resembled the maples on her wooded lot back home.

In Boulder she was surrounded by trees, and she wondered if there had once been more landscaping here. If so, the trees had died or people had cut them for firewood.

The building was in worse shape than the yard. The structure's concrete corners had chipped off. Orange rust in vertical and horizontal streaks showed through. The place looked like an early Mondrian.

"I never imagined life in such a place," Neeltje said, waving an arm. "We don't have such places in Holland."

"It's hideous," Anna said.

"Welcome to the gulag." Neeltje lifted her long skirt and started up the stairs.

Anna felt squeamish about touching the dirty handrail. Painted and rusty and utilitarian, it looked like a handrail in a warehouse. "Does Peter live here?"

"Americans have better places."

"What does being American have to do with it?"

"Americans have money." Neeltje turned, looking down. "I'm sorry. I have a lot on my mind. If you want to know more, you have to come with me."

"What floor do you live on?" Anna asked.

"The fifth," Neeltje said.

"Is there an elevator?"

"It's broken."

"Unless you know Peter, I'd rather not," Anna said.

"I have a good memory for faces."

"Okay, then." Anna put her head down and climbed to the second landing. "But you're sure you met my son?"

"Yes, of course," Neeltje said. "I can picture his face."

When she reached the fifth landing, an open-air space that was fifteen feet wide and dark at its far end, Anna felt lightheaded and leaned against the wall.

Neeltje unlocked a door.

"I want you to see how I and my baby live," Neeltje said. "Then, maybe you agree to help us."

"But what about my son?" Anna said.

"You are offering a reward for information, aren't you?"

"Yes, of course," Anna said. "Three hundred dollars."

"The exchange rate is bad," Neeltje said.

"Three hundred Euros, then."

"Okay," Neeltje said. "I will try to remember."

Anna entered a room with a rose-colored couch and a high-backed, wooden chair. An old woman sat on it. Her knees were spread and her stockings rolled. She wore a kerchief that covered her forehead, and her lips sank in, like one of the poverty-stricken, sickly women in Käthe Kollwitz's prints. Behind the woman, Anna saw a futon mattress on the floor. White sheets were jumbled. There was a worn, figured carpet, but the colors had bled. In the middle of the carpet sat a drawer. Neeltje gave the old woman money, and the woman left.

On her way to the couch, Anna glanced in the drawer. Inside was the kind of doll the school nurse used for teaching CPR. The doll's head moved.

"My God!" Anna said. "There's a baby in there!"

"Yes, of course," Neeltje said. "That's what I told you. I live here with my son."

The baby had a round head and fuzzy, blond hair that stuck straight up like a baby chick's. He was sleeping on his back, and his arms were thrown up in a pose that reminded Anna of Laughing Buddha. Despite the heat, a blanket covered the baby's legs, and she fought an urge to uncover him; he must be hot. She was. Hot and thirsty. Forcing herself to take her eyes away from the child, she looked around.

Behind the door, Anna saw the rest of the dresser. Neeltje had arranged a sort of kitchen on the dresser's top, and she was wiping the rims of two teacups with a rag. "I never wanted a baby, but..." she snapped her fingers "...you miss your period and think it's just because you don't eat and then you have no money, it's a Catholic country you're stuck in, and it's too late."

Neeltje put down the cups, opened the apartment door, and went out to the hall. There was no water in the room, as far as Anna could see. There must be a common bath and kitchen. Maybe Peter's biological mother had lived in a place like this.

In the early nineties, white babies flooded out of eastern Europe. There were big problems with Romanian orphans, kids with attachment disorder because they'd spent so long in cribs and never been held or comforted. A lot of the Russian babies had fetal alcohol syndrome because their mothers were drunks. Anna stood, looked down at the baby, around at the room, then moved the chair closer to the drawer and sat down.

Neeltje returned with a plastic jug of water. She plugged a wire coil into an outlet and plunged it into two cups of water until they steamed. She brought Anna a cup of tea, and Anna wiped the rim with her handkerchief.

"I'll be right back." Neeltje went out again, leaving the door wide open.

Flies buzzed in, and Anna got down on her hands-and-knees to brush them off the baby. He stirred, eyelids fluttering. He had a complexion so pale that, between his eyes, she could see a tiny, throbbing vein. His ears were cowry shells.

"Hello, little baby. Look at your hair." It was almost white. A blanket covered him, and Anna pulled it back. His faded snappy-suit was soaked. She pressed his bottom. His diaper squeaked.

Closing the door, Neeltje held up a diaper. "I begged a neighbor for this. Until you came, I wasn't having a very good day but you changed my luck."

The man Neeltje lived with had left that morning and taken her money. She'd hidden it in the sugar jar, where her mother always hid her household money. Wanting sugar for his tea, he'd raised the lid and found it. Not a lot, just what she earned at the station.

More like begged, Anna thought.

Sitting on the floor beside the baby, Neeltje sighed. She lifted him out and placed him on the rug to change his diaper.

Anna leaned over. "How old is he?"

"Three months," Neeltje said, "but he's not big like a normal Dutch baby. Some are giants."

"Is his father Dutch?"

Neeltje shrugged. "I don't know." Living like this, she said, wasn't the same as having a settled life with a husband and women friends who would have a baby party. And the Czechs didn't help. They'd help their own kind, but not a foreigner. The woman who babysat was Bulgarian. "As you can see, she does nothing for my son except sit in that chair."

Anna got to her feet. The girl needed money. She wanted the reward. It was very unlikely she knew Peter.

"Maybe you've seen my son's work in a gallery," Anna said. She had been to all Prague's galleries. None of the owners had recognized Peter's face.

"I don't go see art," Neeltje said. "It's false."

"False!" Anna said. "Why do you think that?"

"Art bores me. No one can tell me what it means." Sitting with her feet tucked beneath her, Neeltje unbuttoned her blouse. She picked up the baby. He rooted blindly, his nose bouncing against the breast. Neeltje pinched the brown aureole of her nipple and slid it in his mouth.

Anna sat down again, resting her elbows on her knees. The baby sucked noisily.

"He's taking the last ounce of my energy," Neeltje said.

"Oh, yes! I remember that feeling," Anna said, "but even though I was forty-five when I got my son, I was lucky because I've always had ten times more energy than the average person."

"You were old to get a baby," Neeltje said.

"He was adopted," Anna said. She told Neeltje about Boulder, right in the heart of the Rockies. It was the perfect place to raise a child: year-round, outdoor activities and excellent public schools, not just academics, but art. "That's how my son developed as an artist," Anna said. "I taught him."

Neeltje frowned. "Are you a painter?"

"I teach high school art," Anna said.

"Oh," Neeltje said, her face relaxing. "I thought you might be a painter. They're awful."

"Was the man who left a painter? A friend of Peter's perhaps?"

"No," Neeltje said. "He was just someone who lived here."

Neeltje shifted the baby to the other side.

Anna, sitting rigid, a hand on each knee, leaned forward to see if there was milk in the other breast. Not much. As the baby sucked, the balloon deflated.

Neeltje looked up. "You must be very proud of your son." Her knee began to jiggle. "His name was Peter, wasn't it? An artist. It might have been in Wenceslas Square that I talked to him. Only for a few minutes. I am always asking Americans for change, and I can't remember them all specifically, but he seemed very openhearted."

That would be Peter. Anna could feel the question she did not want to ask coming out like a soap bubble. "Was he high?"

"High?" Neeltje reached up to stabilize her unruly nest of hair.

"Yes, high. You know what I mean."

Neeltje's eyes turned to slits. She pulled the baby away from her breast and held him out. "Would you mind burping him?"

Anna took him, gasping with pleasure to hold a baby after all these years. Pressing his cheek against her shoulder, she thumped his back. While Neeltje was looking for a spit-up towel, a sweet little burp erupted. The baby had his fingers inside his mouth. His lips were wet.

"I need to buy diapers before the store closes," Neeltje said. "Would you mind staying with him for half an hour?"

"Not at all," Anna said. "I don't get to hold babies very often."

"It is good to have someone I can trust." Neeltje explained that she needed other things—milk, eggs, yogurt. She was very hungry, and the baby was taking all its nourishment from her body. "If I could fix a meal for myself, I could think of the next step to take, for myself and the baby. I don't need much." Neeltje stood there waiting.

"How much do you need?" Anna said.

"A hundred Euros?"

She probably should say no, but holding the baby, whose skin smelled so sweet, even unwashed as he probably was, feeling his back arch and his floppy head bang rhythmically against her shoulder, Anna thought, why not? This little boy looked like the blond babies her body had rejected and the grandchildren she might have had. She opened her purse. "I can let you have fifty."

Neeltje counted the money and went to the door. "I'll be back in half an hour."

"Fine," Anna said. "I'll amuse myself."

Holding the baby on her hip, she sprang up and opened drawers until she found a saucepan. She poured in water from the plastic jug and warmed it with the heating coil, then, remembering an old trick, flicked a few drops on her wrist. Not too warm. There was a dishtowel to dry the baby with and a clean suit to dress him in. She assembled all the ingredients for the bath and carried them to the drawer, pausing a moment to look at the little boy on her hip. His eyes were so intelligent and blue, an alert personality already evident. She unsnapped his suit and removed his diaper, laying it carefully aside. Seeing his pipe-cleaner legs, she realized the truth of what Neeltje said. The baby was not getting enough to eat. The child's ribs looked like wishbones. He was uncircumcised. Like a tiny, pink thumb, the tip of his penis showing through the foreskin. While she bathed him, he looked at his hands; his eyes were on the verge of focusing. She wondered if he could see her. She clicked her tongue. His eyes turned toward the sound, and he smiled. Probably only a reflex, she thought, pleased nonetheless.

"Hi, baby," she said, drying him with the dishtowel. "My name is An-na."

She re-taped the diaper and put on a clean outfit. "An-na rhymes with Ma-ma."

His eyes followed the sound of her voice. The corner of his

mouth flickered. There was a little person in there. Then, she remembered. His name was Peter, Neeltje had said.

"Hello, little Peter." Anna picked him up and held him against her breasts. He smelled like Herbal Essence, the shampoo she used at home.

THE FIRST WEEK of July, Peter's last communication, and the one she most wanted to forget, had come in the mail. She had immediately gone on Priceline to find a cheap fare to Europe. Inside the envelope he had sent, she found a pen-and-ink drawing of Alois Dryák's Hotel Europa in Wenceslaus Square. There was none of the abstraction of Peter's usual art, nor of the diagonal lines that often slashed through his paintings. This was purely representational, a drawing for tourists.

> Forget I ever existed. Okay? Don't come looking for me. I'm learning the language. I have friends. I have enough money to get by. I feel at home here. ~~Peter~~

She had no idea why he'd crossed out his name. That implied a complete erasure of self. If she could just talk to him and get some reassurance he was still alive, then maybe, yes, he could put college off for a year while he did his European walkabout. He was barely eighteen. She didn't see how she could return to Boulder and leave him here.

THE BABY TENSED, and his knees drew up. She remembered the spasms of a colicky baby and the hours from 4:00 to 9:00 that were Peter's fussiest. With a hand on the chair, she pushed herself up. My goodness, she thought, the old knees sure have gotten creaky. Sitting down again, she laid the baby across her lap and rubbed his back. "There, there little Peter," she said. "You're going be okay."

He whimpered, and his whimpers turned to cries. The cries

grew angrier. He was like a porpoise, arching his back, then curling over her knees to let out another scream. She put him on her shoulder. His mouth opened wide. His screams echoed off the walls. Wahhh! Wahhh! Wahhh! Wahhh!

All right, now, all right, she thought. We're going to be just fine. She walked in circles around the room, bouncing him and cradling his head. "There, there, Peter. Don't cry."

Peter arched his back and tossed his head. His fists pounded her shoulder. He was heavier than he looked. She'd been walking on cobblestones all morning, and her back ached. She wished she hadn't had that tea because now she had to go to the bathroom. The toilets were those squat things. She couldn't very well take him with her. Bending down, she put him in the drawer. He drew his knees up, and then his feet shot out. His fists were tight. Tears tinier than raindrops squeezed from his eyes, and a rage-cry rang out.

"Oh, dear," she said, looking around. Maybe he would calm down if she gave him some sugar water. On the dresser, she lifted the top of the sugar bowl. She moistened her finger and tapped the white powder, touching it to her tongue. Yes, it tasted sweet; she would not be poisoning him with some sort of powdered drug. She picked up the plastic jug. Not even a teaspoon of water left. First, she needed a baby bottle. She opened a drawer. Two little outfits. In another, Neeltje's underwear. In the bottom drawer were wool socks. She might use a sock, moisten it in sugar water, and let him suckle. He was used to a teat. Anything to make the crying stop! It was frightful how a crying baby could eat at one's nerves.

Propping open the door with the chair, Anna looked out in the corridor. Although Neeltje had said she'd gotten a diaper from a neighbor, it didn't seem possible that anyone other than the desperate Dutch girl would pay rent to live here. If she did pay rent. Maybe the building was occupied by squatters. There were two doors across the way. Anna knocked at one. No one answered. She put her ear to the door. Nothing. She stood at the second door. Inside, she heard voices. "Hello?" she said, rapping loudly. "Can you tell me where the kitchen is?" Peter's screams were surely audible to the people behind the door. Maybe they were calling the police to complain about the noise. She tried the door. The voices went quiet. She banged her fist. "Open up! Please! I just need to know where the water is!"

Then she noticed the peephole. A shadow darkened the lens. Standing on tiptoe, she put her eye right up to it. "I know you're in there," she screamed. "Open. The. Door." Backing away, she held up the jug and mimed drinking a glass of water.

Behind her, Peter's cries were dying down. Thank God, she thought. Maybe he'd just cry himself to sleep, and she could sit on the sofa and not worry about feeding him. But she did still have to go to the bathroom.

Back in the apartment, she put the jug on the chair and seeing the peephole on the way out, thought, I must be crazy because anyone could be living in there: the Russian Mafia or gypsies. The hostel's desk clerk had warned her not to go out at night alone. Gangs of gypsies roamed the subways, attacking like feral dogs and robbing unsuspecting tourists. She thought of her son Peter, wondering if he had inherited criminal tendencies, and what kind of people he'd fallen in with.

Heading toward a dark alcove at the end of the hall, she discovered that the corridor jogged to the right, forming an open balcony that faced the hills. She walked down it, hoping to find a door that said WC. Instead, there were half a dozen identical doors, spaced like those in a hospital. Suddenly, she knew: the building had been a dormitory, a place to warehouse factory workers. That meant there had to be a communal toilet. She looked over the balcony. Down below, she saw cans, bottles, and bags of garbage. The humid air formed an opaque glaze that reminded her of Monet's atmospheric light and turned the scene of squalor into something almost beautiful. Then, she heard slow, deliberate footsteps above her head. The footsteps halted. She held her breath. Smoke drifted down.

The people who lived here must be the dregs of society—ruffians, beggars, and thieves—but even lowlifes needed a bathroom. It had to be in that shadowy alcove she'd avoided. That would make sense, a bathroom right there at the end of the hall. Returning to the alcove, she saw a door. She twisted a knob. It fell off in her hand. "Ew!" she said, letting the knob drop to the floor. The space smelled like every drunk in the building had used it as a urinal. The corners were black, and there were white rivulets that reached all the way to a center drain, where the door knob had rolled. Breathing through her mouth, she hiked up her skirt and squatted. Pee spattered her shoes. She stood partway up, said, "Oh, well," and wiped herself with her skirt. She wasn't going to be able to stand herself if she didn't get back to Prague soon.

A puppyish whimper echoed down the hall. She hurried back to the apartment, picked up the jug, and pushed aside the chair. Peter had wedged himself into a corner of the drawer. Poor little fellow. She picked him up. Unsnapping his suit, she stuck her fingers in his diaper. Fluorescent-green shit squirted out. It smelled like ammonia.

She placed Peter on the dishtowel, still damp from his bath. Anna saw the used, rolled-up diaper by the door. A wet diaper was definitely better than a poopy one. She used it to clean his bottom. It had turned red. His stomach was concave. Looking back at the dresser for something she could use as a diaper, she noticed the hand towel beneath the tea things. She moved them to the floor. On her knees, folding and refolding, she tried to tuck in the towel so it would stay closed; the frantic gestures of Peter's little arms frustrated her efforts. With her free hand, she lunged for the dresser and pulled out his clothing drawer. She found another outfit, fastened him into it, and put him back in his bed. His eyes rolled back and his eyelids closed. For a moment, she thought, Oh, no! He's dying on me! But he was just going to sleep. She was tired, too. Dead tired. She was desperate to get back to the hostel, wash her hands, and throw her skirt in the garbage. Old Town was twenty minutes away.

She got to her feet again.

Adjusting the straps of her knapsack and putting it on, she

looked down at the drawer. Peter's eyes were closed, and his hands were as loose as the paws of a sleeping cat. He should be okay for a minute. She checked her watch, then opened the door and listened for footsteps. Neeltje had been gone an hour. Surely, she'd come home soon.

Anna looked around at the open drawers, the tea things on the floor, and the disheveled sheets. She couldn't very well leave him here. Sighing, she bent over and spread the baby-blanket on the rug. Folding down a corner, she placed Peter in it, then bundled him tight as a burrito. Going downstairs would be tricky. He was heavy, and she worried she might trip.

She grabbed the sheet off the mattress, put Peter in the middle, and made a sling. Maybe Neeltje had decided to take advantage of the free babysitting to go back to the train station, Anna thought, closing the door behind her. She felt guilty leaving the place a mess, but then Neeltje had promised to come back, and she hadn't. The best thing was to meet her on the platform. Neeltje would have diapers and food. Anna could tell her about the diarrhea. The baby needed to see a doctor.

With the sling around her neck, holding the baby tight in one arm and clutching the handrail, Anna descended the stairs. At the third landing she stopped to rest. Someone had spray-painted three, fat blue letters—LUV—on the boarded-up windows. Anna stood and looked at them, feeling the baby's weight on her arm. He shifted and whimpered. In the distance, a tram was coming toward the suburb. Commuters were packed like sardines. Probably Neeltje had to run around to several places to buy what she wanted. It wasn't convenient to shop here, not like in America. Anna hurried down the remaining flights, picturing Neeltje, with her long determined strides, coming through the tunnel and up the steps.

At ground level, out of breath, Anna stopped and looked around. The tram was speeding away. Across the tracks, she saw a woman in a pink, spring coat. The woman walked quickly along the gravel embankment beside the tracks and dropped out of sight. There must be stairs, Anna thought, and possibly another housing development on land that sloped down to the river.

In the shade of the plane tree, she took off her knapsack and, cradling the baby in his sling, crossed the steppingstones to the platform. Looking back, she saw that the building next door didn't have boarded windows. Beyond it stood a two-story, salmon-colored house with a vegetable garden. Beans grew up poles. There were fruit trees. This wasn't a totally bad neighborhood. She shifted the sling to her back. The knot had rubbed a raw spot on her skin.

She returned to the tree, untied the sheet, and retied it around a branch. She looked in. The baby's eyes were open. He was turning his hands and staring at them. She held out a finger. His hand moved slowly; then his fingers grasped her index finger. He looked at her, his bright, blue eyes focusing on her face.

"Are you okay?" she said.

He held tight, a death grip, as he moved her finger toward his mouth.

"No, baby." She pulled her finger free. "I need to wash my hands." He was such a lovely baby, but he wasn't the baby she loved.

She gave the sling a push and stepped back. It swung like a hammock. The breeze would cool him. She picked up her knapsack and returned to the platform. A tram was coming, heading back into Prague. The headlight flashed. Brakes screeched as it came to a stop. Anna boarded. Through the windows of the tram, she saw Neeltje coming up the embankment that the woman in the pink coat had earlier descended. The conductor barked out something in Czech and motioned impatiently.

Anna punched her ticket. The tram picked up speed. She bent to look out the window, and in the distance she saw Neeltje emerge from the tunnel beneath the tracks. Neeltje stopped, dropped her grocery sacks, and ran. She reached the tree, where a branch arched like the neck of a stork, holding a triangle of white. Sitting down, Anna sighed. Fingerprints streaked the glass, and her mind rattled like the tram's unsteady wheels. Really, she thought, you can only do so much, and then you have to quit.

BOOK CLUB QUESTIONS

1. Which characters did you identify with the most? Were there some you didn't like but whose actions you found plausible?

2. Pick one character and describe how his/her physical appearance or background shaped that character's life.

3. Which stories felt the most tense? Did the tension arise from the characters' actions or from their internal struggles?

4. What do you think about the characters' moral choices (Billy Rippelmeyer, for instance, in "Proud To Be An American")? How conscious was he of his choice to betray his boss, or was this an "inadvertent action?" Can you think of a story where a character makes a moral choice that seems ill considered?

5. What role does setting play in these stories? How are the characters' decisions affected by where they are? Consider the ice storm and the isolation of the farm in "The Bean Grower." Think about Prague as a backdrop for Anna's quest to find her son. What about Baltimore as a backdrop for Terrell and his friends?

6. Imagine how these stories might have turned out if the setting had been different. Can you think of a setting that might have reduced the pressure on the protagonist?

7. In which stories could you most easily identify with the main character? Were there some stories where you didn't necessarily identify with the character, but where you felt compassion for his/her plight?

8. Describe the dynamics between the couple in "Regret." Do the power struggles seem familiar? Think about what they might have wanted when they first got together versus the routine they'd settled into as they aged.

9. How much time passes in the present time of each story? Is the author showing you a slice of life or a whole life?

10. Pick a story where memory plays an important role. Does the character's memory help you understand her or his present state of mind?

11. You might think about memory as baggage that the characters are lugging in from the past. Can you think of examples where the suitcases of memory felt especially heavy and hard to handle?

12. What was your experience reading a series of short stories compared to the experience of reading a novel? Were you glad to finish a story and then find yourself in a different world, or did it take time to make the transition from one story to the next?

ACKNOWLEDGMENTS

———o———

FINANCIAL SUPPORT FROM the Illinois Arts Council and writing residencies at the Vermont Studio Center for the Arts, Footsteps for Creativity, and Hawthornden Castle gave me time to write. My writing groups in Evanston, IL and Tempe, AZ have provided the support every writer needs. Thanks, as well, to the literary magazines that have published these stories.

"A Weekend in Baltimore," published as "What Am I Doing Here?" in *Blue Moon Literary & Art Review*

"Almost Paradise," winner of the Matt Clark Prize, published in *New Delta Review*

"Bonds of Love & Blood," winner of the Jeanne M. Leiby Memorial Chapbook Award, published in *The Rug Bazaar*, University of Central Florida

"Finding Peter," winner of the ALR 2009 Fiction Contest, published in *The American Literary Review*, University of North Texas

"Key West," published in *North Atlantic Review*

"Oregano," published in *Superstition Review*, Arizona State University East

"The Bean Grower," Finalist for the Lamar York Prize, published in *The Chattahoochee Review*, Georgia Perimeter College

"Two Trains in Manmad," published as "Regret" in *Ruminate Magazine*

"Pancho Villa's Coin," winner of the 2011 Barry Hannah Prize, published as "The Pancho Villa Coin," *The Yalobusha Review*, University of Mississippi

"Proud To Be An American," Third Runner-up in the William Faulkner-William Wisdom Short Story Competition

"Teşekkür," winner of the Ron Rash Award, published as "Tea and Sugar," *Broad River Review*

"The Ambassador of Foreign Affairs," published in *The Briar Cliff Review*, Briar Cliff University

ABOUT THE AUTHOR

—————◦—————

BEFORE TURNING TO fiction, Marylee MacDonald worked as a carpenter and magazine editor. She has five kids, loves gardening and taking long walks in the foothills of Sonoma County, and hanging out with her family.

Every author depends on readers for encouragement. If you enjoyed *Bonds of Love & Blood*, please take a moment to post a review in your favorite online bookstore. You can also leave comments on Goodreads, the online book club.

www.goodreads.com

To learn about forthcoming books, please visit her webpage or find her on another social media site.

www.maryleemacdonald.com

Bookbub
Marylee MacDonald

Facebook
MaryleeMacD

Twitter
MaryleeMacD

CPSIA information can be obtained
at www.ICGtesting.com
Printed in the USA
LVHW111410251020
669761LV00004B/865

9 781951 479183